Blanche

A Story for Girls

By
Mrs. Molesworth

Blanche

Chapter One.

The Sunny South.

About a quarter of a century ago, a young English girl—Anastasia Fenning by name—went to pay a visit of a few weeks to friends of her family, whose home was a comfortable old house in the pleasantest part of France. She had been somewhat delicate, and it was thought that the milder climate during a part of the winter might be advantageous to her. It proved so. A month or two saw her completely restored to her usual health and beauty, for she was a very pretty girl; and, strange to say, the visit of a few weeks ended in a sojourn of fully twenty years in what came to be her adopted country, without any return during that long stretch of time to her own home, or indeed to England at all.

This was how it came about. The eldest son—or rather grandson of her hosts, for he was an orphan—Henry Derwent, fell in love with the pretty and attractive girl, and she returned his affection. There was no objection to the marriage, for the Derwents and Fennings were friends of more than a generation's standing. And Henry's prospects were good, as he was already second in command to old Mr Derwent himself, the head of the large and well-established firm of Derwent and Paulmier, wine merchants and vine-growers; and Anastasia, the only daughter of a widowed country parson of fair private means, would have a "dot" which the Derwents, even taking into account their semi-French ideas on such subjects, thought satisfactory.

Mr Fenning gave his consent, more readily than his friends and his daughter had expected, for he was a devoted, almost an adoring father, and the separation from him was the one drawback in Anastasia's eyes.

"I thought papa would have been broken-hearted at the thought of parting with me," she said half poutingly, for she was a trifle spoilt, when the anxiously looked for letter had been received and read. "He takes it very philosophically."

"Very unselfishly, let us say," her *fiancé* replied, though in his secret heart the same thought had struck him.

But the enigma was only too speedily explained. Within a day or two of the arrival of her father's almost perplexingly glad consent came a telegram to Mr Derwent, as speedily as possible followed by a letter written at his request by the friend and neighbour who had been with Mr Fenning at the last. For Anastasia's father was dead—had died after but an hour or two's acute illness, though he had known for long that in some such guise the end must come.

He was glad for his "little girl" to be spared the shock in its near appallingness, wrote Sir Adam Nigel; he was thankful to know that her future was secured and safe. For he had no very near relations, and Sir Adam himself, though Anastasia's godfather, was an old bachelor, living alone. The question of a home in England would have been a difficult one. And in his last moments Mr Fenning had decided that if the Derwents could without inconvenience keep the young girl with them till her marriage, which he earnestly begged might not be long deferred, such an arrangement would be the wisest and best.

His wishes were carried out. The tears were scarcely dried on the newly orphaned girl's face, ere she realised that for her husband's sake she must try again to meet life cheerfully. And in her case it was not difficult to do so, for her marriage proved a very happy one. Henry Derwent was an excellent and a charming man, an unselfish and considerate husband, a devoted though wise father. For twelve years Anastasia's life was almost cloudless. Then, when her youngest child, a boy, was barely a year old, the blow fell. Again, for the second time in her life, a few hours' sharp illness deprived her of her natural protector, and she was left alone. Much more alone than at the epoch of her father's sudden death, for she had then Henry to turn to. Now, though old Mr Derwent was still living, the only close sympathy and affection she could count upon was that of her little girls, Blanche and Anastasia, eleven and nine years of age respectively, when this first and grievous sorrow overtook them.

For some months Mrs Derwent was almost totally crushed by her loss. Then by degrees her spirits revived. Her nature was not a very remarkable one, but it was eminently healthy and therefore elastic. And in her sorrow, severe as it was, there was nothing to sour or embitter, nothing to destroy her faith in her fellow-creatures or render her suspicious and distrustful. And her life, both as her father's daughter and her husband's wife, had been a peculiarly bright and sheltered one.

"Too bright to last," she thought sometimes, and perhaps it was true.

For trouble *must* come. There are those indeed from whom, though in less conspicuous form than that of death, it seems never absent—their journey is "uphill all the way." There are those again, more like Anastasia Derwent, whose path lies for long amid the flowers and pleasant places, till suddenly a thunderbolt from heaven devastates the whole. Yet these are not, to my mind, the most to be pitied. The happiness of the past is a possession even in the present, and an earnest for the future. In the years of sunshine the nature has had time to grow and develop, to gather strength against the coming of the storm. Not so with those who have known nothing but wintry weather, whose faith in aught else has but the scantiest nourishment to feed upon.

And the new phase of life to which her husband's death introduced Mrs Derwent called for qualities hitherto little if at all required in her. Her father-in-law, already old and enfeebled, grew querulous and exacting. He had leant upon his son more than had been realised; his powers could not rally after so tremendous a shock. He turned to his daughter-in-law, in unconscious selfishness, demanding of her more than the poor woman found it possible to give him, though she rose to the occasion by honestly doing her best. And though this "best" was but little appreciated, and ungraciously enough received, she never complained or lost patience.

As the years went on and in some ways her task grew heavier, there were not wanting those who urged her to give it up.

"He is not your own father," they said. "He is a tiresome, tyrannical old man. You should return to England with your children; there must still be many friends there who knew you as a girl. And this living in France, while *not* French, out of sympathy with your surroundings in many ways, is not the best school for your daughters. You don't want them to marry Frenchmen?"

This advice, repeatedly volunteered by one friend in particular, the aged Marquise de Caillemont, herself an Englishwoman, whose own marriage had not disposed her to take a rose-coloured view of so-called "mixed alliances," was only received by Mrs Derwent with a shake of the head. True, her eyes sparkled at the suggestion of a return to England, but the time for that had not come. Blanche and Stasy were too young for their future as yet to cause her any consideration. They were being well educated, and if the care of their grandfather fell rather heavily on them — on Blanche especially — "Well, after all," she said, "we are not sent into this world merely to please ourselves. I had too little of such training myself, I fear; my children are far less selfish than I was. Still, I will not let it go too far, dear madame. I do not want their young lives to be clouded. I cannot see my way to leaving the grandfather, but time will show what is right to do."

Time did show it. When Blanche, on whose strong and buoyant nature Mr Derwent learned more and more to rely, till by degrees she came almost to replace to him the son he missed so sorely, and whom she much resembled — when Blanche was seventeen, the old man died, peacefully and gently, blessing the girl with his last breath.

They missed him, after all, for he had grown less exacting with failing health. And while he was there, there was still the sense of protectorship, of a masculine head of the house. Blanche missed him most of all, naturally, because she had done the most for him, and she was one of those who love to *give*, of their best, of themselves.

But after a while happy youth reasserted itself. She turned with fresh zest and interest to the consideration of the plans for the future which the little family was now free to make.

"We shall go back to England, of course, shan't we, mamma?" said Stasy eagerly, as if the England she had never seen were the land of all her associations.

"Of course," Mrs Derwent agreed. "The thought of it has been the brightest spot in my mind all through these last years. How your father and I used to talk of the home we would have there one day! Though I now feel that *anywhere* would have been home with him," and she sighed a little. "He was really more English than poor grandfather, for he had a regular public school education."

"But grandfather only came to France as a grown-up man, and papa was born here," said Blanche. "Of the two, one would have expected papa to be the more French, yet he certainly was not. Perhaps it was just that dear old gran was a more clinging nature, and took the colour of his surroundings more easily. We are just the opposite: neither Stasy nor I could be called at all French, could we, mamma?"

She said it with a certain satisfaction, and Mrs Derwent smiled as she looked at them. Blanche, though fair, gave one the impression of unusual strength and vigour. Stasy was slighter and somewhat darker. Both were pretty, and promising to grow still prettier. And from their adopted country they had unconsciously imbibed a certain "finish" in both bearing and appearance, which as a rule comes to Englishwomen, when it comes at all, somewhat later in life.

"We are *not* French-looking, mamma; now, are we?" chimed in the younger girl.

"Well, no, not in yourselves, certainly," said Mrs Derwent. "But still, there cannot but be a little something, of tone and air, not quite English. How could it be otherwise, considering that your whole lives have been spent in France? But you need not distress yourselves about it. You will feel yourselves *quite*English once we are in England."

"We do that already," said Blanche. "You know, mamma, how constantly our friends here reproach us with being so English. One thing, I must say I am glad of — we have no French accent in speaking English."

"No, I really do not think you have," Mrs Derwent replied. "It is one of the things I have been the most anxious about. For it always sets one a little at a disadvantage to speak the language of any country with a foreign accent, if one's *home* is to be in the place. How delightful it is to think of really settling in England! I wonder if I shall find Blissmore much changed. How I wish I could describe my old home, Fotherley, better to you—how I wish I could make you*see* it! I can fancy I feel the breeze on the top of the knoll just behind the vicarage garden; I can *hear* the church bells sometimes—the dear, dear old home that it was."

"I think you describe it beautifully, mamma," said Stasy. "I often lie awake at night making pictures of it to myself."

"And we shall see it for ourselves soon," added Blanche; "that is to say, mamma," she went on with a little hesitation, "if you quite decide that—"

"What, my dear?" said her mother.

"Oh—that Blissmore will be the best place for us to settle at," said Blanche, rather abruptly, as if she had been anxious to get the words said, and yet half fearful of their effect.

Mrs Derwent's face clouded over a little.

"What an odd thing for you to say, my dear?" she replied. "You cannot have any prejudice against my dear old home, and where else could we go which would be so sure to *be* home, where we should at once be known and welcomed? Besides, the place itself is charming—so very pretty, and a delightful neighbourhood, and not very far from London either. We could at any time run up for a day or two."

"Ye-es," said Blanche; "the only thing is, dear mamma, I have heard so much of English society being stiff and exclusive—"

"It's not as stiff and exclusive as French," Mrs Derwent interrupted; "only you cannot judge of that, having lived here all your life, and knowing every one there was to know within a good large radius, just as *I* knew everybody round about Blissmore when I was a girl."

"But all these years! Will they not have brought immense changes?" still objected Blanche. "And it is not as if we were very rich or important people. If we were going to buy some fine château in England and entertain a great deal, it would be different. But, judged by English ideas, we shall not be rich or important. Not that I should wish to be either. I should like to live modestly, and have our own poor people to look after, and just a few friends—the life one reads about in some of our charming English tales, mamma."

"And why should we not have it, my dear? We shall be able to have a very pretty house, I hope. I only wish one of those I remember were likely to be vacant; and why, therefore, should you be afraid of Blissmore? Surely my old home is the most natural place for us to go to: I cannot be quite forgotten there." Blanche said no more, and indeed it would have been difficult to put into more definite form her vague misgivings about Blissmore. Her knowledge of English social life was of course principally derived from books, and from her mother's reminiscences, which it was easy to see were coloured by the glamour of the past, and drawn from a short and youthful experience under the happiest auspices. And Blanche was by no means inclined to prejudice; there was no doubt, even by Mrs Derwent's own account, that her old home had been in a peculiarly "exclusive" part of the country.

"I should not mind so much for ourselves," she said to Stasy, that same afternoon, as they were walking up and down the stiff gravelled terrace in the garden at the back of their house—their "town house," in Bordeaux itself, where eight months of the year had been spent by the Derwent family for three generations. "But I do feel so afraid of poor mamma's being disappointed."

Stasy was inclined to take the other view of it.

"Why should we get on *less* well at Blissmore than anywhere else?" she said. "Of course, wherever we go, it will be strange at first, but surely there is more likelihood of our feeling at home there than at a totally new place. I cannot understand you quite, Blanchie."

"I don't know that I quite understand myself," Blanche replied. "It is more an instinct. I suppose I dread mamma's old home, because she would go there with more expectation. It will be curious, Stasy, very curious, to find ourselves really in England. There cannot be many English girls who have reached our age without having even seen their own country."

"And to have been so near it all these years," said Stasy, "Oh, it is too delightful to think we are really going to live in England—dear, dear England! Of course I shall always love France; we have been very happy in many ways, except for our great sorrows," and her bright, sparkling face sobered, as, at April-like sixteen, a face can sober, to beam all the more sunnily the next moment—"we have been very happy, but we are going to be still happier, aren't we, Blanchie?"

"I hope so, darling. But you will have to go on working for a good while once we are settled again, you know. And I too. We are both very ignorant of much English literature, though, thanks to papa's library and grandfather's advice, I think we know some of the older authors better than some English girls do. I wonder what sort of teaching we can get at Blissmore; we are rather too old for a governess."

"Oh dear, yes. Of course we can't have a governess," said Stasy. "We must go to *cours* — 'classes,' or whatever they are called. I suppose there is something of the kind at Blissmore."

"I don't know that there is. I don't know what will be done about Herty," said Blanche. "I'm afraid he may have to go to school, and we should miss him so, shouldn't we?"

"There may be a school near enough for him to come home every evening," said Stasy, who was incapable of seeing anything to do with their new projects in other than the brightest colours. "There he is — coming to call us in. — Well, Herty, what is it?" as a pretty, fair-haired boy came racing along the straight paths to meet them.

"The post has come, and mamma has a letter from England, and dinner will be ready directly, and — and — my guinea-pigs' salad is all done, and there is no more of the right kind in the garden," said the little boy. "What shall I do?"

"After dinner you shall go with Aline to the vegetable shop near the market place and buy some lettuce — that is the proper word — not 'salad,' when it is a guinea-pig's affair," said Stasy.

For it was early summer-time, and the evenings were long and light.

Blanche smiled.

"My dear Stasy, your English is a little open to correction as well as Herty," she said. "You must not speak of a vegetable shop — 'greengrocers' is the right name, and — there was something rather odd about the last sentence, 'a guinea-pig's affair.'"

"Well, you can't say 'a guinea-pig's business,' can you?" said Stasy. "Let us ask mamma. I am, above all, anxious to speak perfect English. Let us be most particular for the next few weeks; let us pray mamma to correct us if we make the slightest mistake."

"I wonder what the letter is that has come," said Blanche. "I think we had better go in now. Mamma may want us. After dinner, perhaps, she will come out with us a little. How difficult it is to picture this dear old house inhabited by strangers! I think it is charming here in summer; we have never been in the town so late before. I like it ever so much better than Les Rosiers — that is so modern. I wish we were going to stay here till we leave."

She stood still and gazed on the long, narrow house — irregular and picturesque from age, though with no architectural pretensions at all — which for seventeen years had been her home. The greyish-white walls stood out in the sunshine, one end almost covered with creepers, contrasting vividly with the deep blue sky of the south. Some pigeons flew overhead on their way to their home high up in the stable-yard, the old coachman's voice talking to his horses sounded in the distance, and the soft drip of the sleepy fountain mingled with the faint noises in the street outside.

"I shall often picture all this to myself," thought Blanche. "I shall never forget it. Even when I am very old I shall be able to imagine myself walking up and down, up and down this path, with grandpapa holding my arm. And over there, near the fountain, how well I remember running to meet dear papa the last time he came back from one of his journeys to Paris! I suppose it is best to go to what is really our own country, but partings, even with things and places that cannot feel, are sad, very sad."

Chapter Two.

Fogs.

The old house in Bordeaux was not to be sold, but let for a long term of years. An unexpectedly good offer was made for it, and a very short time after the evening in which in her heart Blanche had bidden it a farewell, the Derwents gave up possession to their tenants. For the few months during which Mrs Derwent's presence was required in France on account of the many and troublesome legal formalities consequent upon her father-in-law's death and the winding-up of his affairs, the family moved to Les Rosiers, the little country-house where they had been accustomed to spend the greater part of the summer months.

They would have preferred less haste. It would in many ways have been more convenient to have returned to Bordeaux in the autumn, and thence made the final start, selecting at leisure such of the furniture and other household goods as they wished to take to their new home. But the late Mr Derwent's partner, Monsieur Paulmier, and his legal adviser, Monsieur Bergeret, were somewhat peremptory. The offer for the house was a good one; it might not be repeated. It was important for Madame, in the interests of her children, to neglect no permanent source of income.

Their tone roused some slight misgiving in Mrs Derwent, and she questioned them more closely. Were things not turning out as well as had been expected? Was there any cause for anxiety?

Monsieur Paulmier smiled reassuringly, but looked to Monsieur Bergeret to reply. Monsieur Bergeret rubbed his hands and smiled still more benignly.

"Cause for uneasiness?" Oh dear, no. Still, Madame was so intelligent, so full of good sense, it was perhaps best to tell her frankly that things were not turning out *quite* so well as had been hoped. There had been some bad years, as she knew—phylloxera and other troubles; and Monsieur, the late head of the firm, had been reluctant to make any changes to meet the times, too conservative, perhaps, as was often the case with elderly folk. Now, if Madame's little son had been of an age to go into the business—no doubt he would inherit the excellent qualities of his progenitors— *that* would have been the thing, for then the family capital might have remained there indefinitely. As it was, by the terms of Monsieur's will, all was to be paid out as soon as possible. It would take some years at best, for there was not the readiness to come forward among eligible moneyed partners that had been expected. The business wanted working up, there was no doubt, and rumour exaggerated things. Still—oh no, there was no cause for alarm; but still, even a small certainty like the rent of the house was not to be neglected.

So "Madame" of course gave in—the offer was accepted; a somewhat hurried selection of the things to be taken to England made, the rest sold. And the next two months were spent at Les Rosiers, a place of no special interest or association, though there were country neighbours to be said good-bye to with regret on both sides.

The "letter from England" which little Hertford Derwent had told of the evening he ran out to his sisters in the garden, had been a disappointment to their mother, for it contained, returned from the dead-letter office, one of her own, addressed by her some weeks previously to her old friend, Sir Adam Nigel, at the house near Blissmore, which she had believed was still his home.

"Not known at Alderwood," was the curt comment scored across the envelope.

"I cannot understand it," she said to her daughters. "Alderwood was his own place. Even if he were dead—and I feel sure I should have heard of his death—some of his family must have succeeded him there."

"I thought he was an old bachelor," said Blanche.

"Yes, but the place—a family place—would have gone to some one belonging to him, a nephew or a cousin. He was not a *nobody*, to be forgotten."

"The place may have been sold," Blanche said again. "I suppose even old family places are *sometimes* sold in England."

But still Mrs Derwent repeated that she could scarcely think so; at least she felt an instinctive conviction that she would have heard of it.

"It may possibly be let to strangers, and some careless servant may have sent back the letter without troubling to inquire," she said. "Of course I can easily find out about it once we are there, but I feel disappointed. I had counted on Sir Adam's helping me to find a suitable house."

"How long is it since you last heard from him?" said Stasy.

"Oh, a good while. Let me see. I doubt if I have written to him since—since I wrote to thank him for writing to me when—soon after your father's death," replied Mrs Derwent.

"That is several years ago," said Blanche gently. "I fear, dear mamma, your old friend must be dead."

"I hope not," said her mother; "but for the present it is much the same as if he were. Let me see. No, I cannot think of any one it would be much use to write to at Blissmore. We must depend on ourselves."

"Who is the vicar at Fotherley now — at least, who came after our grandfather?" asked Blanche.

Mrs Derwent looked up.

"That is not a bad idea. I might write to him. Fleming was his name. I remember him vaguely; he was curate for a time. But that is now twenty years ago: it is by no means certain he is still there, and I don't care to write letters only to have them returned from the post-office. Besides, I have not an altogether pleasant remembrance of that Mr Fleming. His wife and daughter were noisy, pushing women, and it was said the living was given to him greatly out of pity for their poverty. Sir Adam told me about it in one of his letters: he regretted it. Dear Sir Adam! He used to write often in those days."

"I daresay it will not make much difference in the end," said Blanche. "No one can really choose a house for other people. Nothing could have been decided without our seeing it."

"No; still it would have been nice to know that there were any promising ones vacant. However, we have to be in London for a short time, in any case. We must travel down to Blissmore from there, and look about for ourselves."

The Derwents' first experience of their own, though unknown country was a rather unfortunate one. Why, of all months in the year, the Fates should have conspired to send them to London in November, it is not for me to explain. No doubt, had Mrs Derwent's memories and knowledge of the peculiarities of the English climate been as accurate as she liked to believe they were of everything relating to her beloved country, she would have set the Fates, or fate, at defiance, if such a thing be possible, by avoiding this mysteriously doleful month as the date of her return thither. But long residence in France, where, though often without any spite or *malice prepense*, people *are* very fond of taunting British foreigners with the weak points in their national perfection, had developed a curious, contradictory scepticism in her, as to the existence of any such weak points at all.

"People do talk such *nonsense* about England," she would say to her daughters, "as if it were always raining there when it is not foggy. I believe they think we never see the sun at all. Dear me! when I look back on my childhood and youth, I cannot remember anything *but* sunshiny days. It seems to have been always summer, even when we were skating on the lake at Alderwood."

She smiled, and her daughters smiled. They understood, and believed her — believed, Stasy especially, almost too unquestioningly. For when the train drew up in Victoria Station that mid-November afternoon, the poor girl turned to her mother with dismay.

"Mamma," she exclaimed, "it isn't three o'clock, and it is quite dark. And such a queer kind of darkness! It came all of a sudden, just when the houses got into rows and streets. I thought at first it was smoke from some great fire. But it can't be, for nobody seems to notice it — at least as far as I can see anybody. And the porters are all going about with lanterns. Oh mamma, can it be — surely it isn't always like this?"

And Stasy seemed on the point of tears.

Poor Mrs Derwent had had her unacknowledged suspicions. But she looked out of the window as if for the first time she had noticed anything amiss.

"Why, yes," she replied, "it is rather unlucky; but, after all, it will be an amusing experience. We have made our début in the thick of a real London fog!"

Herty, who had been asleep, here woke up and began coughing and choking and grumbling at what he called "the fire-taste" in his mouth; and even the cheerful-minded Aline, the maid, looked rather blank.

Blanche said nothing, but from that moment a vague idea that, if no suitable house offered itself at Blissmore, she would use her influence in favour of London itself as their permanent headquarters, was irrevocably dismissed from her mind.

"We should die!" she said to herself; "at least mamma and Stasy, who are not as strong as I, would. Oh dear, I hope we are not going to regret our great step!"

For they had left Bordeaux in the full glow of sunshine — the exquisite "autumn summer" of the more genial south, where, though the winter may not infrequently be bitingly cold, at least it is restricted to its own orthodox three months.

"And this is only November," proceeded Blanche in her unspoken misgivings. "Everybody says an English spring *never* really sets in till May, if then. Fancy fully five months of cold like this, and not improbable fog. No, no; we cannot stay in London: the cold must be faced, but not the fog."

Yet she could scarcely help laughing at the doleful expression of her sister's face, when the little party had disentangled themselves and their belongings from the railway carriage, and were standing, bewildered and forlorn, trying to look about them in the murky air.

"Mustn't we see about our luggage, mamma?" said Blanche, feeling herself considerably at a disadvantage in this strange and all but invisible world. "It is managed the same way as in France, I suppose. We must find the — what do they call the room where we wait to claim it?"

"I — I really don't know," said Mrs Derwent. "It will be all right, I suppose, if we follow the others."

But there were no "others" with any very definite goal, apparently. There were two or three little crowds dimly to be seen at different parts of the train, whence boxes seemed to be disgorging.

"It is much more puzzling than in France," said Blanche, her own spirits flagging. "I do hope we shall not have long to wait. This air is really choking."

She had Herty's hand in hers, and moved forward towards a lamp, with some vague idea that its light would lessen her perplexity. Suddenly a face flashed upon her, and a sense of something bright and invigorating came over her almost before she had time to associate the two together.

The face was that of a person standing just under the lamp — a girl, a tall young girl with brilliant but kindly eyes, and a general look of extreme, overflowing youthful happiness. She smiled at Blanche, overhearing her last words.

"You should call a porter," she said. "They are rather scarce to-night, the train was so full, and the fog is so confusing. Stay — there is one. — Porter! — He will see to your luggage. You won't have as long to wait as in Paris."

A sort of breath of thanks was all there was time for, then the girl turned at the sound of a name — "Hebe" — through the fog, and was instantly lost to view. But her face, her joyous face, in its strange setting of dingy yellow-brown, streaked with the almost dingier struggling gas-light, was impressed upon Blanche's memory, like a never-to-be-forgotten picture.

"Hebe," she said to herself, as she explained to her mother, just then becoming visible, that the porter would take charge for them — "Hebe: how the name suits her!"

An hour later saw them in their temporary haven of refuge — a private hotel in Jermyn Street. In this hotel Mrs Derwent had once spent a happy week with her father when she was eighteen, and she was delighted when, in reply to her letter bespeaking accommodation for herself and her family, there came a reply in the same name as she remembered had formerly been that of the proprietor.

"It *is* nice that the landlord is still there: I wonder if they will perhaps recollect us," she said. "Your grandfather always put up there. They were such civil people."

"Civil" they still were, and had reason to be, for it is not every day that a family party takes up its quarters indefinitely in a first-class and expensive London hotel. And it had not occurred to Mrs Derwent to make any very special inquiry as to their charges.

So in the meantime ignorance was bliss, and the sitting-room, though small, with two bedrooms opening out of it on one side and one on the other, looked fairly comfortable, despite the insidious fog lurking in every corner. For there was a good fire blazing, and promise of tea on a side-table. But it was all so strange, so very strange! A curious thrill, almost of anguish, passed through Blanche, as she realised that for the time being they were — but for this — homeless, and as if to mock her, there came before her mental vision the dear old house — sunny, and spacious, and above all familiar, which they had left for ever! Had it been well to do so? The future alone could show.

But a glance at her mother's face, pale and anxious, under a very obtrusive cheerfulness, far more touching than expressed misgiving, recalled the girl to the small but unmistakable duties of the present.

"I mustn't begin to be sentimental about our old home," she said to herself. "Mamma has acted from the very best possible motives, and I must support her by being hopeful and cheerful."

And she turned brightly to Stasy, who had thrown herself on to a low chair in front of the hearth, and was holding out her cold hands to the blaze.

"What a nice fire!" said the elder girl. "How beautifully warm!"

"Yes," Stasy agreed. "I am beginning already to understand the English devotion to one's own fireside. Poor things! There cannot be much temptation — in London, at least — to stray far from it. Imagine walking, or even worse, *driving* through the streets! And I had looked forward to shopping a little, and to seeing some of the sights of London. How do people ever do *anything* here?"

Her extreme dolefulness roused the others to genuine laughter.

"My dearest child," said her mother, "you don't suppose London is always like this? Why, I don't remember a single fog when I was a girl, and though I did not live in London, I often paid visits here, now and then in the winter."

"Oh, but, mamma, you can't remember anything in England but delightfulness," said Stasy incredulously. "Why, I know one day you told us it seemed to have been summer even when you were skating. And I daresay fogs have got worse since then. Very likely we shall be told that they are beginning to spread all over the country. I know I read or heard somewhere that they were getting worse."

"Only in London," said Blanche, "and that is because it is growing and growing so. That does not affect the rest of England. The fogs are the *revers de la médaille* of these lovely, hot coal-fires, I suppose."

She stooped and took up the tongs to lift a red-hot glowing morsel that had fallen into the grate, taking advantage of the position to whisper into her sister's ears a word of remembrance.

"Do try to be a little brighter, Stasy, for mamma's sake."

The entrance of tea at that moment did more perhaps in the desired direction than Blanche's hint. Stasy got up from her low chair and looked about her.

"How long has there been fog like this?" she asked the waiter, as he reappeared with a beautifully toasted tea-cake.

"Yesterday, miss. No, the day before, I think," he replied, as if fog or no fog were not a matter of special importance.

"And how long do they last generally?" Stasy continued.

"As bad as this — not often over a day or two, miss," he replied. "It may be quite bright to-morrow morning."

"There now, Stasy," said her mother. "I told you so. There is nothing to be low-spirited about. It is just — well, just a little unlucky. But we are all tired, and we will go to bed early, and forget about the fog."

"Besides," said Blanche, quietly, "we are not going to live in London. — Herty, you had better come close to the table; and if you mean to have any dinner, you had better not eat *quite* as much as you can, at present."

"I don't want any dinner," said Herty. "English boys don't have late dinner. They have no little breakfast, but a big one, early, and then a dinner instead of big breakfast, and just tea at night. Don't they, mamma? And I am going to be quite English, so I shall begin now at once. Please may I have some more bread-and-butter, mamma?"

Mrs Derwent looked at him rather critically.

"Yes," she said, "you may have some more if you really mean what you say. But it won't do for you to come, in an hour or two, saying you are so hungry, you really must have some dinner, after all."

"No," said Herty, "I won't do that."

"And remember," said Stasy severely, "that this is a hotel, not our own house. Whatever you eat here has to be paid for separately. It's not like having a kitchen of our own, and Félicie going out and buying everything and cooking for us. *Then* it didn't make much difference whether you ate a great deal or not." Herty took the slice of bread-and-butter, in which he had just made a large semicircular hole, out of his mouth, and looked at Stasy very gravely. This was a new idea to him, and a rather appalling one.

"Yes," his sister repeated, nodding her head to give emphasis to her words, "you'll have to think about it, Herty. Mamma isn't as rich as she used to be; we haven't got vineyards and great cellars all full of wine now. And when you go to school, that will cost a lot. English schools are very dear."

Herty slowly turned his head round and gazed, first at his mother, then at Blanche. The round of bread-and-butter had disappeared by this time, so he was able to open his mouth wide, which he proceeded to do preparatory to a good howl.

"Mamma," he was beginning, but Blanche stepped in to the rescue.

"Stasy," she said, though she could scarcely help laughing, "how can you tease him so?"

For it was one of Stasy's peculiarities that, in a certain depressed mood of her very April-like temperament, the only relief to her feelings was teasing Herty. The usual invigoration seemed to have followed the present performance; her colour had returned, and her eyes were sparkling.

"Blanchie, Blanchie," said Herty, wavering for moment in his intention, "is it true? Will poor mamma have to pay a great lot of money if I eat much bread-and-butter?"

"No, no; of course not. Can't you see when Stasy's teasing you, you silly boy?" said Blanche caressingly. "Why, you are eight years old now! You should laugh at her.

Mamma has plenty of money to pay for everything we need, though of course you mustn't be greedy."

"But hotels *are* dear," persisted Stasy calmly.

"Well, we are not going to live at a hotel for ever," said Blanche.

"Nor for very long, I hope," added her mother. "I do look forward to being settled. Though, if the weather were pretty good, it would be nice to be in London for a little. We must get to know some of the shops, for living in the country makes one rather dependent upon writing to London for things."

Blanche was silent for a few moments. Then she looked up suddenly.

"Have you no friends to go to see here, mamma? Is there nobody who can give us a little advice how to set about our house-hunting?"

"I scarcely thought it would be necessary to have any," said Mrs Derwent. "My plan was simply to go down with one or both of you to Blissmore for a day, and look about for ourselves. You see, I shall feel quite at home once I am there, and it would be easy to ask at the inn or at the principal shop — old Ferris's — if any houses are vacant. They always used to have notice of things of the kind."

"But mamma, dear," said Blanche softly, "all that is more than twenty years ago."

Mrs Derwent was giving Herty a second cup of tea, and did not seem to catch the words.

Chapter Three.

Then and Now.

Negatively, the waiter's prediction was fulfilled the next morning. That is to say, the fog was gone; but as to the "quite bright" — well, opinions vary, no doubt, as to "quite brightness." Stasy stood at the window overlooking the street, when she felt a hand on her shoulder, and, glancing round, saw that it was her sister's.

"Well, dear," said Blanche, "it is an improvement on last night, isn't it?"

"I don't know," said Stasy dubiously. "It's certainly better than fog, but then, fog isn't *always* there; and this sort of dull grey look is the regular thing in London, I suppose. I have often heard it was like that, but I don't think I quite believed it before."

"But we are not going to live in London," said Blanche, "and the country in some parts of England is very bright and cheerful. Of course, this is the very dullest time of the year; we must remember that. Perhaps it is a good thing to begin at the worst; people say so, but I am not quite sure. There is a great deal in first impressions — bright ones leave an after-glow."

Just then their mother came into the room.

"Isn't it nice that the fog has gone?" she said. "And to me there is something quite exhilarating in the sight of a London street! Dear me, how it carries one back — "

She stood just behind the two girls, and as Blanche glanced round at her, she thought how very pretty her mother still was. Her eyes were so bright, and the slight flush on her cheeks made her look so young.

"You have slept well, mamma, haven't you?" she said affectionately. "You seem quite fresh and energetic."

"Yes, I feel so; and hungry too. I always think London air makes me hungry, even though people abuse it so. Here comes breakfast. — You look well too, Blanchie. — But Stasy, have you not got over your fatigue yet?"

"I don't know," said Stasy. "Perhaps not; everything feels so strange. I don't think I like London, mamma."

Mrs Derwent laughed, but she seemed a little troubled too. Stasy, like herself, was very impressionable, but less buoyant. She had been full of enthusiastic delight at the thought of coming to England, and now she seemed in danger of going to the other extreme.

Blanche darted a somewhat reproachful look at her sister.

"Mamma," she said, "are you going to make some sort of plans? It would be as well to do so at once, don't you think? For if we are to be settled in a home of our own by Christmas, as we have always hoped, there is not much time to lose about finding a house. And if there was nothing at Blissmore—"

"Oh, but there *must* be something at Blissmore," said Mrs Derwent confidently. "And I quite agree with you, Blanchie, about not losing time. I wonder what is the best thing to do," she went on, consideringly.

The waiter just then entered the room.

"Can you let me see a railway guide?" she asked.

"A Bradshaw, ma'am, or a 'Hay, B, C'?" said the man.

"A *what*?" enquired Mrs Derwent, perplexed.

"A 'Hay, B, C,'" he repeated. "They are simpler, ma'am, more suited to ladies, begging your pardon."

"Please let me see one, then.—It must be some new kind of guide since my time, I suppose," she added, turning to the others. "I must confess, Bradshaw would be a labyrinth to me. I want to see exactly how long it takes to Blissmore, and if we could get back the same evening." And as the waiter reappeared with the yellow-paper-covered guide in one hand, and the *Morning Post* in the other, she exclaimed, as soon as she had glanced at the former, "Oh, *what* a nice guide! B—'Blackheath,' 'Blendon'—yes, here it is, 'Blissmore.'"

There was silence for a moment or two. Then Mrs Derwent spoke again:

"Yes, I think we can manage it in a day—the first time, at any rate. There is a train at—let me see.—Blanchie, do you hear?"

But Blanche was immersed in the newspaper. The outside column of houses to let had caught her eye.

"Mamma," she said suddenly, "is there more than one Blissmore?" And her fair face looked a little flushed. "If not, it is really a curious coincidence. Look here," and she held the paper for her mother to see, while she read aloud:

"Shire. Country residence to be let unfurnished, one mile from Blissmore Station. Contains" — and then followed the number of rooms, stabling for three horses, ending up with "quaint and well-stocked garden. Rent moderate. Apply to Messrs Otterson and Bewley, house-agents, Enneslie Street, Blissmore."

"Otterson and Bewley," Mrs Derwent repeated. "Who can they be? I don't remember the name at all. Enneslie Street? Let me see; that was —"

"Never mind about that, mamma dear," said Stasy, who had brightened up wonderfully as she listened to her sister; "I do feel so excited about this house. It seems the very thing for us. Shall we go down to Blissmore at once to see it? I do hope it won't be taken."

"That is not likely," said Blanche. "It is not everybody that has any peculiar attraction to Blissmore. And just look at the list of houses to let!" she added, holding up the paper as she spoke. "But I do think it would be well to write about it, don't you, mamma?"

"Certainly I will. And I am glad to know the name of a house-agent, though it seems strange that there should be such a person at a tiny place like Blissmore. I can't even remember Enneslie Street, though there seems — oh yes, that must be why the name seems familiar. There was a family called Enneslie at a pretty place a short way from Blissmore — Barleymead — yes, that was it. The Enneslies must have been building some houses, I suppose."

And as soon as the obliging waiter had removed the breakfast things, Mrs Derwent got out her writing materials, and set to work at a letter to Messrs Otterson and Bewley.

It was just a little difficult to her to write anything of a formal or business-like nature in English. For as a young girl, nothing of the kind had been required of her, and since her marriage, though the Derwent family had been faithful to their own language among themselves, all outside matters were of course transacted in French. So Blanche and Stasy were both called upon for their advice and opinion.

"How do you begin in English, when it is to a firm?" said Blanche. "In French it is so easy — 'Messieurs' — but you can't say 'Sirs,' can you?"

Mrs Derwent hesitated.

"I really don't know," she said frankly. "You sometimes wrote for your grandfather to bankers and such people, didn't you, Blanche? Can't you remember?"

Blanche considered.

"I don't recollect ever writing anything but 'Sir' or 'Dear sir,'" she said.

The three looked at each other in perplexity.

Suddenly a bright idea struck Mrs Derwent.

"I will write it in the third person," she said. "Mrs Derwent will be obliged, etc."

"That is a capital plan," said Blanche, and in a few minutes the letter was satisfactorily completed.

It read rather quaintly, notwithstanding the trouble that had been taken with its composition. The clerk in Messrs Otterson and Bewley's small back office, whose department it was to open the letters addressed to the firm, glanced through it a second time and then tossed it over to young Mr Otterson, who was supposed to be learning the business as a junior in his father's employ.

"Foreigners, I should say," observed the clerk.

"Better show it to the governor before you send an order to view," replied the other.

Mr Otterson, senior, looked dubious.

"Send particulars and an order," he said, "but mention that no negotiations can be entered upon without references. We must be careful: this school is bringing all sorts of impecunious people about the place."

So the reply which found its way to the private hotel in Jermyn Street, though, strictly speaking, civil, was not exactly inviting in its tone.

Mrs Derwent read it, then passed it on to her elder daughter. She felt disappointed and rather chilled. They had been looking for the letter very eagerly, for time hung somewhat heavy on their hands. They had no one to go to see, and very little shopping to do, owing partly to their still deep mourning. And the noise and bustle of the London streets, even at this dead season, was confusing and tiring; worst of all, there was an incipient fog about still, as is not unusual in November.

"What do you think of it?" said Mrs Derwent, when Blanche had read the letter.

"It is dear, surely," said Blanche. "Let me see — one hundred and twenty pounds; that is, three thousand francs. I thought small country-houses in England were less than that."

"So did I," her mother replied. "Still, we can afford that. Of course, if it had not been for my own money turning out so much less than was expected, we could have bought a little place, which would have been far nicer."

"I don't know that," said Blanche. "At least, it would not have been wise to buy a place till we had tried it. And you have still a little money, mamma, besides what we get from France. We shall have quite enough."

Mrs Derwent's "own money," inherited from her father, had been unwisely invested by him; when it came to be realised after his death, it proved a much less important addition to Henry Derwent's income than had been anticipated.

"Oh yes, we shall have *enough*," she replied, fingering the agents' letter as she spoke. "I don't understand," she went on again, "I don't understand what they mean by the 'recent rise in house rents owing to the improvements in the town.' What improvements can there be?"

"Gas, perhaps, or electric light," said Blanche.

"*Gas*, my dear child!" repeated her mother. "Of course, there has always been gas there. It was not such a barbarous, out-of-the-way place as all that. Still, I scarcely think they can have risen to the heights of electric lighting yet. But we must go down and see for ourselves. These agents ask for references, too: I wonder if that is usual in England? No doubt, however, it will be all right when I tell them who I was."

"But if they did want formal references," said Blanche hesitatingly, "have we any one whose name we could give?"

"My bankers," Mrs Derwent replied promptly. "Monsieur Bergeret opened a private account for me with the firm's bankers here. I do wish I could identify the house," she added. "I am sure I never heard the name before — 'Pinnerton Lodge' — and yet I have a vague remembrance of 'Pinnerton.'"

"Just as you had of 'Enneslie,' mamma," said Stasy. "Well, when are we to go to see it? To-morrow?"

"Yes; I see no use in delaying it," said Mrs Derwent.

So the next morning saw the mother and daughters again at Victoria Station, Master Herty having been given over with many charges to the care of the faithful Aline.

They were in more than good time; their train was not due for some twenty minutes or so, and as they walked up and down the platform, the picture of their first arrival there returned to Blanche's mind.

"Did you see that girl the other night, mamma?" she said. "The girl who hailed a porter for us. No, I don't think you did. The fog was so thick. I never saw such a charming face: the very incarnation of youth and happiness she seemed to me;" and she related the little incident to her companions.

Stasy sighed.

"I daresay she has got a lovely home somewhere, and relations who make a great pet of her, and—and—oh, just everything in the world she wants," she said.

Blanche looked at her sister doubtfully.

"Perhaps she has, but perhaps not," she replied. "It isn't always those lucky people who are the happiest. But, Stasy, I do wish you wouldn't be so lugubrious: the air of London doesn't seem to suit you."

"I am not lugubri— what a dreadful word!—I am quite cheerful to-day. It is so interesting to be going to choose our new house. Mamma, shall we have to buy a lot of furniture, or will there be enough of what we had at home?"

"My dear Stasy—of course not. What a baby you are! Don't you remember that we sold by far the greater part to the Baron de Var? Dear me, yes; we shall have to buy all sorts of things."

Stasy's eyes sparkled.

"That will be delightful," she said. "I *am* so glad. So if we settle to take the house at once, we shall be ever so busy choosing things. That's just what I like."

Her good spirits lasted, and, indeed, increased, to the end of the journey. It was exhilarating to get out of the murky London air, even though in the country it was decidedly cold, and even slightly misty. As they approached her old home, Mrs Derwent grew pale with excitement.

"To think," she said to her daughters, "of all that has happened since I left it, a thoughtless girl, that bright October morning, when my father drove me in to the station, and gave me in charge to the friend who was to take me to Paris, where young Madame de Caillemont, as we called her—the daughter-in-law of our old friend— met me, to escort me to Bordeaux. To think that I never came back again till now—

with you two, my darlings, fatherless already in your turn, as I was so soon to be then."

"But not *motherless*?" said Stasy, nestling in closer, "as you were, you poor, dear, little thing. And you hadn't even a brother or sister! Except for marrying papa, you would have been very lonely. But I wish you'd look out of the window now, mamma, and see if you remember the places. We must be getting very near Blissmore."

The train was an express one, which in itself had surprised Mrs Derwent a little: express trains used not to stop at Blissmore. They whizzed past some roadside stations, of which, with some difficulty the girls made out the names, in one or two instances familiar to their mother. Then signs of a more important stopping-place began to appear; rows of small, "run-up" cottages, such as one often sees on the outskirts of a town that is beginning to "grow;" here and there a tall chimney, suggestive of a brewery or steam-laundry, were to be seen, on which Mrs Derwent gazed with bewildered eyes.

"This surely cannot be Blissmore," she exclaimed, as the train slackened. "I have not recognised the neighbourhood at all. It must be some larger town that I had forgotten, or else the railway comes along a different route now."

But Blissmore it was. Another moment or two left no room for doubt; and, feeling indeed like a stranger in a strange land, Mrs Derwent stepped on to the platform of what was now a fairly important railway station.

"A fly, ma'am—want a fly?" said several voices, as the three made their way to the outside, where several vehicles were standing, and some amount of bustle going on.

Mrs Derwent looked irresolutely at her daughters. "I had thought of walking to the house-agents'," she said; "but now I doubt if I should find the way. It all seems so utterly changed."

"We should need a carriage in any case to get to the place we have come to see," said Blanche. "It is a mile or more from the station, they said."

"Pinnerton Lodge," said Mrs Derwent to the foremost of the flymen; "do you know where that is?"

"Pinnerton Lodge," repeated the man. Then, his memory refreshed by some of the standers-by, he exclaimed: "Oh, to be sure—out Pinnerton Green way. There's two or three houses out there."

"Then I shall want you to drive us there; but go first to Enneslie Street—Messrs Otterson and Bewley, the house-agents," said Mrs Derwent, as she got into the fly, followed by her daughters.

"Pinnerton Green," she repeated as they were driving off. "Oh yes; I remember now. That was what was in my mind. It was a sort of little hamlet near Blissmore, with an old-world well in the middle of the green. They must have built houses about there. How they have been building!" she continued, as the fly turned into the High Street of the little town. "I know where I am now; but really—it is almost incredible."

Blanche and Stasy were looking about them with interest. But in comparison with London and Paris, and even Bordeaux, Blissmore did not strike them as anything but a small town. They had not their mother's associations with grass-grown streets, and but one thoroughfare worthy the name, and two or three sleepy shops, whose modest windows scarcely allowed the goods for sale to be seen at all.

"It is a nice, bright, little place, I think," said Blanche, as some rays of wintry sunshine lighted up the old church clock, which at that moment pealed out noon, sonorously enough, eliciting the exclamation, "Ah yes; there is a familiar sound," from Mrs Derwent.

A moment later and they had turned into a side-street, to draw up, a few yards farther on, in front of a very modern, spick-and-span-looking house, half shop, half office, with the name they were in quest of, "Messrs Otterson and Bewley, House-agents, Auctioneers, etc," in large black-and-gold letters, on the plate-glass.

"Enneslie Street," said Mrs Derwent. "Why, this used to be Market Corner! There were only about half-a-dozen cottages, and, on market days, a few booths. Dear me! I feel like Rip Van Winkle."

Chapter Four.

Pinnerton Lodge.

Mr Otterson received the strangers with formal and somewhat pompous civility, and a somewhat exaggerated caution, not to say suspiciousness of manner, which struck disagreeably on Mrs Derwent and Blanche, accustomed to have to do with people who knew as much about them as they did themselves.

The house could be seen at once, certainly; as to that there was no difficulty. But before entering further into the matter, Mr Otterson begged to be excused, but might he remind the ladies that his client empowered him to deal with no applicants whose references were not perfectly sufficient and satisfactory. Clear understanding in such cases was, according to his experience, the best in the end, even if it should cause a little delay at the outset.

"No delay need be caused in *my* case," said Mrs Derwent, with a touch of haughtiness which her daughters enjoyed. "My references will be found perfectly satisfactory. Is this—this ultra caution, *usual* in such transactions," she continued, flushing a little, "may I ask?"

And as she spoke, she drew out of her bag and deposited on the table two letters she had had the foresight to bring with her—one from the firm at Bordeaux, enclosing an acknowledgment to them of the money placed to the credit of "Mrs Anastasia Derwent" with their London bankers.

Mr Otterson's keen eyes took in the nature of their contents even while scarcely seeming to glance at them. His manner grew a trifle less stilted.

"Cautious we have to be, madam," he replied, "though you will not find us exaggeratedly so, I trust. And in the interests of our clients, we naturally feel it our duty to give the preference to the most desirable among the constantly increasing applications for houses here. In your case, possibly, being foreigners, a little extra—"

"We are *not* foreigners," said Blanche; "and if we were? I certainly am not surprised at the small number of upper-class 'foreigners' who come to England, if this is the sort of thing they have to go through."

The house-agent glanced at her with a mixture of annoyance and admiration. She looked beautiful at that moment. Her fair face flushed, her usually gentle eyes sparkling.

"You—you misunderstand, madam," he was beginning, when Mrs Derwent in her turn interrupted him.

"On the contrary, sir," she said very quietly, "I think, it is distinctly you who have misunderstood us. As my daughter says, we are not foreigners. Beyond the statement of that fact, which you seem to consider important, I do not think we need waste time by entering into further particulars. The matter is a purely business one. If you do not find my references satisfactory, be so good as to say so at once, and I will apply to London agents about a house."

In his heart Mr Otterson had no wish to let these really very promising applicants for the honour of inhabiting Pinnerton Lodge escape him. On the contrary, they struck him as just the sort of people its owner would approve of—not unwilling to lay out a little money on repairs and improvements, etc.

"I have in no way implied, madam, that the names you have submitted to me are unsatisfactory references," he said, not without a touch of dignity. "As you observe, it is a matter of business, and if you approve, I will send a clerk at once to the house to have it all open for you."

"He can go on the box of our fly," said Mrs Derwent, with a glance out of the window; "I understand it is some little way off." And as Mr Otterson touched a hand-bell standing beside him on the table, Mrs Derwent addressed him again.

"What has caused this increased demand for houses here?" she said. "What has led to the many changes in the place—the sudden growth of it?"

Mr Otterson raised his eyebrows in surprise.

"Naturally, of course, in the first instance, the school," he replied. "And the breweries—the two large companies of brewers have brought a great many working men to the place, and the school even more. It has led to an immense amount of building—private houses of all classes, as the advantages and cheapness of the education to be got here are now almost unparalleled."

Mrs Derwent looked surprised.

"I do not remember any school here in the old days," she said. "At least—there was a small old school—but—"

"That is the same, no doubt," said the house-agent. "The foundation has been altered, by Act of Parliament, of course. The accumulated funds were very large: it is now a first-rate school for middle-class, indeed for upper-class boys, where economy is a consideration. Families have been in consequence flocking to Blissmore. But the last year or two has cooled down the rush a little. At one time it was almost alarming; but things are settling themselves now."

Just then the clerk appeared. Mr Otterson opened the door, speeding the parting guests with more urbanity than he had received them.

"I will look in here on my return," said Mrs Derwent, with a sufficiently courteous bow, "and tell you what we think of the house."

"Oh mamma," exclaimed Stasy, as soon as the three found themselves again in the privacy of the fly, "how *horrid* England is—how horrid English people are! How dared that common man speak to you like that, when you think how Monsieur Bergeret, who was far, *far* more a gentleman than he, used to treat you, as if you were a queen! Why, he used to look as proud as anything if you shook hands with him! Oh Blanchie, do let us go back—go home again. I have been feeling it ever since we arrived, that first night with the dreadful fog, though I didn't like to say so."

And poor Stasy looked up with tearful and beseeching eyes as she repeated:

"Oh, do let us go home again."

Mrs Derwent was sorry and distressed. But, on the whole, Blanche took it more seriously. For her mother was still to some extent under the glamour of her old associations, and "After all," thought the elder girl to herself, "she must know better than we can. Perhaps it will come right in the end."

So she said nothing, resolutely crushing back the strong inclination she felt to join in the cry, "Oh, do, mamma, do let us go home," while she listened to her mother's expostulations with poor Stasy.

"There are vulgar-minded and disagreeable people everywhere, my dear child. And perhaps, after all, the man only meant to do his duty. I daresay now, if we were going over to France for the first time, inexperienced and strange, we should find just as much to complain of there. You will feel quite different when we are settled in a pretty house of our own. And think how interesting it will be to choose the furnishing and everything. Do try, dear, to be more cheerful—for my sake, too."

Stasy wiped off such of her tears as had found their way to the surface, and swallowed down the others, though the choking in her throat prevented her speaking for a moment or two. But she took hold of her mother's hand and stroked it.

"I think," said Blanche, smiling a little at the remembrance, "the man got as good as he gave. I hope that isn't a very vulgar expression, mamma? I have read it often, though I never heard it. Was I too scornful to him? I did feel *so* angry; perfectly boiling for a moment or two. I don't often feel like that."

Stasy began to smile too.

"You were splendid, Blanchie. He was *shaking*; he was, really. I am so glad I was there to see it. And he had begun to look ashamed when mamma laid the letters on the table in that nice grand way. Oh yes, I do hope the house will be pretty. Are we getting near it, do you think, mamma? The road seems quite country now."

Mrs Derwent looked out of the window scrutinisingly.

"I think we must be nearly there," she replied, "but I do not know this side of Blissmore nearly as well as *our* side. I am glad to see there is not so much building hereabouts. Oh yes," as the fly rather suddenly turned down a lane, "I know where we are now; it is all coming back to me. This lane comes out on to Pinnerton Green. There is an old well in the centre, and five or six cottages, and the church, and a pretty little vicarage. I will shut my eyes, and you girls tell me if I am not right. The church stands right opposite the side of the green, where we come out — now, doesn't it?"

Mrs Derwent was quite excited; the two girls scarcely less so. And as the fly emerged on to the opener ground, for a moment or two no one spoke. Then Blanche exclaimed, half hesitatingly:

"Yes, there is the church. A dear old church, just across the green, all covered with ivy. And the vicarage. But the cottages — where can they be? And mamma, there are ever so many big, or *rather* big houses, with gardens opening on to the green. Oh, you must open your eyes, dear. I can't make it out." Mrs Derwent did as she was told, and looked about her.

What a metamorphosis! There remained the church and the vicarage and the old well as landmarks certainly, but beyond these, everything was new.

The houses struck her herself less pleasantly than Blanche. They were of the essentially English modern "villa" class, a class really unknown in France, in old-world France especially. She gave a little gasp of surprise and disappointment, but without speaking. And the next moment she felt more than glad that she had not put her impression into words, when poor Stasy exclaimed brightly:

"Oh, what nice cheerful houses; so fresh and new looking. And what pretty, neat gardens. I do wonder which is Pinnerton Lodge! I feel quite happy again about living in England, mamma."

Mrs Derwent smiled back at her, of course, though her own heart was going down a little. Blanche's face expressed nothing but gentle and resigned expectancy.

They were not long left in doubt as to "which" was their destination. The fly, after some fumbling on the part of Messrs Otterson and Bewley's clerk at a rusty padlock on the chain, which fastened a gate, turned in at a short but shady drive, and Pinnerton Lodge in another moment stood full before them.

Mrs Derwent's heart went up again. And glancing at her, Blanche's face too relaxed into less constrained, or restrained lines; her eyes brightened, and looked ready for a smile.

It was several degrees better than the obtrusively smart villas, though, very possibly, less materially convenient and complete. It was nothing more nor less than an enlarged and transmogrified cottage. The gable end and deep-eaved roof were still to be seen at one side; the faithful, clinging, all-the-year-round ivy; the more fitful summer friends—old-fashioned climbing roses, honeysuckle, and the like—would reappear again in due season, one felt instinctively. And the additions had not been badly managed; there was no glaring incongruity between the new and the old, and already the busy, patient ivy was doing its utmost to soften with its veiling green all offensive contrasts.

"A nice little place of its kind," the boyish-looking clerk ventured to remark to the three strangers, gazing before them in silence. "What you call 'quaint;' but some admire that style. It's not up to the mark of the other houses on the green, but that's not to be expected. You see it was the first start here, and the owner added on to the two old cottages, instead of pulling them down and building all new, like the rest;" and he jerked his thumb in the direction of the villas.

"Thank Heaven he did nothing of the sort," ejaculated Mrs Derwent. And the clerk stared at her so, that she checked herself with a smile. "I like it just as it is," she said by way of explanation. "It is a picturesque-looking house; but it seems very small, I fear. From the rent named, I expected a larger place."

"Rents have gone up about Blissmore quite astonishing," said the young man. "And these odd houses are sometimes roomier than you'd think. You'd like to see through it, no doubt. I have all the keys."

He moved forward, as he spoke, to the front of the house.

"Perhaps you wouldn't mind waiting in the porch for a minute or two," he said. "The quickest way for me to get in is by the back door; the front one is barred inside."

The porch was charming. Deep and shady, and with tiny lattice-windows high up at each side, through which the wintry sun was sending a few rays. There were seats and a red-tiled floor. The two girls gave a quick exclamation of pleasure.

"It is like a little room," said Stasy. The clerk's face brightened. He seemed to feel a personal interest in the matter.

"There is no one living in the house, then, to take care of it?" inquired Mrs Derwent. "Is that not necessary?"

"Not in the fine season," was the reply. "We were just thinking of putting some one in against the winter, if nothing came of the advertisement. But in the summer it's very dry — very dry, indeed."

He turned away towards the back premises, and soon they heard his footsteps returning through the passages. Then some unbolting and unbarring ensued, and the door was thrown open.

They all entered eagerly. It was rather dark, but this their guide explained was partly the result of unnecessarily closed shutters and untrimmed ivy round some of the upper windows, though partly owing, no doubt, to the oak wainscoting of the small square hall itself.

"It would look much cheerfuller with a nice paper — picked out with a little gold, perhaps. But the woodwork has a style of its own; the late owner was all for the antique."

"The *late* owner," repeated Mrs Derwent. "Is he dead, then? Has the house been long uninhabited?"

"Only since last spring. Mr Bartleman scarce lived in it himself. He found the winters too cold. Then it was let to Major Frederic, and he and his family lived here five years, till the young gentlemen had finished their schooling. There were several after it in the summer, but they mostly objected to the distance from the school."

"But how is it, then, that the villas are all let?" asked Blanche. "At least, I suppose they are."

"They're not let, Miss. They're mostly lived in by their owners — parties from the town, who have moved out, finding they could get a good rent for their houses near the school. There's Mr Belton, the principal draper at Blissmore, lives next door; and

Mr Wandle, junior partner in Luckworth and Wandle's brewery. The neighbours are highly respectable."

Mrs Derwent did not speak. Stasy was smothering a laugh. Blanche led the way into the rooms opening on to the hall.

They were nice—decidedly tempting, though not large. But they were depressingly out of repair. The Frederic schoolboys had evidently bestowed upon the house more than the legitimate "wear and tear" during their five years' occupancy. The drawing-room, especially, was scarcely deserving of the name: it looked as if it had been a playroom *pur et simple*. The attentive clerk was ready with his explanations.

"Major Frederic never furnished this room," he said. "It was kept empty for the young gentlemen."

"It might be a very pretty room," said Blanche, "but it needs *everything* doing to it."

The dining-room, though it had been furnished and used in a nominally orthodox way, was in not much better case. Still, a dining-room never, to ladies especially, seems such a serious matter. The library was the best-cared-for room, and it opened into a small boudoir or study, which was really charming. There were great capabilities about the house, though hitherto these had but scantily been made available. Up-stairs it was brighter. There was a sufficient number of rooms, though everywhere the same story of needful repair and embellishment.

Outside, to somewhat inexperienced eyes, it looked in fair order, for it needs the full luxuriance of summer vegetation to show how, in a neglected or semi-neglected garden, the weeds grow apace with or outrun the orthodox inhabitants of the soil.

The clerk was very patient. The minute attention bestowed by the visitors upon the little place seemed to him to savour of hope, and it was in his own interests, poor fellow, to secure a "let," as it would increase his chances of promotion in the office. But at last Mrs Derwent and her daughters seemed satisfied.

"We shall miss our train to London," said the former, "if we stay any longer; for I must see Mr Otterson on our way through the town."

So saying, she led the way out, turning, as she stepped on to the drive, to give a last look at the house, with already a slight sense of prospective proprietorship. But she said nothing, and the two girls were quick-witted enough to follow her lead.

The flyman, for reasons best known to himself, had seen fit to drive out into the road again, and was waiting, more than half asleep, at the gate.

Blanche glanced round, and an idea struck her.

"Mamma," she said, "if you are not tired, might we walk on a little way? I should like to have some idea of the neighbourhood, and to look in at the church for a moment."

"Certainly," said Mrs Derwent; "it cannot make five minutes' difference. And, after all, even if it did, we could wait for a later train."

"You won't find the church open, madam, I'm afraid," said the clerk. "But you might like to walk round it. From the other side there's a nice view, Alderwood way. On a clear day you can see right across. And at the other end of the lane there's one of the lodges of East Moddersham, Sir Conway Marth's place—one of *the* places. You can see it any Thursday. The avenue is half a mile long by this approach."

Chapter Five.

The Girl with the Happy Face.

As Derwent did not seem to feel any *very* lively interest in East Moddersham, and proud little Stasy reared her head at the very idea of going to see a show, like tourists, when, of course, they would there as guests!

But the mention of Alderwood had a different effect.

"Alderwood," repeated Stasy's mother, ignoring the young man's last words. "Do you mean Sir Adam Nigel's place? Why, it is quite at the other side of Blissmore, unless there are two Alderwoods. But that could scarcely be."

"Sir Adam Nigel," repeated the clerk in his turn, shaking his head. "I don't recollect the name. Alderwood is the residence of Mrs Lilford — that's to say, it is her property, but it has been let on a long lease to Lady Harriot Dunstan."

"Ah," said Mrs Derwent, turning to her daughters, "that explains it, then. Poor Sir Adam must be dead, for Mrs Lilford is a niece of his, a favourite niece, his brother's only child. I am surprised at her letting a family place like that; and yet it must be the same. Only I can't understand its being at this side of Blissmore."

"It is three or four miles off, quite the other way," said the young man, "but there is a view of it from this. It stands high, and I believe there is a short cut to it across the fields, skirting the town."

"I see," said Mrs Derwent consideringly. "Then you have never heard Sir Adam Nigel's name? Perhaps you are not a native of the place, however."

"No; I come from Yorkshire," replied he. "I have only been down here a few months."

"Ah; that explains it," the lady said again.

They strolled round the church, and gazed over to where they were told Alderwood *should* be seen, if it were clearer. But a slight mist was already rising, and there was a mist over the older woman's eyes too.

"Alderwood was close to my old home, you know," she whispered to Blanche.

Then they walked round the green and down the short bit of lane separating it from the high-road, the clerk staying behind to tell the flyman to follow them.

"How does it all strike you, Blanchie dear?" said Mrs Derwent, with some anxiety in her tone.

"I like the house very much indeed," the girl replied. "It might be made *very* nice. Would all that cost too much, mamma?"

"We must see," Mrs Derwent replied. "But the place — the green, and all these other new houses. What do you think of the neighbourhood, in short?"

"They are pretty, bright little houses," said Blanche, not fully understanding her mother's drift. "But I think, on the whole, I like the old-fashionedness of —"

"Of *our* house?" Stasy interrupted, clearly showing how the wind was setting in *her* direction.

Blanche smiled.

"Of *our* house, best," she concluded.

"Yes, oh yes, most decidedly," agreed Mrs Derwent. "But that was not exactly what I meant. I was wondering if the close neighbourhood of this sort of little colony may not be objectionable in any way."

"I scarcely see how," Blanche replied. "Of course, they are not the sort of people we should *know*; but still, these other houses make it less practically lonely. And once you look up all your friends, we shall be quite independent, you see, mamma."

"Of course," said Mrs Derwent, and she was going on to say more, when at that moment the sound of a horse or horses' feet approaching them rapidly, made her stop short and look round.

They were just at the end of the lane. A few yards higher up the road, on the opposite side, large gates, and the vague outline of a small house standing at one side of them, were visible. This was the entrance to the great house — East Moddersham — of which the clerk had spoken with bated breath. The sounds were coming towards where the Derwents stood, from the direction of the town, so, though they naturally turned to look, they in no way associated them with the near neighbourhood of the East Moddersham lodge.

There were two riders — a lady, and not far behind her, a groom. They were not going very fast; the horses seemed a little tired, and were not without traces of cross-country riding through November mud. Still they seemed to go by quickly, and as the first comer — a girl evidently, and quite a young girl — passed, a slight exclamation made both Mrs Derwent and Stasy start slightly.

"Did you speak, Blanchie?" said her sister; and as she glanced at Blanche's face, she saw, with surprise, that she was smiling.

In her turn, Blanche started.

"I—I really don't know if I said anything, or if it was she who did," she replied. "Did you see her, Stasy? Did you, mamma? It was the girl at the station—the girl with the happy face."

But neither her mother nor Stasy had known the little episode at the time, though they remembered Blanche's telling them of it afterwards.

"I wish I had looked at her more," said Stasy regretfully. "I didn't notice her face; I was so taken up in looking at her altogether, you know—the horse, and the whole get-up. It *did* look so nice! Shall we be able to ride when we come to live here, mamma? It is one of the things I have longed to be in England for."

"I hope so," said Mrs Derwent. "At least we can manage a pony and pony-carriage. I think you could enjoy driving yourselves almost as much as riding. I wonder who the girl is. Did she look as happy this time, Blanche?"

"Yes; it seems the character of her face. I couldn't picture her anything else," Blanche replied. "I wonder, too, who she is."

"She rode in at those big gates a little farther on," Stasy said.

Just as she spoke, the clerk came up to them again, followed by the fly. He overheard Stasy's last words, and ventured, though quite respectfully, to volunteer some information.

"That lady who just rode past," he said, "is Lady Hebe Shetland; she is a ward of Sir Conway's. A very fine-looking young lady she is considered. She has been hunting, no doubt. She is a splendid horsewoman."

"Of course, there is a great deal of hunting hereabouts," said Mrs Derwent. "It was my own part of the country in my young days."

And something in her tone, though she was too kindly to indulge in "snubs," made the young man conscious that the ladies were of a different class to most of the applicants for houses at the office in Enneslie Street.

They soon found themselves there again; Mr Otterson receiving them with urbanity, which increased when he found Mrs Derwent a prospective tenant, likely to do more than "nibble."

"I should have *preferred* a house on the other side," she said, "nearer Alderwood and Fotherley. Fotherley was my own old home."

"Indeed," said the agent, with secret curiosity. "I fear there is nothing thereabouts — really *nothing*. The new building has all been in the town, or quite close to it, with the exception of Pinnerton Green."

"Ah well, then there is no use in thinking of another neighbourhood," said Mrs Derwent.

And she went on to discuss the house that there *was* use in thinking of, after a very sensible and practical fashion, which raised Mr Otterson's opinion of her greatly.

There would be a good deal to do to it; of that there was no doubt. And repairs, and alterations, and embellishments are not done for nothing. Mr Otterson looked grave.

"The first thing to be done," he said, "is to get at an approximate idea of the cost."

"You cannot make even a guess at it?" said Mrs Derwent, glancing at the clock.

For it had been already explained to her that all but the most absolutely necessary work must be at her own expense.

The agent shook his head.

"Not till to-morrow morning," he said. "I have a very clever builder close at hand, who could give a rough idea almost at once, but not this evening. You are not staying the night at Blissmore, I suppose, madam?"

"We had not thought of doing so," Mrs Derwent replied doubtfully.

"It would save a good deal of time, and indeed the man would almost need to see you to receive your personal instructions," said Mr Otterson. "If it is impossible, perhaps you can manage to come down again next week."

Blanche looked at her mother, as if to ask leave to speak.

"Yes, my dear?" said Mrs Derwent inquiringly.

"I think, mamma, it would be a good plan to stay the night," she said. "It would be less tiring for you, and we should feel more settled if we knew a little more."

"I think so too," said Mrs Derwent. "We can telegraph to Jermyn Street, so that Herty and Aline will not be frightened. I suppose there is a good hotel here?"

Mr Otterson hesitated.

"There are one or two fairly comfortable, but not exactly what I should recommend for ladies," he said.

"It is not very often hotel accommodation is needed here. People come down for the day. I did not know — I thought perhaps you had friends in the neighbourhood."

"No, no one I could go to suddenly," said Mrs Derwent. "I daresay we shall manage well enough," and she was turning away, when a bright idea struck the agent.

"There are lodgings — private apartments — in the High Street," he said, "where you could certainly be accommodated for the night, and though it might be in a plain way, it would be quieter and more retired for ladies alone than the hotels. It is at number — What is Miss Halliday's number in the High Street, Joseph?" he called out to an invisible somebody in the inner office.

There was a moment's delay. Then the invisible somebody replied.

"Twenty-nine, sir — number twenty-nine."

"Exactly — twenty-nine. Miss Halliday has a small millinery establishment, but has more rooms than she wants — it is a good-sized house — and lets them to lodgers. And I happen to know that they are vacant at present."

"Thank you," said Mrs Derwent more cordially than she had yet spoken to the house-agent; "I think that sounds much better. We will drive round there at once."

"Mamma," said Blanche, when they were again in the fly, "it may be a very good thing to know of these rooms; for we may find it a convenience to come down here before the house is ready, to superintend its getting into order."

"Yes, that is a good idea," her mother agreed; "for I may find the hotel in London very dear. I really don't know. I could not get them to say anything very definite, but English hotels are always dearer than abroad, I believe. Yes, I really think we are very lucky."

This opinion increased when, in reply to the flyman's knock at Miss Halliday's door, it was opened by a neat, old-fashioned looking, little servant-maid of twelve or thirteen, who replied that her missis was in the shop, but she would see the ladies at once. It was evidently a case of lodgings, not bonnets, and the small damsel appreciated its importance.

Mrs Derwent and Blanche left Stasy, rather to her disgust, to wait for them in the fly, while they were shown into Miss Halliday's best sitting-room. A very nice old sitting-room it was, at the back of the house, looking out upon a long strip of walled-in garden, which in summer bade fair to be quaintly pleasant. And Miss Halliday matched her house. She was small and neat, with a certain flavour of "better days" about her, though without the least touch of faded or complaining, decayed gentility. On the contrary, she was briskly cheerful, though the tones of her voice were gentle and refined. She took in the situation at a glance, was honoured and gratified by the application, much obliged to Mr Otterson, and anxious at once to take upon her small shoulders the responsibility of making her visitors as comfortable as their sudden advent would allow.

"Tell Stasy to come in, Blanchie dear," said Mrs Derwent. "I have no doubt Miss Halliday will make us a cup of tea quickly, for we are cold and rather tired. — Will your servant ask the flyman his fare?" she added, turning to the little landlady; "and, oh, by-the-by, I forgot. Can I easily send a telegram?"

"The post-office is only two doors off," Miss Halliday replied. "Deborah shall run with it at once. And this room will soon be warm — the fire burns up very quickly once it is lighted — but if the ladies would honour me by stepping into my own little parlour across the passage. It is nice and warm, and tea shall be ready directly. Dear, dear, down from London to-day, and such cold weather! You must be tired, and longing for tea."

Now that they were free to rest, they *did* begin to feel tired, and very glad to escape the dark journey back to town, and the cold drive from the station. The bedrooms upstairs were aired and ready, as Miss Halliday was expecting visitors next week for a few days.

"There's a good deal of coming and going at Blissmore, nowadays," she said. "It's a very improving place by what it used to be, every one says," as she hospitably bustled about.

"You have not been here many years, I suppose," said Mrs Derwent. "I cannot remember this house. I don't think it used to be a shop in the old days, otherwise I should recollect it. There were not many shops here when I was a girl."

Miss Halliday looked deeply interested, but she was too well-bred a little woman to ask questions.

"If you were here a good many years ago, madam," she said, "you may remember my aunt, Mrs Finch, whom I succeeded. She had a nice little millinery business, and I came to her as a learner. Things had gone badly at home, after my dear old father died, and I was very glad to have the chance my aunt offered me. That was about seven years ago. There's been many changes here even since then, but the most of the building had begun before I came."

"Yes," said Mrs Derwent, "I had not heard anything of it. I was quite astonished to find how the school had increased. Mrs Finch, did you say? Oh yes, I remember her very well, but she did not live here—not in this house."

"No," said Miss Halliday, "my aunt lived in the Market Place—a small corner house. But we got on pretty well, and then we moved here to join apartments to the millinery. So many ladies disliked the hotels: they were noisy and rough. And it's answered pretty well on the whole."

"Then your aunt is dead, I suppose," said Mrs Derwent. "She must have been a good age, for when I remember her, she had already quite white hair and stooped a good deal. She used to retrim and alter my hats very nicely, and I remember how interested she was when my new ones came down from London. I was—my unmarried name was Fenning. My father was the rector of Fotherley, the village near Alderwood."

Miss Halliday looked delighted at having her curiosity thus satisfied.

"Oh indeed, madam," she said. "I'm sure I've heard my aunt speak of the late Mr Fenning. When I first came to Blissmore, the vicar of Fotherley was a Mr *Fleming*, and I recollect my aunt drawing a contrast, if you'll excuse my naming it, between that gentleman and his predecessor."

Mrs Derwent smiled.

"Yes," she said, "by all accounts there was a very marked contrast."

Then Deborah appeared to say that the fire was burning up nicely in the best parlour, and thither the ladies repaired to rest and talk. Blanche, the foreseeing, had taken the precaution of bringing a bag with a few necessary articles "just *in case* we were kept too late," and Miss Halliday was only too ready to lend anything she could, so the prospects for the night were not very alarming.

Altogether, the spirits of the little family improved; and when Miss Halliday's neatly prepared little supper made its appearance, they drew their chairs round the table, prepared to do full justice to it.

"I really think," said Mrs Derwent for the second time that day, "that we have been very lucky. It is nice to have found out these lodgings. We could stay here quite comfortably for a few weeks while the house is getting ready."

"It would certainly be much less expensive than a London hotel," said Blanche. "Yes, I do hope we may get to like Blissmore, if all goes through about the house."

"You mean you hope we shall like Pinnerton Lodge," said Stasy. "We needn't have anything to do with Blissmore, except, of course, that it will be our station and post-town. And I suppose we shall do a little shopping here. But, *of course*, we shall not know any Blissmore people. Mamma, I wish you'd begin to look up some of your old friends. That big place now, near us—East Moddersham. Didn't you know those people long ago?"

Mrs Derwent shook her head.

"It was as good as shut up in those days," she said. "The Marths were scarcely ever there, as the then Lady Marth was very delicate.—Do the present owners of East Moddersham live there much, do you know?" she inquired of Miss Halliday, who just then re-entered the room to see that her guests had all they wanted.

"Sir Conway and Lady Marth?" she replied. "Oh yes, they are there most of the year; they have several sons, some grown up and some still at school, and one quite little daughter. They are very much liked and highly thought of in the county."

"And," began Blanche, "there is a grown-up girl, is there not? A niece or a ward of Sir Conway's?" Miss Halliday's face grew still brighter.

"Lady Hebe, Miss, you must mean; Lady Hebe Shetland. Yes, she is their ward, and Sir Conway's niece too. A great heiress, and to my mind the most beautiful and charming young lady in all the country round. Her face makes one think of everything sweet and pleasant."

"And happy," said Blanche. "I never did see any one look so happy."

"She has everything to make her so," said Miss Halliday. "But that wouldn't do it without a happy *nature*."

"How old is she?" asked Stasy abruptly.

"Nineteen, I think, Miss. They do say she is engaged to young Mr Milward, a fine young gentleman, and well suited to her. But I don't know if it is true."

"Do you mean the Milwards of Crossburn?" said Mrs Derwent.

"Yes; that is where they live, I believe," was the reply.

"I hope it's not true that that girl of Blanche's is engaged," said Stasy, later in the evening, after she had been sitting silent for some time.

"Why?" said her sister, looking up in surprise; "what difference could it make to us?"

"All the difference. If she were married, she'd go away to a home of her own, and we would never see her. But living there, so near, she would be a nice friend for us. She is just about your age, Blanchie."

"Well," said Blanche, "we shall see. It is not even certain yet that we are going to live at Pinnerton at all."

"I'm sure we shall. I have a presentiment that we shall," said Stasy oracularly.

Chapter Six.

The Doctor's Wife.

Stasy's presentiment came true. The reports of the builder the next morning, when he called to enter into particulars with Mrs Derwent, were favourable; and later in the day the mother and daughters returned to London with very little doubt in their minds as to their future home being Pinnerton Lodge.

London looked very grim and dreary after the clear fine sky in the country, and Stasy shivered at the thought of how many days must yet forcibly be spent there, before they could install themselves in their new quarters.

But the things we dread are not always those that come to pass. Mrs Derwent, as I have said, was in some ways extremely inexperienced in English life and rates of expenses. Busy and eager about the arrangements for their new house, she put off asking for her hotel bill till fully a fortnight after the little party's arrival in London. And when she received it and glanced at the total, she was aghast!

"Blanche, my dear," she exclaimed, "just look at this. Is it not tremendous? Why, we might have lived at a hotel at home for nearly a year for what this fortnight has cost us!"

"Not quite that, mamma," said Blanche, smiling, though her own fair face was flushed with annoyance. "But, no doubt, it is very dear. And yet we seem to have lived plainly enough. Mamma," she went on decidedly, "we mustn't stay here; that is quite certain. All you have got in reserve for furnishing our house and paying for the alterations will be wasted, and what should we do then?"

Mrs Derwent sat silent, considering.

"You are quite right, dear," she said at last. "We must look out for lodgings. But I have a horror of London lodgings. They are so often detestable."

"Why stay in London at all?" said Stasy suddenly from her corner of the room, where, though engrossed with a story-book, her quick ears had been caught by the sound of vexation in her mother's voice. "I am sure it is horrid — so dull, and knowing nobody. Why shouldn't we go down to Blissmore, to that nice little Miss Halliday's, and stay there till the house is ready? We meant to go there for the last week or two, anyway."

Blanche's face lighted up, and she looked at her mother anxiously. But Mrs Derwent hesitated.

"It would certainly be comfortable enough," she said; "quite as comfortable as here. But to stay there for so long—for several weeks? Is it not rather lowering? I don't want to get mixed up with Blissmore people: they must be a very heterogeneous society; not like in the old days when there were just a very few thoroughly established people living in the town, whom everybody knew and respected."

"I don't see that we need know people we don't want to know, any more when living in the town than in the neighbourhood," said Blanche. "We can keep quite to ourselves; unless, of course, you can look up some of your old friends, who would understand how we were placed."

Mrs Derwent seemed perplexed.

"I wish I could," she said, "but I scarcely know how to begin. There seems nothing but changes. It is such a disappointment about dear old Sir Adam to start with."

"Still we are gaining nothing in that way by remaining in London," said Blanche. "And when at Blissmore you can find out about the people you used to know, and perhaps write to them."

"I can find out about them, certainly," Mrs Derwent agreed. "But I don't think I should actually write or suggest any one's calling, till we are in our own house, and have everything nice and settled. People are so prejudiced. They would immediately begin saying we lived poorly or messily because we had been so long in France."

"I don't think any one could live 'messily' in Miss Halliday's house if they tried. It is so beautifully neat," said Stasy, who had taken a great fancy to their little landlady. "Do let us go there, mamma. I am so tired of being here. London is horrid in winter, especially if you have no friends. And why should you and Blanche worry about the hotel bills, when there is no need, and none of us want to stay?"

And in the end, as not unfrequently happened—for there was often a good deal of wisdom in her suggestions—Stasy's proposal was adopted; so that about three weeks after their first arrival in England, the Derwents found themselves settled for the time being at Number Twenty-Nine in the old High Street of Blissmore.

It was not exactly the beginning of life in England which Mrs Derwent had pictured to herself. It was a trifle dreary to be back again, really back again in the immediate neighbourhood of her old home, with no one except Miss Halliday—herself a new-comer in the place—to welcome her and her children, or take the slightest interest in their advent.

"If there had been even one or two of our old servants left somewhere near," she could not help saying to Blanche that night, when Stasy and little Hertford had gone to bed, in high spirits at having really got away from "that horrid London," as they both called it. "But every one seems gone that I had to do with," she concluded, in a depressed tone.

"You really can't judge yet, mamma," said Blanche. "You haven't looked up anybody except Sir Adam Nigel, and you said you would rather wait till we were settled in our own house."

"I know I did. Oh yes, I daresay it will all be right enough. I am going to make out a list of all the friends I remember, and inquire about them by degrees. Some day soon we must drive over to Fotherley, Blanchie. Just think, I have never even seen your dear grandfather's grave! I am tired to-night, and everything seems wrong when one is tired."

Things did brighten up even by the next morning. The weather, though cold, was clear and bracing; very different from the murkiness of London, which had been peculiarly trying to nerves and lungs accustomed to the pure smokeless air of southern France. And the work at Pinnerton Lodge was already begun. It was most interesting to go all over the house again with the delightful sense of proprietorship, planning which rooms should be for what and for whom; how the old furniture would "come in," and what it would be necessary to add to it. And an occasional day in London, with definite shopping for its object, made Stasy allow that for some things, and in some ways, the great city was not altogether a bad place after all.

Still, though they were not "dull" in the sense of having nothing to do, and feeling in consequence listless and dreary, the little family felt curiously lonely.

Miss Halliday was no gossip — that is to say, she drew the line at the concerns of her visitors, and sternly refused to tell any of her cronies anything about them. And though this rule of hers was well known, still it added a slight element of mystery to her present lodgers, which, in reality, led to more gossip about them than they were in the least aware of. It was not often that visitors stayed so long at Miss Halliday's; as a rule, her rooms were merely taken as a half-way house for a very few days, by families pitching their tents in the now sought-after little town. And for some time no one knew anything about Pinnerton Lodge, as the distance between it and Blissmore was sufficient, in winter especially, to prevent much passing by. Added to which one of the good qualities of the Otterson and Bewley firm was discretion carried to the limits of surliness, in their determination that all knowledge of their clients' affairs should be confined to the office itself.

So Blanche and Stasy walked up and down the Blissmore streets, intent on such amount of shopping as Mrs Derwent would allow them to do there, or marched out bravely to Pinnerton and back, however cold it was, rejoicing in the "delightful English freedom," as Stasy called it, which made it possible for them to do so without any breach of accepted rules, innocent of the remarks and comments their appearance in public called forth.

"I *can't* make them out," said the wife of one of the doctors—Blissmore now rejoiced in four or five, though formerly one and an assistant had been all that was required—the wife, unluckily, of *the* doctor whose house in the High Street was nearest to Miss Halliday's. "I *can't* make them out. Do they never mean to know anybody or tell who they are? People who have come from abroad *should* tell all about themselves, or how can they expect any one to notice them."

Which was, to say the least, a begging-the-question kind of reproach, seeing that in no way had the Derwent family expected, or seemed to expect, the "notice" of Mrs Burgess or any of her coterie!

But it is not only the brave that chance sometimes favours. It favours the idle and inquisitive and the busy-bodies too, now and then. And I am afraid, without judging her too harshly, Mrs Burgess might come under these heads.

The chance was that of Stasy getting a sore throat. It was not a very bad one, but she was rather subject to sore throats, and the change of climate made Mrs Derwent extra cautious about her. It got suddenly worse one evening, and though Stasy was not cowardly or impatient when she was ill, she had to own to feeling pretty bad, and depressing visions of a quinsy she had had on one or two occasions rose before her.

"We must not trifle with it," her mother decided, and Miss Halliday was summoned and consulted as to sending for the doctor. Her own doctor, the one of oldest standing in the place, was unfortunately away for a few days, she happened to know. But there were others. Mr Meyrick was considered second best, but he lived quite at the other side of the town, and—

"I do not think it is anything complicated," said Mrs Derwent. "If we were at home"—and she sighed just a little—"I should know how to treat it myself. But I have forgotten the names of English medicaments, and, indeed, I doubt if we could get the herbs and simple drugs here at all. No, it is best to have a doctor. Who is the nearest, Miss Halliday?"

"Mr Burgess lives only a few doors off," the little woman replied. "And he is clever, I believe."

"But you don't like him, I see," said Mrs Derwent. "Is there anything against him?"

"Oh dear, no. But they — Mr Burgess and his wife — are not like Dr Summers and Miss Summers. Mrs Burgess has the name of chattering a great deal, and rather spitefully sometimes," Miss Halliday admitted.

The Derwents only smiled.

"That really does not matter," said the mother. "We shall have nothing to do with the wife. I think you had better send round for Mr Burgess and ask him to look in at once."

The throat was not a quinsy, but still rather troublesome and painful. Mr Burgess doctored it — or Stasy rather — skilfully enough, and being pleasant and good-tempered, a certain amount of friendliness naturally sprang up between himself and his new patient's family, including Stasy herself.

"*He* is not his wife, and you can say anything to a doctor," she replied to Blanche, when, some days later — by which time Stasy was almost quite well again — the elder sister was remonstrating with her for talking too fast to her new friend, considering the warning they had been given. "Besides, there is no secret about who we are, and where we come from, or anything about us."

"Certainly not," said her mother, "but we do not want these Blissmore ladies to begin calling upon us simply out of curiosity, and I did hear you saying to the doctor this morning that it was very dull not to have any friends here. I daresay he will have sense enough not to pay any attention to it, otherwise, it almost sounded like asking his wife to call."

But Stasy was sure she could not have been so misunderstood, and the subject dropped. Only, however, to be revived more disagreeably when, two days later, Mrs Burgess *did* call. Her husband was really not to blame for it, but he was an easy-going man, and, by a great show of sympathy "with the poor things," feeling so lonely as they must be doing, she extracted from him a reluctant half-consent to her taking advantage of his professional acquaintance with the ladies, whose doings had so occupied her empty head.

They were at home, and Deborah, somewhat overcome by the honour of a call from Mrs Burgess, admitted and announced her without hesitation. It was not in lady nature, certainly not in Mrs Derwent's nature, to be other than perfectly courteous in her own house to any visitor, however little desired, and, as was almost a matter of course with a woman of Mrs Burgess's calibre, she mistook the gentle gravity with which she was received for somewhat awe-struck gratification at her visit, and speedily proceeded to make herself very much at home, very much at home indeed.

This process consisted of several stages. In the first place, after ensconsing herself in the most comfortable chair—Mrs Burgess had a quick eye for a comfortable chair—and amiably waving her hostess to one conveniently near, and, as she expressed it, on her "best side"—for the doctor's wife was deaf—she loosened her cloak, remarking that, though cold out-of-doors, it was rather "warm in here," the ceilings were low, and low rooms get quickly "stuffy."

"Indeed," said Mrs Derwent. "I am sorry you find it so. We think these rooms very well ventilated. Old-fashioned, thick-walled houses are often warm in winter as well as cool in summer."

"Pr'aps so," said Mrs Burgess, "but I'm all for modern improvements. We've done a deal to our house; we'd almost better have rebuilt it. But you've been living abroad, I believe. Foreign houses are quite another style of thing, I suppose? Very rough compared with English."

Mrs Derwent could not repress a smile.

"'Foreign' is a wide word," she said, "if you mean it in the sense of anything or everything not *English*. No, I cannot say that we have been accustomed to living in very rough ways, and there are many beautiful houses in the south of France."

"Oh, the south of France!" repeated her visitor, who had not very clearly caught the rest of Mrs Derwent's speech. "Yes, I suppose that's very much improved by so many English going over there for the winters. And was it for health, then, that you lived there? These young ladies don't look so very strong. I must tell Mr Burgess to keep his eye on them—living so near, it would be quite a pleasure. But, oh, I was forgetting. You're thinking of living out of town a bit?"

"Yes," said Mrs Derwent. "I have taken a house at Pinnerton Green—Pinnerton Lodge."

Mrs Burgess screwed up her lips.

"Damp," she said oracularly. "I don't hold with all these trees. And these delicate girls—"

"Thank you, you are very kind," said Mrs Derwent, more stiffly; "but my daughters are *not* delicate, and—"

The only word that caught Mrs Burgess's ears was the objectionable adjective.

"Of course, of course," she repeated; "I could see it in a moment. But I'll tell you what you must do — have the trees thinned. That's what the Wandles did in their grounds at Pinnerton; they had the trees *well thinned*, especially at the side of the house, where the children's windows look out. Mrs Wandle is most kind. I'm sure a word from me, and she'd come to see you and tell you all about it. You don't know her, of course? Never mind; I'll ask her to call. You see this is a great tree country, and if you're not used to — "

"I know all about this part of the country very well, thank you; and I think it particularly healthy. I was brought up here, and we are not the least afraid of Pinnerton being damp," said Mrs Derwent, in her irritation adding more than she need have done, or had meant to do.

Mrs Burgess, in her eagerness at some volunteered information, had listened with extra attention.

"You were brought up here?" she exclaimed. "Where? Here, at Blissmore?"

"No; at Fotherley," Mrs Derwent replied, in a sort of desperation, thinking, perhaps, that the best policy would be to tell all there was to tell, and so get rid of this unwelcome visitor. "My father, Mr Fenning, was the vicar of Fotherley, and I lived there with him till a short time before his death. I married abroad, and have never been in England since."

"Dear, dear, how very interesting!" Mrs Burgess exclaimed. "I have heard the name, Mr Fleming of Fotherley; though, of course, it was before my time."

"*Fenning*, not Fleming," said Mrs Derwent, who had reason for objecting to this mistake.

"Ah yes; *Fleming*," responded Mrs Burgess serenely.

And Mrs Derwent, afraid of beginning to laugh out of sheer nervousness and irritation, gave up the attempt to set her right.

Then followed more cross-questioning, in which the doctor's wife was almost as great an adept as the smartest of great ladies. She varied her inquiries skilfully from mother to daughters, and back to mother again, till none of the three felt sure what sort of correct or "crooked" answers they had been beguiled into giving, and finally took leave in high good-humour, reiterating at the last that she would not forget to speak to Mrs Wandle; Mrs Derwent might depend upon her. "A word from me will be enough: we are such great friends. I am sure she will call as soon as she hears how anxious you are to see her."

As the door closed upon her, Mrs Derwent and Blanche looked first at each other, then at Stasy, who put on an expression of extra innocence and indifference. This hardened Blanche's heart.

"Well, Stasy," she said, "I hope you are satisfied. See what you have done by telling Mr Burgess we felt dull, and so on."

"*I* don't mind her having called," said Stasy, determined to keep up a brave front. "I think she is most amusing; and what possible harm can she do us?"

"Every harm of the kind; though, of course, I suppose one should try to be above those things," said Blanche doubtfully. "But still, we didn't come to live in England to have as our only friends and companions people we *cannot* feel in sympathy with. It is not wrong not to want to live among coarse-natured, vulgar-minded people, if it isn't one's duty to do so."

"There are vulgar minds in every class, I fear," said Mrs Derwent. "Still, that is a different matter. I do wish this had not begun; for I do not like to seem arrogant or ill-natured. And it is very difficult to keep a pushing woman like this Mrs Burgess at a distance, without being really disagreeable to her."

"We could stand *her* even," said Blanche, regretfully. "There would be a sort of excuse for it, as she is the doctor's wife; but it is all these other awful people she is going to bring down upon us, 'butchers and bakers and candlestick-makers,' like the nursery rhyme you used to say, mamma! And if other people — refined people — hear we are in the midst of such society as that, *they* won't want to know us. I wish we hadn't come to Blissmore."

It was not often that Blanche was so discomposed. Her mother tried to soften matters.

"It will only call for a little tact, my dear," she said. "I am sure we shall be able to make them understand. It is not as if we were going to live in the town."

"But Pinnerton Green is a nest of them," said Blanche.

"That won't matter so much. Once we are in our own house we can draw our own lines. And when other people — better people — come to see us, these good folk will keep out of the way," said Mrs Derwent.

"Well, I wish you would look up some of them, mamma," said Stasy. "For my part, I would rather amuse myself with the Goths and Wandles, than know nobody at all."

The others could not help laughing; but, nevertheless, Blanche still felt not a little annoyed. She was more concerned for her sister than for herself; for there was a vein in Stasy's character which sometimes caused her mother and Blanche uneasiness — a love of excitement and amusement at all costs.

"She *must* have some really good companions," thought the elder girl.

And that very evening she persuaded her mother to write to Mrs Lilford, Sir Adam Nigel's niece, recalling herself to that lady's memory. The letter was addressed to Alderwood, and marked "to be forwarded."

"I hope something will come of it," said Blanche. "And you must try to remember some other nice people, mamma; though, if Mrs Lilford is kind, she can do a good deal in the way of introducing us, even though she no longer lives here herself."

Chapter Seven.

Mrs Lilford's Tenant.

In the increasing interest of getting the house at Pinnerton Green into order, the arrival of the furniture from Bordeaux, the unpacking of various precious belongings which had been left to come with the heavy things by sea, all of which necessitated almost daily expeditions to the new home, Mrs Derwent and her daughters forgot to think much of Mrs Burgess and her unwelcome offers of introductions.

And as Mrs Wandle did not present herself, they began to hope that perhaps the doctor's wife was as short of memory as she was hard of hearing.

Still the latent fear was there, though what was to be done to evade the acquaintance, it was difficult to say.

One afternoon—a dull, December afternoon, when the air was misty and penetratingly cold, and one could only feel thankful it had not the addition of smoke to turn it into fog of the first quality—the little family was sitting in Miss Halliday's well-warmed, best parlour, glad that the walk to Pinnerton Lodge had taken place that morning, before the day had become so ungenial; and Stasy was proposing that, to cheer them up a little, they should have afternoon tea rather earlier than usual, when suddenly a sharp rat-tat-tat at the front door—for the house owned both knocker and bell—followed by a resounding tinkle, made them all start.

"Who can it be?" said Blanche. "It isn't often that any one both rings and knocks."

"A telegram," said Mrs Derwent. "No; that isn't likely. There is no one to telegraph to us."

Then Deborah was heard hurrying along the passage; her footsteps sounded as if she were somewhat flurried with the anticipation of a visitor of more importance than the postman or milkman. The ladies listened with curiosity, as a colloquy ensued between Deborah and some person or persons unknown, ending, after some little delay, by footsteps slow and heavy, following the small servant's patter along the passage.

Blanche glanced at her mother.

"Mrs Wandle," she ejaculated in a stage whisper.—"Stasy, jump up. For goodness' sake, let us be dignified to her."

For Stasy was sitting on a low footstool on the hearthrug, doing nothing, as was rather a favourite occupation of hers, and greatly enjoying the agreeable glow of the fire, which had sunk down to the pleasant redness preceding the sad necessity of "fresh coals," and the consequent "spoiling it all" for the next half-hour.

"Coal-fires are very interesting, I find," she had just been saying. "It almost makes up for the pleasure of turning the logs and seeing the sparks fly out, to watch the pictures in a coal-fire. The fairy castles and the caverns, and the— Oh, there is Monsieur Bergeret's nose! Do look, Blanche. Did you ever see anything so exactly like?"

But "Jump up, Stasy," was all the reply she got, and as the door slowly opened, a repeated whispered warning—"Mrs Wandle."

The name was not clearly audible which Deborah announced, but she announced *something*, and to the prepossessed ears of her audience it sounded as like "Mrs Wandle" as anything else. And in trotted, with as much dignity as a stout, short person can achieve, a lady enveloped in furs and wraps, who, after glancing round her with a sort of "nonchalant" curiosity, held out a somewhat limp hand to Mrs Derwent.

"How de do?" she began. "I heard from Mrs—" (afterwards, with a sensation of guilt and self-reproach, Blanche had to own to herself that the name had *not*sounded like "Burgess") "that you—I mean that she would like me to call, though it's quite out of my way to come into Blissmore. Are these your daughters?—How de do? how de do?"

And then she sank into a chair, apparently at an end of her conversational resources.

"What an impertinent, vulgar old cat!" thought Stasy, shivering prospectively at the "all your doings" which she felt sure were in reserve for her.

But aloud, of course, she said nothing, only sat motionless, her great dark eyes fixed on the stranger with a peculiar expression which Blanche knew well.

For a moment or two there was silence. Then Mrs Derwent's clear, quiet tones sounded through the room.

"I am sorry you should have inconvenienced yourself by coming out of your way to see us," she said. "I trust you will not dream of giving yourself the trouble a second time."

"Well, no, I don't think I shall," the visitor replied calmly. "I hear you are going to live at Pinnerton. I should be glad to show you the pictures, and anything else you care to see, if you come over some day. It's not a very long walk over the fields."

"Some of us go to Pinnerton nearly every day," said Mrs Derwent, "but it is too far for me to walk. When I go, I drive. But I did not know there was a short cut to Pinnerton. We have always gone by the road."

"I didn't say to Pinnerton," said the visitor. "I said *from* Pinnerton. *I* don't live there, but I heard you were going to live there."

"So we are," Mrs Derwent replied, rather bewildered.

Evidently this could not be *the* Mrs Wandle, the Pinnerton Green Mrs Wandle, that was to say, and yet—she had distinctly said that she had been *asked* to call upon them.

"You used to live in our neighbourhood, I hear," the stout lady proceeded. "Fleming, I think that was the name?"

"No," Mrs Derwent replied rather sharply. If there was one thing in the world she cordially detested, it was to be confused with the Fleming family, whom she remembered, before they came to Fotherley, as very objectionable. "No, my name was *Fenning*. My father was vicar of Fotherley, and Mr Fleming, who succeeded him there, and was once his curate, had a small living in the neighbourhood."

"Oh, indeed—yes, Fenning or Fleming. I knew it was some such name. Well, Mrs Flem— I beg your pardon, Mrs Derwent. If you like to come over some day when you are at Pinnerton, you can see through the house, even if I am not at home. I will leave orders. I can't promise to go to see you at Pinnerton, for it's quite out of my way. Even when I am at East Moddersham, I always go and come by the other side."

"At East Moddersham?" said the Derwents to themselves, more completely perplexed than ever. "Did the Wandles visit *there*?"

"East Moddersham is Sir Conway Marth's, is it not?" said Blanche. "Can you tell me if that charming-looking girl whom I have seen riding about there is his niece?"

The visitor looked at her for a moment without speaking. It was a calm, deliberate taking stock of her, of which Blanche felt the extreme though, quite possibly, not intended rudeness, and her cheeks grew crimson. On the whole, the taking stock seemed to result favourably.

"No, but she is his ward," the stout lady replied; "I suppose you mean Lady Hebe Shetland. She is very lovely," and a softer and more genial expression came over the plain face as she spoke. "You have lived a great deal in France, I hear," she went on, continuing to address Blanche. "It must have been a great advantage to you. I suppose you speak French *quite* well—without any accent?"

"Naturally," said Stasy, and her clear, rather shrill voice almost made the others jump. "How could we help speaking it perfectly, when it was the language of the country we were born and brought up in?" She got no reply. The lady glanced at her for half an instant, as if to say, "What an impertinent child!"—then turned again to Blanche. "I should like you to come to luncheon with me some day. I will let you know a day that I shall be quite alone, so that we could talk French all the time. I want to rub up my French. Mr Dunstan and I go abroad every year, and I like to speak French perfectly."

Then, quite satisfied that she had made herself most agreeable, the visitor rose, and saying as she shook hands, "I shall tell Mrs Lilford I saw you. And you must come over to see the pictures some day," she slowly made her way to the door, which Blanche had scarcely presence of mind enough left to open for her. There was no need to ring for Deborah, who was waiting in the passage, in a state of flutter.

"Deborah," said Blanche, as soon as the front door, disclosing a view of a ponderous-looking carriage in attendance, had finally closed, "Who is that lady? Is it a Mrs Wandle, or who?"

"Lor, Miss—Mrs Wandle! No indeed, Miss; its Lady Harriot Dunstan—the lady as lives at Alderwood Park."

Blanche went back into the sitting-room, and shut the door.

"Mamma," she said, "do you know who that was? It was Mrs Lilford's friend—at least I suppose she is her friend, as well as her tenant—Lady Harriot Dunstan."

"And we thought she was Mrs Wandle, the brewers wife!" said Stasy, going off into a fit of laughter. "Whoever she is, she is a vulgar, impertinent old cat.—Oh, mamma, are all English people so stupid and horrid? Why, she's worse than Mrs Burgess."

The mention of Mrs Burgess brought a look of annoyance to Blanche's face.

"It has all come of your hinting to Mr Burgess that we should like his wife to call, Stasy," she said. "Lady Harriot may not be the most charming or intelligent of human beings, but still, if we hadn't had our heads full of Wandles and Burgesses, we should have met her differently, and perhaps got on better with her. She must have thought us very stiff and queer in our manners."

"Yes," agreed Mrs Derwent, "I am sorry about it, certainly. This Lady Harriot seems the only direct link I have, as she is evidently an intimate friend of Mrs Lilford, Sir Adam's niece. It must be in consequence of my letter to Mrs Lilford that she has called. But—she surely cannot have been told much about us, or she would not have been so—so—"

"So horribly rude and patronising," said Stasy. "Oh, mamma, whoever she is, and even if we were never to make any friends at all, don't let us have anything to do with such people as that. And I—I used to think English people were all so nice and refined!"

The tears rose to her eyes—tears partly of disappointment and mortification, partly of vexation with herself. And instantly, as was always the case where Stasy was concerned, the hearts of her mother and sister softened to her again.

"My dear child, how you do rush at conclusions!" Mrs Derwent exclaimed. "Because we have come across two commonplace, perhaps I must say vulgar-minded women, you make up your mind that English society is composed of such people."

"And," Blanche added eagerly, "did you notice, mamma, how even Lady Harriot's dull face lighted up when she spoke of Lady Hebe? Mamma, I am perfectly certain that girl is as good as she is charming. It refreshes me merely to think of her face— Stasy, I wish you had seen her better."

"I did see her well enough. I thought she was lovely, and she looked as if she'd never had a trouble in her life. Oh, I daresay there are some nice people in England, but I don't believe *we* shall know any of them," said Stasy very lugubriously.

The next morning threw more light on the visit of the day before, for it brought a letter from Mrs Lilford. Mrs Derwent, guessing who was the writer, opened it with interest and some curiosity, but she had not read far before she startled her daughters with a sudden exclamation.

"What is it, mamma?" said Blanche.

"It is from Mrs Lilford, Sir Adam Nigel's niece," she said; "and, fancy, Blanchie—I am so delighted—he is *not* dead. Dear old Sir Adam, I mean. Listen. I may be hearing from him before very long."

And she went on to read aloud from the letter.

"I am glad to say that you have been misinformed about my uncle. Though he left Alderwood several years ago, at which time he gave it up to me, he is still living. His health would not stand English winters, and he spends eight or nine months of the year in Algeria. When I write to him next, I will tell him of your return to England. In the meantime I have asked my friend and tenant, Lady Harriot Dunstan, to call upon you, and I have no doubt she will be glad to be of any little neighbourly service in her power." Then followed Sir Adam Nigel's address, and a few sufficiently cordial words. But the tone of the whole was barely "friendly," though ladylike and courteous.

Mrs Derwent, however, was too pleased with the news of Sir Adam to think much of anything else.

"I am so delighted," she repeated — "so glad to think I shall see him again."

Blanche took up the letter, and toyed with it in her fingers. The distant Sir Adam seemed to her and Stasy of less importance than matters nearer at hand. Her silence caught her mother's attention.

"It is a nice letter," Mrs Derwent said.

"Oh yes," said Blanche; "but she doesn't seem very interested in us, mamma. And then, of course, as she has let Alderwood, she is not going to live here; so perhaps it doesn't very much matter. But I wish that Lady Harriot had been nicer."

Mrs Derwent's face lost its joyous expression.

"I wish Sir Adam were going to be at Alderwood again," she said with a little sigh. "*That* would have made all the difference. Mrs Lilford did not know me well. She was four or five years older, and she married and went to India before I was grown up. She only remembers me as a child more or less. But now I can write to Sir Adam himself, and he will be sure to ask some old friends to come to see us."

And that very day she did so.

But the result was not what she had hoped. A few thoroughly kind words from her old friend came in response in the course of a week or two, hoping to see her and her children on his return to England the following spring, but evidently not "taking in" the Derwents' present loneliness. "I hear from Amy Lilford that she has asked her tenants to look after you a little," he said. "I don't know them personally, but you will like to have the run of the old place again."

And Mrs Derwent could not make up her mind to trouble him further. "Men hate writing any letters that are not business ones," she said to Blanche. "We must just wait till he comes back in the spring, and make ourselves as happy as we can till then; though, of course, I hope some people will call on us as soon as we are settled. The Marths at East Moddersham could scarcely do less."

To some little extent her expectations were fulfilled. The wife of the vicar of Blissmore called. The vicar was a younger son of the important Enneslie family, enjoying the living in his father's gift after old-fashioned orthodox fashion, and Mrs Enneslie was a conscientious "caller" on all her husbands parishioners. She had perception enough to discern the Derwents' refinement and superiority at a glance, but she was a very busy woman, with experience enough to know that to be accepted by the "County," much more than these qualities was demanded. And she contented herself with such kindly attentions to the strangers as lay in her own power. She did a little more. She spoke of them to her brother, the Pinnerton Green parson, who promised that his wife should look them up as soon as they came under his clerical wing.

"They seem nice girls," she said, with perhaps some kindly meant diplomacy. "It would be good for them to do a little Sunday-schooling or something of that kind."

So the weeks passed, bringing with them the exasperating delays which every one in the agonies of house changing thinks peculiar to one's own case; and Christmas came and went before the Derwents could even name a time with any certainty for taking possession of their new home. It was a dull Christmas. Not that, with their French experience, the young people were accustomed to Yule-tide joviality; but they had heard so much about it—had pictured to themselves the delights of an overflowing country-house, the glories of a real English Christmas, as their mother had so often from their earliest years described it to them.

And the reality—Miss Halliday's best sitting-room, with some sprigs of holly, a miniature (though far from badly made) plum-pudding, no presents or felicitations except those they gave each other!

"Another of my illusions gone," said Stasy, with half-comical pathos, which drew forth a warning whisper from Blanche of "Don't, Stasy. It worries mamma," and aloud the reminder:

"Everything will be quite different when we are in our own house, you silly girl."

And when at last the own house did come, and the pleasant stage began of making the rooms home-like and pretty with the old friends so long immured in packing cases, and the new dainty trifles picked up in London, in spite of the fogs, for a short time they were all very busy, and perfectly happy—satisfied that the lonely half-homesick feeling had only been a passing experience.

"I am really glad not to have made new friends till now," said Mrs Derwent. "It does look so different here, though we have been very comfortable at Miss Halliday's, and she has been most good to us."

"Yes," Blanche agreed; "and I think we should make up our minds to *be* happy here, whether we know many nice people or not, mamma. The only thing I really care about is a little good companionship for Stasy."

"She must not make friends with any girls beneath her — as to that I am determined," said Mrs Derwent.

"Far better have none. Not that anything could make *her* common, but it would be bad for her to feel herself the superior; and I can picture her queening it over others, and then making fun of them and their homes and ways. She has such a sense of the ridiculous. No; Stasy needs to be with those she can look up to. I am sure, Blanche, it is better not to think of her going to that day-school at Blissmore."

For Stasy was only sixteen, and the question of her studies was still a question. At Blissmore, under the shadow of the now important public school for boys, various minor institutions for girls were springing up, all, as might have been expected, of a rather mixed class, though the teaching in most was good.

And Stasy, for her part, would have thought it "great fun" to go to school for a year or so.

The matter was compromised by arrangements being made for her having private lessons at home on certain days of the week, and joining one or two classes at the best girls' school at Blissmore on others, to which she could be escorted by Aline when she took little Herty to his day-school.

Chapter Eight.

Old Scenes.

By March the Derwents felt quite at home in their new abode; in one sense, almost too much so. The excitement of settling had sobered down; the housekeeping arrangements were completed, and promising to work smoothly. For Mrs Derwent had profited by her twenty years of French life in becoming a most capable and practical housewife, and being naturally quick and able to adapt herself, she soon mastered the little difficulties consequent on the very different ideas as to material questions of her own and her adopted country.

So that, in point of fact, time was in danger of hanging rather heavily on their hands; there was really so little to do!

Their peculiar position cut them off from many of the occupations with which most of us nowadays are only too heavily burdened. They had few letters to write, for Frenchwomen are not great correspondents—in the provinces, at least—and when the Derwents left Bordeaux, their old friends there extracted no promises of "writing very often—very, very often."

"Notes," of course, which in London seem to use up hours of each day, there was never any occasion for. They had no calls to pay, beyond a rare one at the vicarage; no visitors to receive. For the Pinnerton Green folk had not followed suit, as the Derwents had feared, after Mrs Burgess's invasion. Nothing had been heard of Mrs Wandle, and—probably through some breath of the great Lady Harriot Dunstan's visit, and Mrs Enneslie's introduction of the new-comers to her relations at Pinnerton Vicarage—the immediate neighbours had held back: the "butchers and bakers and candlestick-makers" had left them in peace. Mrs Burgess having been called away to a sick sister or niece early in the winter, and not yet having returned, even the excitement of watching her tactics had been wanting.

In short, the Derwents, socially speaking, were very distinctly in the position, to use a homely old saying, of "falling between two stools."

And though Stasy was the least to be pitied, for her lessons kept her pretty fairly busy, and she managed to find food for amusement and material for mimicry among her class companions—some of whom, too, she really liked—at Mrs Maxton's school, she was the readiest to grumble.

"What is the use of making the house pretty when there is no one to see it?" she said to her sister one afternoon, when the two had been employing themselves in hunting for early violets and primroses in the woods, with which to adorn the library, their favourite sitting-room. There were not many of these spring treasures as yet, for the season was a late one, but they were laden with other spoil, as lovely in its way — great trails of ivy and bunches of withered or half-withered leaves of every shade, from golden brown to crimson, which in sheltered nooks were still to be found arrested in their beautiful decay.

"What is the use of making the house pretty when there is never any one to see it?" Stasy repeated, as she flicked away an unsightly twig from the quaint posy she was carrying, for Blanche had not at once replied.

"There is always use in making one's home as pretty as possible. There are ourselves to see it, and the — the thing itself," replied Blanche a little vaguely.

"What do you mean by the thing itself?" Stasy demanded.

"The being pretty, or the trying to be — the aiming at beauty, I suppose, I mean," said Blanche. "Can't you imagine a painter giving years to a beautiful picture, even though he knew no one would ever see it but himself? or a musician composing music no one would ever hear?"

"No," said Stasy, "I can't. That sort of thing is flights above me, Blanchie. I like human beings about me — lots of them; they generally interest me, and often amuse me. I like a good many, and I am quite ready to love *some*. I want sympathy and life, and — and — well, perhaps, a little admiration. And I do think it's too horribly dull here; at least, I'm afraid it's going to be. I would rather leave off being at all grand, and get some fun out of the Wandles, and the Beltons, and all the rest of them."

"Mamma is still looking forward to Sir Adam's return in the spring — well, soon, it should be now. It *is* spring already," said Blanche, rather at a loss, as she often was, how to reply to Stasy's outburst.

"I don't believe he'll come to see us; or if he does, I don't suppose it would do us much good. He has been away so long, and is no use to the neighbourhood; and I believe that's all that most people care about," said Stasy cynically. "These families round about here live their own lives and have their own circles. They'll all be going up to London directly, I suppose, for the season. They don't want us, or care about quiet, not very rich, people like us. England isn't a bit like what I thought it would be."

"We can't quite judge yet," said Blanche. "And — I am sure you are too sweeping, Stasy. Mamma may have been too sanguine, and have seen things too much through rose-coloured spectacles, but she cannot be altogether mistaken in her pleasant remembrances of her old friends — the 'best' people — among whom she lived."

"Would you give Lady Harriot Dunstan as a specimen?" said Stasy snappishly.

"No; she would be a common-minded, inferior woman in *any* class," said Blanche. "I believe that is the truth of it all: there are refined and charming natures to be found in every class, and there are the opposite."

"Well, then, let us hunt up a few among the Blissmore *bourgeoisie*, and content ourselves with them," said Stasy.

"No," said Blanche again. "It is one's duty to live in one's own class unless one is plainly shown it is necessary to leave it. And that reminds me, speaking of Lady Harriot, I really think mamma should call there, now we are settled. She did not *mean* to be impertinent, we must remember."

"*I* don't need to go, as I'm not out," said Stasy. "Besides, one of us would be enough in any case. I would have liked to see Alderwood, though, but I *won't* go the way those Blissmore girls go, on a 'show' day — 'open to the public' — faugh!" with great disgust.

Blanche could not help laughing.

"How consistent you are," she said. — "Well, Herty," as at that moment her little brother came flying out of their own gate to meet them, "why didn't you come with us to the woods to gather leaves and hunt for violets?"

"I meant to come," said Herty regretfully, "but when I'd finished my lessons for Monday, you were gone, and I couldn't see you, though I ran as far down the road as I could. Oh, Blanchie," he went on, "I met such a nice lady riding. She saw I was looking up and down, and she stopped her horse and spoke to me. I asked her if she'd seen two girls like you and Stasy, and she said no, but if she did, she'd tell you I was looking for you. She said she knew you by sight, and she hoped we liked living at Pinnerton."

"Was it a young lady?" asked Blanche.

"Yes," said the boy, "and she came out of those big gates, nearly opposite the lane, you know. She had a nice face, not as pretty as *yours*, Blanchie, but about as pretty as —" And he glanced at his younger sister dubiously. "No, she wasn't like Stasy. She had a more shiny face."

"Thank you," said Stasy. "Perhaps she uses Pears's soap, which I *don't*."

Herty looked puzzled.

"That's not what I mean," he said. "It was a pretty, shiny way—out of her eyes, too. Not *soapy*. You are silly, Stasy."

"I know," said Blanche with interest, and not sorry to divert the quarrel, which she saw impending between the two—"I know who it was. It must have been the girl with the happy face—Lady Hebe. That was what Herty was trying to describe. You might say 'sunshiny,' instead of 'shiny,' Herty."

"Yes, that's what I meant," he said. "Her face smiled all over."

"And did you say we *did* like Pinnerton?" inquired Stasy with some eagerness.

"I said I did, except when I'd too many lessons; and I said Blanchie did, but Stasy said it was very dull."

Stasy looked uncertain whether to be pleased or vexed.

"What did she say?" she asked.

"She said it wasn't so bright here as in France, and she'd been there all this time since Christmas, and then she nodded and trotted away," was Herty's reply.

"I thought she must be away," said Blanche.

"Why—because she has not called upon us?" said Stasy, with what was meant for extreme irony.

"No," said Blanche quietly. "She could not call unless her friends did, of course, and I don't think the Marths are old acquaintances of mamma's. But I had a feeling that she was away. We should have met her, riding or walking about."

"I don't suppose she ever walks," said Stasy.

"Nonsense, Stasy! English girls are not like that. And don't you remember Mrs Harrowby, the vicar's wife, saying the other day that some of the girls in the neighbourhood were very good about the poor people, but that, unluckily, the most influential were seldom here. It was when she was telling us about the classes she wants to get up for some of the older girls."

"No," said Stasy, "I didn't pay attention. I suppose I thought she was speaking of the Miss Wandles and the Miss Beltons, and all the other Miss Somebodies or Nobodies. I don't care about poor people: it's not my line—excepting making a *quête*. I used to like doing that when I was a little girl."

Blanche said nothing. She had considerable experience of Stasy's contrariness.

But a certain pleasurable though vague sense of anticipation had made its way into her mind since hearing of Herty's meeting with Lady Hebe.

"I do feel so *sure* she is good and unselfish and thoughtful for others," she said to herself. "She may not have much in her power, but I feel as if she would like to be kind to us. I don't care so much for myself, of course, though it *would* be nice to know her; but it is for Stasy. I am so afraid of the friends she may make if she has not nice ones."

And Blanche's face looked anxious and perturbed as they re-entered their own little domain, laden with their pretty spoils.

Two things happened in the course of the next few days, which somewhat broke the monotony of the Derwents' daily life. The first was a drive to Alderwood, to return Lady Harriot's call. Blanche impressed upon her mother that whether the visit was expected of them or not, it was due to their own dignity to make it, notwithstanding the unfavourable impression that Mrs Lilford's tenant had left with them.

"If we don't call, she will think us fair game for patronising and condescending to. Of course we must, and we should have done so before."

"I have kept hoping to hear again from Sir Adam or Mrs Lilford," said Mrs Derwent. "I should much have preferred not to meet Lady Harriot till she understood better about us."

"She will probably ring the bell and tell the housekeeper to show us the pictures," said Stasy. "*You*, not 'us,' I should say, for, of course, I needn't go."

"You can go with us for the drive and wait in the fly outside," said Blanche.

For though they had been talking of a pony-carriage "in the spring," they had not yet heard of a suitable steed; and on the whole, perhaps Mrs Derwent was not sorry to defer for a little any avoidable expense, the installation at Pinnerton Lodge having cost, as is always the case in such matters, much more than she had anticipated.

Stasy received her sister's proposal with a laugh. "All right," she said. "Anything for a spree. I'll come."

Something in her tone slightly grated on Blanche.

"Stasy," she said, "I do hope even the little you see of those girls at Mrs Maxton's is not doing you any harm. You—you seem to be catching up their expressions."

"What b— nonsense!" said Stasy, quickly substituting the second word, though she could not help reddening a little. "Mamma, you know better than Blanche. Is there anything unladylike in 'all right,' or 'a spree?'"

"I can scarcely say, my dear," said her mother. "But I know what your sister means. It is the *tone* we—"

Stasy ran across the room and stopped her mother saying more, by a kiss.

"Don't be afraid," she said. "I'm not going to get vulgar and horrid. And some of those girls are really quite nice, mamma. I'll tell you what—I wish you'd let me invite one or two here one afternoon to tea. Oh, might I? It would be so nice. I'd like them to see you and Blanchie, and then you can judge for yourselves if the ones I bring aren't quite ladylike. It is so dull sometimes, mamma. Do say I may."

"I will think about it, dear," said Mrs Derwent. "It is not that I have any prejudice against the girls. I daresay there are among them truly refined and charming natures, but I do not want to open a visiting acquaintance in Blissmore. I did not bring you to live in England to fall into a lower social position than is naturally ours. It was not for that we left our dear old home at Bordeaux."

There was a slight catch in the mother's voice as she said the last words, that made both her daughters look at her anxiously.

"Mamma dear," whispered Stasy, "do you sometimes wish we *hadn't* left it?"

"I can't say, dear. I did it for the best, and we must be patient still," she replied.

But when the sisters were alone, Stasy confided to Blanche that she thought "mamma" just a trifle prejudiced and narrow-minded.

"Si on n'a pas ce qu'on aime," she said in her half-laughing, half-grumbling way, "*il faut aimer ce qu'on a*. If we can't have grand friends, much better content ourselves with common ones. We are not put into the world to live alone: anything is better than dullness."

"I am not so sure of that," said Blanche.

The next day they went to call at Alderwood.

It was a real spring afternoon, and though the air had still a touch of keenness in it, it was full of the exhilaration which is the essential charm of the childhood of Nature's year. In spite of some anticipatory shivers, Stasy persuaded her mother and Blanche to have the carriage open, filling it with shawls and rugs, "in case *they* should be cold," though as regarded herself, she felt sure that would be impossible.

The first part of the road was familiar to them, as they had to go some considerable part of the way to Blissmore before reaching the cross-country route to Alderwood, which lay on the other side of the town. But once they had turned in the Alderwood direction, a lovely view was before them, and the girls burst into expressions of pleasure; while to their mother, every cottage, every milestone almost, recalled her happy youth.

"I am so glad to find I remember it all so well," she said. "It makes me feel more at home than I have done yet. Is it not really a charming country? I wish we could have found a house near Alderwood."

"*I* don't," whispered Stasy, with a private grimace for Blanche's benefit.

When they reached the lodge gates and were driving slowly up the avenue, Mrs Derwent became perfectly silent, and her daughters respected her mingled feelings. For Alderwood in the old days, as they knew, had been almost as much "home" to her as the pretty Fotherley vicarage.

The anticipation of an interview with Lady Harriot Dunstan was a safe tonic against emotion or overmuch sentiment. And on the servant's reply that her ladyship was at home, it was with a perfectly calm and dignified demeanour that Mrs Derwent, followed by Blanche, got out of the fly and made her way up the stone steps and across the tiled hall to the inner vestibule, whence opened the drawing-rooms and morning-room, all of which she knew so well. She felt as if in a dream: every footfall seemed to carry her back a quarter of a century. But for a glance at the grave face of the fair, beautiful girl beside her, she could have fancied all the events of the intervening years to have been imaginary, and herself again "Stasy Fenning," running in with some message from "papa" to her kindly godfather!

Chapter Nine.

Afternoon Meetings.

When the door was thrown open, and the butler's sonorous tones announcing Mrs and Miss Derwent made the occupants of the room turn round, and the short, stout figure of their hostess came waddling towards all illusion was dispelled, and with a little sigh Blanche's mother came back to the very different present.

Lady Harriot, whose manners, as I have indicated, were not exactly "grande dame," looked, and honestly was, a little perplexed.

"How de do?" she said, with as much civility as she was in the habit of showing to any but her immediate cronies, and turning to Blanche, "How de do?"

Blanche happened at the moment to be standing in the full light, and as she looked down in calm response to the little woman's greeting, even obtuse Lady Harriot was struck by her incontestable beauty.

"She stood there like a picture," said one of the others present, when describing the momentary scene, and though the words were childish, they expressed the feeling.

Nevertheless, "the picture" was the first to take in the whole situation.

"Mamma," she said quietly, "I scarcely think Lady Harriot Dunstan recognises us."

"Oh yes, I do; at least I—I'm sure I've seen you before," began Lady Harriot, in a nearer approach to flutter than was usual with her. For, after all, she was "a lady born," as the poor folk express it, and conscious of the obligations of a hostess. "I'm sure I—"

"You were so good as to come to see us when we were staying temporarily at Blissmore," said Mrs Derwent clearly. "I believe you did so at Mrs Lilford's request. And I should apologise for not having returned your call sooner, but till quite lately we have been in the agonies of furnishing and moving into our house."

A light broke over Lady Harriot's face, but with the illumination her slight diffidence disappeared. She relapsed into her stolid, self-satisfied self, and the change was not an improvement.

"Oh yes, I thought I'd seen you before," she said. "I've been away, but you needn't have minded. I told the housekeeper after I saw you that you might be coming over to see the—"

"Aunt Harriot," said a masculine voice, suddenly breaking in at this juncture, "excuse me, but is there any reason why your friends and you should be standing all this time? If you specially want to remain in that part of the room, may I not at least bring some chairs forward?"

And then Blanche, lifting her eyes, saw that a man, a very young man he seemed to her at first sight, was standing not many paces off, behind Lady Harriot, slightly hidden by some intervening furniture or upholstery.

He came forward as he spoke, thus entirely disengaging himself from a little group — two or three women sitting, and another older man, who had also, of course, risen from his chair — at one end of the room, and Blanche's grave eyes scanned him with some interest.

It is sometimes — often — well that we are in ignorance of the unspoken thoughts of those about us, but it is sometimes to be regretted. A link of sympathy would have been quickly forged between the girl and the man in this case, had she known the words which almost forced themselves through his teeth.

"Those confounded pictures! Is Aunt Harriot an utter fool?" he said to himself. "To speak to women like these as if they were her maid's cousins asking to see the house!"

Lady Harriot turned, and a smile — the first of its kind that the Derwents had seen — came over her face, mellowing its plain features with a pleasant glow, for her husbands nephew, Archie Dunstan, owned perhaps the softest spot in her heart.

"Certainly," she said. "Won't you sit down, Mrs— Oh, I know," triumphantly, "Mrs Fleming?" Irritating as it was, Blanche *could* not repress a smile; and the smile, like an electric spark, darted across to Archie Dunstan, and was reflected in his face. Mrs Derwent flushed slightly; she too was more than half inclined to laugh.

"No, Lady Harriot," she said, "I am sorry to contradict you, but in this instance you do not 'know.' My name is Derwent. It used to be *Fenning*, in the old days when this house was almost home to me."

Mrs Derwent's intonation, as has before been mentioned, was remarkably distinct. Her words penetrated to the group of ladies, and a slight rustle ensued. Then a very tall, thin, still wonderfully erect figure came forward, both hands outstretched in welcome.

"Then are you Stasy?" said a tremulous, aged voice—"little Anastasia Fenning? And can this be your daughter? Dear me—dear me! Do you remember me? Aunt Grace—Sir Adam's cousin? I *am* pleased to see you again." And the very old lady stooped to kiss her long-ago young friend on the cheek.

"Aunt Grace!" repeated Mrs Derwent; "oh, I *am* glad to see you;" and her eyes glistened with more than pleasure. It seemed the first real welcome to her old home that she had received.

Lady Harriot stood by, trying to look amiable, but feeling rather bored.

"How very interesting!" she said. "You've met before, then. Isn't it nearly tea-time? Do sit down, Aunt Grace; you will be tired if you stand so long." But Mrs Selwyn would not sit down till she had drawn Mrs Derwent to a place beside her.

"Tell me all about yourselves," she said. "What a lovely daughter! She must know Hebe.—Hebe, my dear," and she turned to look for her.

But "Hebe has gone, Mrs Selwyn," said one or two voices, the older of the two men adding: "She is to be with us to-night, and Norman was to meet her at the lodge, I think."

"Oh, I am sorry," said the old lady; and then seeing the puzzled look on Mrs Derwent's face, she went on to explain. "Hebe Shetland is the grand-daughter of one of my earliest friends. She is an orphan, and lives with the Marths, and she is a delightful girl Lady Harriot is really my niece on the other side, for she is no relation to Sir Adam or Amy Lilford, whom you remember, of course?"

"Yes," said Blanche's mother, "but not very well. Dear Sir Adam, *of course*, I remember as well as I do my father. But I began to think something must have happened to him—he never answered my first letter." And she went on to tell how she had written to ask Mrs Lilford about him, and had at last received a letter from himself. And then she repeated her expressions of pleasure at meeting Mrs Selwyn.

"I am only here for a few days," said the old lady. "In fact, I leave to-morrow. I wish I could have seen more of you, but I fear it is impossible. I shall be back in the autumn again, however, if I am still alive. And you are sure to see Adam when he comes to England."

"I hope so, indeed," said Mrs Derwent fervently.

Mrs Selwyn looked at her with kind and understanding eyes.

"You must feel rather strange," she said, "and perhaps a little lonely, after your long absence and the complete change of life. And some English people are so dull, so slow to take in an idea. She," with a slight inclination of her head towards their hostess, "is a good woman in her way, but intensely dull and narrow. And I don't think you would care much for Lady Marth. However, in this world one has to make the best of one's neighbours, as well as of a good many other things. Now tell me all you can about yourself and your children. But first—Archie, I want to introduce you to my very old friend's daughter—Blanche, did you say her name was, Stasy? How well it suits her!"

"Archie" asked nothing better; and in another moment—for he had a great gift of chatter—he was talking to Miss Derwent in his most charming manner, Blanche listening quietly, with a slight suspicion of condescension in her tone, which greatly amused the young man. For, after all, he was not so young as he looked. It set him on his mettle, however, and made him feel it a positive triumph when he succeeded in drawing out a smile of amusement, which lighted up her blue eyes into new beauty.

All this time—though, in reality, no very great stretch of minutes had passed since the mother and daughter first entered the room—Stasy was waiting in the fly outside. But, after a while, the distractions of wondering how her mother and Blanche were "getting on;" of listening to the observations which the driver from time to time addressed in a sleepy voice to his horse, while he lazily tickled its ears with the end of his whip; or of peering in as far as she could see, in hopes of a gleam of primroses among the thick growing shrubs at one side of the house, began to pall upon her. And the tantalising possibility of the primroses so near at hand carried the day.

Out of the carriage stepped Miss Stasy.

"If any one should meet me, or if mamma and Blanche were vexed, I could say I was getting too cold sitting still, which would be perfectly true," she said to herself.

There was no getting in among the shrubs and trees from the immediate front; but the yellow specks were more clearly visible, and Stasy was not a girl to be easily baffled when she had got a thing in her head. So she made her way round by a side path skirting the house at some little distance, saying to the driver as she passed him, that if the ladies came out, he was to say she would be back immediately. The path was somewhat deceptive; it led her further than she knew, till she suddenly came out on a broader one bearing away towards another drive some way off at the back of the house, ending in a small lodge on the road to Crossburn.

A sort of curiosity led Stasy on.

"I'll look for primroses as I go back," she said. "I do like finding out about places. I wonder if this way would take us back to Pinnerton across the fields somehow."

Everything was perfectly still. She stood some little way up the drive, looking towards the gate, and wishing she dared venture as far as the road without risk of keeping her mother and Blanche waiting. The ground was dry and crisp; last year's leaves were still lying thickly; and at the other side of the drive a small fir-wood was attractively tempting.

"I wish our woods at Pinnerton were more firs than all mixed kinds of trees as they are," thought Stasy. "I do love cones so, and the pricks make such a nice crackle when you walk on them. We used to get tired of the fir-woods at Arcachon, I remember. I think there is something fresher about them in England."

And with a sigh at having to cut short the delights of her exploration, she was turning to retrace her steps, when a sound fell on her ears which made her stop short.

It was a woman's—a girl's—voice, singing softly, but clearly, the old ballad of "Robin Adair." Stasy had never heard it; but she was of a sensitive and impressionable nature, and the indescribable charm of the song fell upon her at once. She stood motionless, till, in another moment, the figure of the singer, advancing towards her, grew visible.

"I knew it was a girl," thought Stasy. "I hope she won't leave off, I wish I could hide."

She glanced round her. There was no possibility of such a thing; and in another moment the new-comer had seen her, and had left off singing. She stopped short as she came up to Stasy, and glanced at her inquiringly, with a slight, half-comical smile.

"Have you lost your way?" she said. "Are you not one of the Miss Derwents? It seems always my fate to be directing one or other of you. I met your little brother a day or two ago, looking as if *he* had lost his way."

"No," said Stasy laughing; "he had only lost *us*. And I have not lost my way either, thank you. I am waiting in the fly at the door for my mother and sister, who are calling on Lady Harriot Dunstan."

"*Are* you?" said Lady Hebe. "*I* should have said, do you know, that you were wandering about the woods at the back of the house, looking for—I don't know what."

Stasy laughed again. There was something infectious about Hebe's comical tone.

"Primroses," Stasy replied promptly. "It was primroses that first lured me out of the fly, I think. But now I'm beginning to be afraid that mamma and Blanche may be waiting for me; perhaps I had better go back."

"They can scarcely be ready yet," said her new friend. "They had not come in when I left the drawing-room, and I have not been long. I only stopped a minute or two to speak to the dogs. There are some dear dogs here. And tea was just about coming in. No; you are safe for a few minutes yet. Would you"—and she hesitated a little—"would you like to walk to the lodge with me, and a little way down the road I can show you another way back to the front of the house?"

Stasy was delighted.

"We know who each other is—or are—oh dear, how can I say it?" she replied as they walked on, "though we have never been introduced. I am only sorry you were not in the house there when Blanche came in. She would have liked to see you so much."

Lady Hebe's face flushed a little.

"I wish I had been," she said. "We must have had the same feeling. I have wanted to meet your sister. I love her face, though I have only seen her twice. Perhaps, some day—" Then she hesitated. "I was rather hurried," she went on; "I promised to meet—a friend, who will walk back to Crossburn with me."

"Then you are not staying here, at Alderwood?" said Stasy.

"Oh no; I am not staying anywhere, except at what is my home—East Moddersham, near you. I came over here this afternoon to see Lady Harriot, or, rather, to see a dear old lady who is staying here. I sent my ponies on to Crossburn, as I am dining there, and shall dress there, and drive home late."

"How nice!" said Stasy. "How delightful to have your own ponies and do exactly as you like! I do think English girls have such nice lives—so much fun and independence. I should have liked England ever so much better than France if I had been brought up in it, but as it is—" And Stasy sighed.

Lady Hebe listened with great interest. "And as it is," she repeated, "do you not like it?"

"It is so very dull," said Stasy lugubriously. "At least, *I* shouldn't find it dull if I might amuse myself in ways mamma and Blanche would not like."

Hebe looked rather startled, but Stasy was too engrossed with her own woes to notice it. "I mean," she continued, "that there are some girls at the school I go to for classes, who are really nice, and there are lots who are very amusing. But mamma and Blanchie don't want me to make friends with them, because, you see—well, they are not exactly refined."

"I see," said Hebe gravely; "and, of course, I think your mother and sister are quite right. But I can quite understand that it must be dull—for your sister too, is it not? She is not much older than you."

"No," said Stasy, "but she is *different* She has always been so very, very good, you see. She *has* never been—well, rather mischievous, and wanting a lot of fun, you know."

"But she doesn't look dull," said Hebe. "She has a very bright expression sometimes in her eyes. I am sure she has some fun in her too. I don't think I could have been so attracted by her if she had not had fun in her; I am so fond of it myself," she added naïvely.

"Oh yes," said Stasy, "Blanchie is *very* quick, and very ready for fun too. But she never grumbles. If things we want don't come, she is just content without I'm not like that. Next to fun, I like grumbling. I couldn't live without it."

Hebe smiled, but in her heart she was thinking that there *were* some grounds for complaint in the present life of these pretty and attractive girls. They attracted her curiously; they were so unlike others—so refined, and yet original; so perfectly well-bred, and yet so unconventional.

"I wish," she began, but then she stopped. What she was going to wish was nothing very definite, and yet it was better, perhaps, left unexpressed.

"When I am married," she thought, "I shall have more in my power in many ways. Norman will understand; he always does. I fear there would be no use in trying to get Lady Marth to be kind to them. She would only think it one of my 'fads.'"

But suddenly Stasy started.

"I am afraid," she said, "that I am going too far, and mamma and Blanche may be looking for me. Perhaps I had better go back now."

"I don't think they are likely to have come out yet," said Hebe. "But I don't want to make you uneasy, so perhaps you had better go back. Good-bye, and—I hope we may meet again soon."

She held out her hand, and Stasy, looking at her as she took it, felt the indescribable charm of the sweet, sunshiny face.

"Yes," she thought, "Blanche was right, and Herty was right. She is lovely."

"I do hope so," she replied eagerly, as they separated. Lady Hebe walked on, thinking. For she thought a good deal.

"Poor little thing," she said to herself, "it must be very dull. Yet they have each other, and their mother: the only things that have ever been wanting to me, they have! But still, the strangeness and the loneliness, and the not having any clear place of their own. I wonder they cared to settle in England; I wonder if there is nothing I can do for them."

She had reached the lodge gates by this time. A little further down the road — scarcely more than a lane — was a stile, on the other side of which lay the field path, which was the short cut to Crossburn.

And leaning by the stile was a figure, which, at the first glimpse of Hebe emerging from the Alderwood grounds, started forward, hastening across with eager gladness; young, manly, full of life and brightness, he seemed almost a second Hebe, in masculine form.

"Norman," she exclaimed, "I haven't kept you long waiting, have I?"

"I enjoyed it, dear: not very long. I liked to watch for the first gleam of you," he said simply.

And together, in the long rays of the soft evening sunshine, the two young creatures made their way across the fields.

"What have I done," said Hebe Shetland to herself — "what have I done to be so very, *very* happy?"

Chapter Ten.

At the Vicarage.

The second event which about this time made a little break in the monotony of the lives at Pinnerton Lodge came out of the first; for it was the result of much consideration on Lady Hebe's part as to what she could do to enliven things for these two girls, who seemed in a sense to have been thrown across her path.

She knew that it was useless to appeal to Lady Marth, her guardian's wife—a woman who had deliberately narrowed her life and her sympathies by restricting all her interests to a small and very exclusive clique, which was the more to be regretted as she was naturally intelligent and quick of discernment, without the excuse of poor Lady Harriot Dunstan's intense native stupidity. But Hebe managed to have a good talk with Mrs Selwyn—"Aunt Grace"—the very morning after the Derwents' visit to Alderwood, and Aunt Grace's own interest in the new-comers being keen, she was delighted to find Hebe's enlisted on their behalf.

"I am very sorry I am leaving so immediately," said Mrs Selwyn. "I might have been of a little use to them, even though very little. You see, no one is altogether to blame in a case like this. Life is short, and there are only so many hours in each day, and no one can be in two places at once, or full of conflicting interests at the same time. People who are half their lives in London, in the thick of the things of the day, all have too much upon them; it *is*difficult to get to know much of those who are quite out of it. And the Derwents are only half English, too."

"Then do you think it a mistake for them to have come to live here?" said Hebe.

"I scarcely know; I can't judge. They have put themselves in a *difficult* position, but there may have been excellent reasons for their leaving France. If they are very high-minded, superior women, they may be happy, and make interests for themselves, and not fret about things they cannot have. Certainly they—the mother, I should say—is far too refined to struggle or strain after society."

"And the elder one is, I do believe, an extraordinarily high-minded girl," said Hebe, with a sort of enthusiasm. "Still, it isn't fair upon her to be shut out from things; and the little one, though she is as tall as I"—with a smile—"says frankly that she finds it woefully dull."

"And she is only sixteen," said Mrs Selwyn; "not out, and with French ideas about young girls. Dear me, it must be very dull indeed for a girl brought up on those lines to think it so."

"She is not the very least French in herself," said Hebe. "Just a touch of something out of the common in her tone and manners, perhaps. But I never met a more thoroughly English girl in feeling. Yes, indeed. What will she think when she *is* grown up?"

"Let us hope that things may improve for them a little, before then," said Mrs Selwyn.

Then the two—the old woman and the young—put their heads together as to what they *could* do; the result being that, three or four days after the drive to Alderwood, a note was brought to Blanche one morning, inviting her and her sister to afternoon tea at the vicarage.

"I expect one or two young friends living in the neighbourhood," wrote Mrs Harrowby, the vicaress, "whom you may like to meet, and who, on their side, have some hopes of getting you to help in their little local charities."

"Humph," said Stasy, when Blanche read this aloud; "I've no vocation for that sort of thing. I think you had better go without me."

"No, I certainly won't," said her sister, without much misgiving. For she saw that, notwithstanding Stasy's ungraciousness, she was secretly pleased at even this mild prospect of a little variety.

Mrs Harrowby's attentions hitherto—though her good offices had been bespoken for the Derwents by her brother at Blissmore—had been less friendly, and more, so to say, professional. She was a very busy woman, almost too scrupulous in her determination to be "the same to everybody," to show no difference between her bearing towards the retired tradespeople of Pinnerton Green, and towards Lady Marth, or other county dignitaries; the result being, that no attention she ever paid to any one was considered much of a compliment. But she was well-born and well-bred, though not specially endowed with tact.

And she was honestly pleased when Lady Hebe appealed to her to suggest *something* that might help to enliven the sisters at Pinnerton Lodge.

"Yes," she agreed, "I have thought it must be very dull for them. And yet I could not exactly take it upon me to suggest their making friends with their neighbours here. Something in their manner has caused a slight prejudice against them. None of the families here have called."

"What neighbours or families are you talking of, Mrs Harrowby?" said Hebe quickly. She knew the vicar's wife very well—knew, too, her peculiar way of looking at social things, and was not in the very least in awe of her. "Lady Harriot has called, though —"

"Of course, I was not speaking of neighbours of that kind," replied Mrs Harrowby, interrupting her. "I meant the Wandles at Pinnerton Villa, and the Bracys: I am sure Adela Bracy is as nice a girl as one could wish to see, and Florence Wandle is good-nature itself. It is much wiser, as well as more Christian, to throw aside those ridiculous ideas of class prejudice, and make the best of the people you live among."

"Then why should not all the county people call upon the Derwents, as well as the Wandles and Bracys?" said Hebe, with a very innocent air.

Mrs Harrowby coloured a little.

"I don't know. I don't see why you should blame them if they don't, as you evidently don't blame the Derwents for standing off from the Green people. But, the fact of the matter is, they would have nothing in common with the Derwents. You know yourself, Hebe, Lady Marth *couldn't* find anything to talk to Mrs Derwent about — now, could she?"

"She could if she chose," said Hebe; "but I don't want to talk about Josephine" — she always called her guardian's wife, who was still a comparatively young woman, by her first name — "she and I don't agree on several points, but she is very good to me. I am not going to urge her calling on Mrs Derwent, for she wouldn't, if I did. And I don't think the Derwents could possibly like the only side of herself she would show them. But putting her aside, I certainly don't see that the *Derwents* would have 'anything in common' with the Wandles and people like that, if you take that ground."

"Then they *should* have," said Mrs Harrowby, who was apt to take refuge in didactic utterances, when she found herself driven into a corner.

Hebe laughed.

"We have not come to the point at all, though we have been talking all this time," she said. "What I was thinking of was some plan for enlivening the Derwent girls a little. *At present,*" and she blushed slightly, "I can do nothing, but supposing we ask them to help us with our girls' guild? You do want to improve it, don't you? The last meetings have been so deadly dull. And we were speaking of some new things — cooking lessons, was it?"

"Yes, we spoke of that, but I think we must wait till one of the professional cooking ladies comes round. We were speaking of millinery lessons — the girls do make such vulgar guys of themselves."

"That would be nice," said Hebe. "I daresay Miss Derwent could help us. And we must have some treats for the girls when the weather is quite warm enough. Let us have a meeting, and talk it all over. You can ask Miss Wandle and Miss Bracy, and I will get Norman's sister to come, though it is rather beyond their part of the country. For she might get leave to invite the guild to Crossburn. Yes, do let us have a nice afternoon-tea meeting *here*, and talk it over comfortably."

Mrs Harrowby consented. There were not many people who could refuse Hebe anything she had set her heart upon. Besides, the vicars wife had no objection to the proposal. She was kind-hearted, if a trifle dictatorial, and not without a pleasant strain of humour, as well as a fair amount of sympathy.

So, on the appointed afternoon, Blanche and Stasy made their way to the vicarage.

"How pretty you look, Blanchie!" said Stasy, with a gush of sisterly enthusiasm. "I do think you are getting prettier and prettier. England suits you, I suppose," with a little sigh.

Blanche laughed.

"Suits my looks, I suppose you mean?" she said lightly. Stasy's admiration amused, but did not much impress her. Indeed she was not of the nature to be much impressed by any admiration. She knew she was "pretty," as she called it to herself, but the subject never dwelt in her thoughts. And she was entirely without vanity. Many a girl of far less beauty, of no beauty at all, gives a hundred times more consideration to the question of outward appearance than would have been possible under any circumstances for Blanche Derwent.

There seemed to be quite a number of people in the vicarage drawing-room when they entered it. Stasy — who, to tell the truth, was feeling a trifle shy, though wild horses would not have drawn such a confession from her — had insisted on coming some minutes later than the hour at which they had been invited.

"I don't want to seem so very eager about it," she said to Blanche. "And if we go early, we are sure to be set down to talk to some of the Green people. It would be horrid."

To some extent, she was caught in her own trap. A chair was offered her between two girls, neither of whom she had seen before, and who, she immediately decided, must belong to the neighbours she certainly had no reason to feel friendliness towards. For, whatever had been the motive, and though very possibly their staying away was from the social point of view more gratifying than their calling would have been, no kindliness of any kind had been shown or attempted by the good folk of Pinnerton Green to the little family who had come as strangers among them.

Stasy glanced cautiously at the girls beside her. One was plain, not to say ugly, and dressed with almost exaggerated simplicity. Her features were heavy and ill-assorted; her nose was large, and nevertheless seemed too short for the curious length of her face; her eyes—no, she was not looking Stasy's way—her eyes could not be pronounced upon.

"She is really ugly," thought Stasy; "I haven't seen any English girl as ugly as she is. And how very plainly she is dressed: I wonder if it is because she knows she is ugly. It cannot be that she's poor: all these common people here are rich. Her dress is only"—Stasy gave another covert glance at the cloth skirt touching her own—"only—no, it's good of its kind, though so plainly made, and yet—"

Yes, there was a "yet," very decidedly, both as to dress, which was the very best of its kind, and, when the girl slowly turned to Stasy with some trivial remark, as to looks. For her eyes were beautiful, quite beautiful, with the touch of pathos in them which one sometimes sees in eyes which are the only redeeming feature of an undeniably plain face.

"Have a little indulgence for me—I cannot help myself," such eyes seem to say, and Stasy, sensitive as quicksilver, responded at once to the unspoken appeal.

"Thank you," she said gently, "I have plenty of room—no, I don't mind being near the window," and then she salved over to herself her suavity to "one of those Wandle or Bracy girls," by reflecting that Blanche had said it would be very wrong indeed to show anything but perfect courtesy and kindliness at a party especially arranged for a charitable object, though a slight misgiving came over her when the owner of the beautiful eyes spoke again in an evidently less conventional and more friendly tone.

"That was your sister who came in with you, was it not? I am so glad to see her more distinctly. She is so—so very lovely."

Stasy, gratified though she felt on one side, stiffened slightly. Miss Wandle should not comment upon Blanche's appearance, however favourably.

"Yes," she said, "every one thinks so. *I* do, I can't deny."

Then she turned to her neighbour on the right. She was a pretty girl, with wavy brown hair, and a charming rosebud of a face. But her dress, though much more studied than the austere but perfectly fitting tweed, jarred at once on Stasy's correct instincts. So did her voice, when in reply to the inquiry as to whether any guild business had yet been transacted, she said:

"Oh no, we always have tea first. Mrs Harrowby says it makes us feel more at" — was there or was there not a suspicion of the absence of the aspirate, instantaneously and almost obtrusively corrected? — "at — at *home*; not so shy about speaking out, you know."

"Oh indeed," said Stasy.

Then she turned again to the heavy face and the luminous eyes, in whose depths she now read a twinkle of fun.

"I like you, whoever you are," she thought. And as at that moment Hebe came up with outstretched hand and cordial "How do you do? You found your way the other day, I hope?" an irrepressible little burst of enthusiasm made its way through her caution.

"Is she not charming? She is always so perfectly sweet and happy," she said.

"Yes indeed," her neighbour replied, and the bright responsive smile on her face made one forget everything except the eyes. "She is — *perfectly* charming. I like to see that she gives the same impression to strangers as to those who have known her long. I can remember her nearly all my life, and yet every time I see her there seems something *new*. She is — I daresay you know? — she is going to be married to my brother Norman. Won't it be delightful to have her for a sister?"

And again the beautiful eyes gleamed with something brighter than their ordinary expression of appeal.

Stasy gasped. Who, then, was this girl? For an instant, a wild, ridiculous idea rushed through her mind that Lady Hebe must be going to marry one of the Wandles or Bracys, so prepossessed was she with her first guess about her plain-featured neighbour. But she dismissed it at once, and she began to feel shocked at her own want of discernment.

The colour mounted into her face as she replied to her companions question.

"I didn't know; at least," hesitatingly, "I am not sure. I think I did hear something, but I can't remember. I— Please don't think me rude, but I don't know your name."

"I am Rosy Milward. We live at Crossburn, the dearest old, old house in the world," said the girl.

"Oh!" said Stasy. "Yes, I have heard your name. It will be delightful to have Lady Hebe for your sister."

But her tone was slightly melancholy. She had been cherishing, half unconsciously perhaps, dreams of special friendship, romantic friendship, between Lady Hebe and herself (though she called it "us," reluctant to leave out Blanche from anything so charming). And now her dreams seemed shattered. She—Hebe—was going to be married, and here was a sister-friend all ready made for her. It was much better never to expect to see or know any more of the future wife of Mr Norman Milward.

Rosy was conscious of the underlying disappointment, though she could not have defined it.

"I wish I could invite them to come to Crossburn," she thought to herself. "I don't like to see such a young girl so subdued and almost sad. But unless grandmamma would call, of course I can't, and I'm afraid there is no use in trying for that."

The Milwards had no mother, and their father's mother, who had to some extent brought them up, was old, and naturally disinclined to make new acquaintances without strong motives for doing so; somewhat narrow and exclusive she was, too, in her ideas, and in this a great contrast to the old friend, with whom, nevertheless, she had much in common—Mrs Selwyn.

Just as Miss Milward was feeling about for some other topic of conversation which might interest her companion, Stasy bent towards her.

"Would you mind telling me who the girl is on my other side—she can't hear, she is speaking to some one else?"

Rosy glanced across Stasy: she had forgotten for the moment who was sitting there.

"Oh yes," she said; "that is—let me see. I often confuse the two families: they are cousins. Oh yes; that is Miss Wandle—Florry Wandle, Mrs Harrowby calls her. She helps a good deal with the guild. She has a nice, pretty face, hasn't she?"

"*Very* pretty," Stasy agreed, and she meant what she said, and something in Miss Milward's tone gratified her. There was a tacit and tactful taking for granted that their little commentary on Miss Wandle was from the same point of view: there was no touch of surprise that Stasy did not already know the girl, or that the Pinnerton Green folk were not of the Derwents' "world."

Then they went on to talk a little of the guild and its interests, till a summons to Miss Milward to help at the tea-table interrupted the *tête-à-tête*. But Stasy's mercurial spirits had risen again, and they rose still higher, when, encouraged by an almost imperceptible signal from Lady Hebe, she ventured to leave her place, and, as one of the youngest present, volunteered her services in handing about bread and butter and cakes.

And Blanche, meanwhile? On entering, she had at once been led over to the other end of the room, which was a long one, by Mrs Harrowby, and ensconced in a corner beside Lady Hebe.

"Now, I want to talk to you very seriously, Miss Derwent," said Blanche's "girl with the happy face."

"Mrs Harrowby and I are counting on your doing great things to help us. You see it is such a disadvantage in any little work of this kind for those who principally manage it to be so much away. And if you *could* take interest in it, it would be such a good thing for the girls. For I suppose" — and she glanced up with a touch of apology — "I suppose you will not be going to London for the season *this* year, as you have come here so lately?"

"No," said Blanche simply, "we shall certainly stay here. I doubt if we shall ever go to London except for a day or two's shopping: we have no friends there."

"It will be different, of course, when you have been longer in England," said Hebe. "And," she added with a smile, "when your sister comes out, I scarcely think *she* would be satisfied with nothing more amusing than Pinnerton, however content *you* are."

Blanche coloured a little.

"You think me better than I am," she said. "I should enjoy — things — too, but if one can't have them? But I think I *should* mind for Stasy more than for myself. She is naturally more dependent on outside life than I. She does feel it very dull and lonely here, and I wish she had some companions." Hebe looked and felt full of sympathy.

"I hope your life here will brighten by degrees," she said. "Don't you think your sister would do something to help us, too? She seems so clever."

"Yes, she is very quick, and she can be very amusing," said Blanche. "We should both be glad to do anything we can. But have you not a good many helpers already? And those other ladies — the residents here — *they* don't go away. Could not they take charge in your absence much better than a stranger like me?"

She glanced across the room to where Miss Adela Bracy, a small, capable-looking, dark girl, was at the moment saying something in a low voice to the rosebud-faced Florry Wandle. Lady Hebe's eyes followed hers.

"They are very good, so far as they go," she replied, "but they are not quite capable of taking the lead. And they have really as much to do as they can manage. It is some one to replace myself when I am away that I want to find. And I could explain it all to you so well, and get advice from you too, I have no doubt."

"I am very ignorant about such things," said Blanche.

"Yes, but you have a good head, and you" — here Hebe smiled and blushed a little — "well, you must know how I mean. It would be so different explaining things to you: you would see them from our point of view. These girls are very good-natured and nice, but I never feel sure that they perfectly understand."

And then she went on to tell Blanche further details about the little work she had inaugurated and carried on — so simply, and yet earnestly, that Blanche's full interest was quickly won, and they went on talking eagerly till tea and interruption came, as Hebe had to help Mrs Harrowby with her hostess duties.

After tea, some of the ladies drew a little closer together: they were the committee, I believe, and Mrs Harrowby read aloud, for the benefit of all present, a short report of the work that had been done during the last three months, and then some one else sketched out what they hoped to do during the summer, and what they were in want of to enable them to carry out these intentions. Then Lady Hebe announced Miss Milwards offer of a day's entertainment for the girls at Crossburn House, and Miss Milward was duly thanked; and there was a good deal of practical and some very unpractical talk, during which Mrs Harrowby and Hebe managed to introduce the Misses Derwent as new members whose assistance would be of great value, Hebe going on to say that Miss Derwent had kindly consented to take her own place during her absence in London. Altogether, it was cheerful and informal, and, to Stasy especially, very amusing.

But just as the Derwents were beginning to feel more at home, and Blanche had been introduced to Rosy Milward, and Stasy was laughing at Miss Wandle's despair about *her* girls' insubordination at the singing class, which was her special charge, there fell a wet blanket on the little party. The door opened, and "Lady Marth" was announced.

Hebe's face sobered. She had not expected her guardian's wife to call for her, as she had promised to be back before the hour at which Lady Marth wished her to drive with her to Blissmore, and Hebe was a very punctual person.

"Josephine!" she exclaimed. "It is not late. You said you did not want me till—"

"Oh no, you are not late," said the new-comer, after shaking hands with Mrs Harrowby and one or two others. "I only came on because Archie"—and here she suddenly turned and looked round her—"where is he? I thought he was behind me—"

"Who—Archie Dunstan?" said Hebe.

"Yes; he wanted to see you about something or other—fishing or something—and he did not venture to come on here alone, when he heard there was a meeting going on. But it's over, isn't it? It doesn't look very solemn."

"Well, I think we have discussed everything we had to settle," said Mrs Harrowby, getting up again from the chair beside Lady Marth, which she had momentarily occupied. "I must say a word or two to Miss— Oh, here he is, Lady Marth—here is Mr Dunstan."

Chapter Eleven.

Ruffled Plumage.

"Yes, here I am," said the young man, as he entered the room and hastened up to Mrs Harrowby, no one suspecting that in his rapid transit he had managed to take in the fact of certain individuals' presence. "Yes, here I am; and I should apologise, I know, but it is all Lady Marth's fault. She dragged me here, and then left me in the lurch with the ponies at the door, quite forgetting I was not the groom. And then, no doubt, she has been wondering 'what in the world has become of that Archie.'"

The few within hearing could not help laughing, he reproduced so cleverly Lady Marth's coldly languid tones.

She laughed herself, and her laugh was a pleasant one.

"You are very impertinent," she said. "And as for dragging you here—you *know* you were dying for an excuse to get in to see what one of Hebe's meetings was like. He reminded me of the legendary female who exists in so many families, you know, whose husband was a Freemason, and she hid herself to overhear their secrets," she went on, to Miss Milward, who happened to be nearest her, Mrs Harrowby by this time having crossed the room to Florry Wandle and her cousin.

"Well, my curiosity has not been rewarded—nor punished," said Mr Dunstan.

And as he spoke he glanced at Blanche, who was standing a little behind Rosy. He had already shaken hands with her, in an unobtrusive, friendly, yet deferential way, which somehow gratified her, simple and un-self-conscious as she was.

"He is such a rattle of a young fellow," she said to herself; "I wonder he remembers having met me before."

"When *will* Hebe be ready?" said Lady Marth, with a sort of soft complaint, as if she had been kept waiting for hours. "Does she need to go on talking confidentially to all those bakers' and brewers' daughters whom she is so fond of?—Can't you give her a hint to be quick, Rosy?"

She half turned, laying her hand on what she supposed to be Miss Milward's arm; but, somehow, Rosy had moved away. The arm Lady Marth actually touched was Blanche's.

Blanche started. She had been watching Archie.

"Can I—" she began; but before she had time to say more, Lady Marth drew herself back.

"Where *is* Rosy?" she said haughtily. "I thought—I thought the meeting was over, and that we were only ourselves. I really must go," and she stood up, drawing her cloak, which had partly slipped off, more closely round her shoulders.

Mr Dunstans face grew stern, all the boyishness died out of it, and he looked ten years older.

"Miss Derwent," he said, in a peculiarly clear and most respectful tone, "I do beg your pardon. I did not notice till this moment that you were standing. If you are going, Lady Marth, you will allow me to move your chair," and, as he spoke, he drew it forward a little.

Lady Marth gave him an icy glance over her shoulder, and moved away. Blanche simply accepted the courtesy.

"I want to go too," she said quietly; "but I must see Lady Hebe for one moment, first."

"Don't hurry," said Mr Dunstan; "she is saying good-bye to those girls now, and she is looking towards you. It will do Lady Marth good to be kept waiting for once, so pray be as deliberate as you like. No one asked her to come here, unless—unless, indeed, I did so myself. I don't— She is quite odious, sometimes," he went on, disconnectedly, looking, for once, *not* equal to the occasion.

Blanche lifted her serene eyes to his face.

"Did you think she was rude to me?" she said. "Please don't mind. She does not know me, or anything about me, so what does it matter? I should mind if any one I knew or cared about was disagreeable or unkind; but when it is a perfect stranger it is quite different."

The young man looked at her with a mixture of admiration and perplexity. Had she not taken in the covert impertinence of Lady Marth's speech?

He smiled a little as he replied. "You are very philosophical and very sensible, Miss Derwent," he said. "But still, I am afraid you must think English people have very bad manners."

"I have not seen many; I can scarcely judge," she said. "But I should not like to say so. I think Lady Hebe and that old lady, Mrs Selwyn, and Mrs Harrowby—oh, and others I could name—have charming manners."

"Why don't you include my aunt—by marriage only—at Alderwood?" he said maliciously.

Blanche laughed a little.

"Some people can't help being awkward, I suppose," she said. "She means to be kind, I think."

Archie's face brightened.

"Now you are better than sensible," he said eagerly—"you are truly kind and charitable. And you are not mistaken. My aunt does mean to be kind, so far as she can understand it. A great many ugly things in this world come from ignorance, after all."

"And from want of imagination," said Blanche, thoughtfully. "Want of power to put one's self in the place of another."

She was beginning to think there was more in this young man, who had struck her at first as a mere boyish rattle; she was beginning to have a touch of the delightful suspicion that he was one who would "understand" her; and her face grew luminous, and her sweet eyes brighter, as she spoke.

He glanced at her again, with a smile in which there was no disappointment for her.

"Yes, I often think so; I have come to think so. But you are very young to have made such a discovery."

Blanche could scarcely help laughing at his tone, she had so completely made up her mind that he was little, if any, older than she.

"Why," she began, "I cannot be much—" But here she suddenly caught sight of Stasy's face looking across at her with a sort of indignant appeal.

"Do come away, Blanchie," it seemed to say.

"Something has rubbed her the wrong way," thought Blanche, and she moved forward at once. "I think my sister wants me," she said, with a little movement of the head, as if in farewell.

Archie Dunstan followed her with his eyes; but he was not long left in peace.

"Can't *you* get Hebe to come away?" said Lady Marth, in a tone that very little more would have rendered querulous. "Rosy has gone now. Everybody has gone. You are as bad as Hebe, Archie. What on earth could you find to talk to that Miss Wandle, or Bracy, or whoever she was, about?"

"She was neither a Miss Wandle nor a Miss Bracy, Lady Marth," said Mr Dunstan. "I thought you had more discernment," and he calmly walked away, entirely disregarding her request that he would summon Hebe.

Lady Marth was angry. She had known that the girl he was talking to was *not* one of the Pinnerton Green tradespeople's daughters, and she had had a strong suspicion that she *was* Miss Derwent. But, of course, she was not going to allow this. She had taken one of her violent and unreasonable prejudices to the Derwents, whom she knew almost nothing about, and would not have felt the slightest interest in, had she not found out that Hebe had come across them, and meant or wished to be kind to them. And she was really very much attached to Hebe, and cared for her good opinion. It annoyed her that she had not been herself appealed to by her husband's ward in the matter, little sympathy though she would have felt about it, as what she called "one of Hebe's fads."

Perhaps, on the whole, it had been a mistake on the girl's part not to have made an effort to enlist Lady Marth's interest in the Derwents. But she had been afraid to do so, knowing by experience how extraordinarily disagreeable "Josephine" could be to any one she considered beneath her. Still, her reticence had aroused deeper prejudice on Lady Marth's side than need have been drawn out; and Mr Dunstan's manner and tone increased it.

Blanche made her way somewhat anxiously to Stasy.

"Do let us go," said the younger girl in a half-whisper. "I am sure mamma will be wondering why we are so long," she added in a louder tone, for Mrs Harrowby's benefit.

"I was only waiting because Lady Hebe wanted to say something to me," said Blanche; and Hebe, who had said good-bye by this time to Miss Wandle and her cousin, came hurrying up.

"I won't keep you any longer just now," she said, for she had an instinctive dread of Lady Marth; "I am so sorry. Just tell me this—can you meet me here alone some afternoon to look over the account-books, so that it may all be quite clear to you?"

Blanche hesitated. Why should they meet "here?" She could understand Hebe's not asking her to go to East Moddersham, considering that Lady Marth had not seen fit to call upon Mrs Derwent, but why should not Hebe offer to come to Pinnerton Lodge herself? She glanced up. Hebe was slightly flushed, her lips were parted, and she seemed a little anxious. The expression was new to Blanche on that usually untroubled face, and it touched her. Blanche's dignity was too simple and true for her to think much about what was "due" to it.

"Yes," she said, "I can easily do so."

"Oh, thank you," said Hebe in a tone of relief.

Then a day and hour were rapidly decided upon, and in another minute or two the sisters found themselves outside the vicarage, on their way home, after saying good-bye to Mrs Harrowby, cordially on Blanche's part, most cordially on that of the vicar's wife, somewhat stiffly on Stasys. Mr Dunstan held the door open for them as they passed out, and his markedly deferential bow somewhat smoothed the younger girl's ruffled plumage.

"*That* man knows how to behave like a gentleman," she said. "Who is he, Blanchie? Have you seen him before?"

"Yes," said Blanche; "he was at Alderwood the afternoon mamma and I called there. I thought he was quite a boy—he looks very young—but I'm not sure about it now. Something in his way of speaking and his manner altogether make me think that perhaps he is older than he looks."

Stasy listened with interest.

"I like him," she said decidedly, and for the moment Blanche forgot the expression on her sister's face which had made her hasten the leave-taking.

"What was the matter, Stasy?" she asked, when it recurred to her. "Why did you look so vexed and uncomfortable?"

"Uncomfortable!" repeated Stasy. "Oh dear, no. I am not afraid of any of those people. They *couldn't* make me uncomfortable. I was only angry—very angry. What do you think Mrs Harrowby said?"

"I'm sure I don't know," said Blanche. "When I looked across at you, I thought you were getting on so well. Lady Hebe said that that was Miss Milward whom you were talking to, and that she is so nice."

"The plain girl—indeed, she is almost ugly—with the beautiful eyes," said Stasy eagerly; "yes, she was awfully nice. But Mrs Harrowby spoilt it all. Just when everybody was standing up to go, she came bustling forward—"

"She doesn't bustle," interposed Blanche.

"Well, never mind—up she came, and began talking to those Wandle girls and me in a patronising sort of way: 'Your roads lie in the same direction; you will be going home together, I suppose?' I stared, and to do them justice, *they* looked uncomfortable. 'Oh no,' I said, 'I think you do not know me. I came with my sister, Miss Derwent. I have not the—' Then she interrupted me. 'You don't mean to say you have not made friends yet? and such near neighbours!' And she was on the point, the very point, Blanche, of insisting on our 'making friends,' as she called it, when Lady Hebe came up about some books or something, and I managed to get out of the way. That was why I was fidgeting so to get hold of you. Blanchie, I *won't* be treated like that. I wish we had never gone to that horrid tea-meeting."

Blanche looked distressed.

"And yet, Stasy," she said, "you were the one to want to make friends out of school, so to say, with some of the Blissmore girls—the very same class as those here, some of them actually relations."

"Not all of the same class," said Stasy; "some of them are much more ladies, only poor. And, besides, that would have been *quite* different, don't you see, Blanchie? It would have been me, or us, being kind to them—not us being put on a level with them, as that Mrs Harrowby wanted to do. But I don't think she will try that sort of thing again, with me, at least."

"How did the girls take what you said?" her sister inquired quietly.

Stasy seemed a little uncomfortable.

"Oh well, you know, it wasn't pleasant for them either. The dark one—she's much cleverer and quicker than the pretty, stupid, fair one—the dark one looked very grave, and I think she got a very little red."

"Poor girl!" said Blanche—and something in her tone made Stasy wince—"I daresay she did. *They* did not deserve to be punished, that I can see."

"I never said they did, unless—well, if they are to be counted the same as us, they should have tried to be kind and 'neighbourly.' How I do detest that word! It is so inconsistent. You seem to think I should have been gushing over with amiability to them, just because they have not even been honestly, vulgarly kind. Not that we wanted anything of the sort, of course. We are completely and entirely independent of them."

"Yes; and for that very reason you could well have afforded to be simply courteous. You may be pretty sure that if they have not called, it has been that they thought we should not like it; and I don't say that we are in any way bound to make friends with people whose interests are quite different from ours, and who would have very little in common with us. But it could have done no sort of harm to have spoken pleasantly to them, and *even* to have walked home together, that I can see."

Stasy did not reply. She was beginning to feel rather ashamed of herself. Had she behaved "snobbishly?" Her cheeks burned at the thought of having appeared to do so: I fear her first misgiving dealt more with this possible "appearing," than with the actual wrong or contemptibleness of her feelings. Blanche walked on silently. She was thinking to herself how the same spirit came out in different positions. There was Stasy, now, sixteen-years-old Stasy, showing already the same worldly narrow-mindedness, which, had not Blanche's own dignity and self-respect been of exceptional quality, might have mortified her not a little when shown to herself by Lady Marth.

"I would not tell Stasy of it at present, on any account," she thought; "but some day I shall let her know how curiously the two incidents came together, and let her draw her own deductions."

But she was sorry for Stasy too. She was at all times very tender of her sister's faults and follies, and intensely sympathising in her troubles. So she exerted herself to disperse the little cloud of mortification which had gathered on Stasy's face; and when the two entered the library, where their mother was waiting for them, they were both bright and cheerful, and ready to relate to her all the incidents of the afternoon which were likely to interest her.

"Lady Marth was there, you say?" she inquired. "I did not know she was likely to belong to the girls' guild, or whatever you call it. I don't know that I should have cared to let you go had I thought she would be there."

Blanche looked rather surprised.

"Why, mamma, what does it matter? Do you mean because she has not called?"

"Not exactly. But she is the sort of woman who, unless she takes it into her head to be civil to people, can be—very much the reverse. And"—Mrs Derwent's face hardened a little—"I don't want you and Stasy, my darlings, to be exposed to that kind of thing. Aunt Grace hinted at something of the kind, and since then I have remembered who Lady Marth is. She belongs to a family of no ancestry, but which has become rapidly prominent through a mixture of cleverness and good luck. They—her people, the Banfleets—are now enormously rich, and pride themselves on their extreme exclusiveness. They are *plus royalistes que le roi*."

"How detestable!" said Stasy, "and how contemptible! I am sure I don't want to know them."

"You can't call them really contemptible," said her mother. "They are a very talented family, in several directions too. And they are very generous and liberal and honourable. But this one weakness—the trying to be just the one thing they are not—spoils them."

"And, very likely, if they *were* of very old descent, they would care less about it," said Blanche reflectively.

"Perhaps so, but that does not always follow. Sir Conway Marth is a much wider-minded man, but not specially clever. And he is of a very old family. I used to know his sisters. They were thoroughly nice; more like that girl you have taken such a fancy to—his ward, I mean," said Mrs Derwent. "But we cannot expect to know her in an ordinary way if she lives with the Marths. I wish—" And then she hesitated, while a troubled look crept over her face.

Blanche, who was sitting next her, took her hand and fondled it softly.

"I know what you are going to say, mother dear," she said, "and you are not to say it. Everything you have done has been for the best, and with the best motives, and you are just not to wish it undone. We have a mass of things to be grateful for and happy about, and why should we worry about things that, through no fault of ours, don't come in our way."

"Some of them may come in our way," said Stasy, whoso versatile spirits had already gone up again. "I shouldn't wonder if that nice, ugly Miss Milward were to call on us, and ask us to go to see her.—Oh Blanchie, there's Flopper rushing about over the flower-beds; he really must be tied up, till he sobers down a little."

"Run out and tie him up, then," said Blanche, and off Stasy set. Flopper was a new acquisition; a very interesting and aggravating retriever puppy, with all the charms and foibles of puppyhood intensely developed in him. Looking after Flopper was very wholesome for Stasy, her sister had discovered.

Blanche turned again to her mother.

"Mamma dear," she said, "I really think we must not get into the way of seeing the worst side of things. If we are a little lonely, any way we have each other, and such a charming home. Could any one picture to themselves a sweeter room than this library? How our French friends would admire it!"

"Yes," said Mrs Derwent, "it is a delightful room. Of course, the name is rather inappropriate, we have so few books."

"We must get some more," said Blanche; "by degrees, of course."

"I fear it must be by degrees," said her mother; "I cannot afford anything for the house at present, it has cost so much more than I expected. And there seems some little difficulty about our income still; the new partners are asking for longer time to pay us out in, and it will make it difficult to get good investments if the capital is realised so irregularly."

"I don't understand about it," said Blanche. "But it doesn't matter for the present. When Stasy is grown up, it would be nice to take her about a little; perhaps to London now and then, if by that time we have made some friends there. Mamma, couldn't we invite some of our old friends to come to stay with us a little — Madame de Caillemont, for instance?"

"She is too frail now, I fear, to come so far," said Mrs Derwent. "And as for any one else — no, I don't feel as if I should like it. Do not think me small or childish, Blanchie, but — you know French peoples ideas? They are all already expecting, from one day to another, to hear of your making some grand marriage; they thought a good deal of us as well-connected English people, you know. And, I confess, it would mortify me for them, any of them, to see how — how completely 'out of it all' we are."

"Poor little mother!" said Blanche caressingly, "you really mustn't get gloomy. *You* don't think I want to marry and leave you, do you? I can't *imagine* such a thing. I cannot in my wildest dreams picture to myself the going away from you and Stasy! Never mind about that; but I do understand that you would feel rather sore at any friends thinking we were more friendless here than in France. There is no need to invite any one at present. I think I had a vague idea that it might cheer you up a little. This house is so pretty; I should enjoy showing it off."

"I should like you to have the pleasure of doing so," said Mrs Derwent wistfully. "You are always so sweet, my Blanchie. I can't help feeling as if nothing and nobody would be good enough for you; the faintest idea of any one in the very least looking down upon you is — "

"Mother dear, it is not that. These people don't know us, or anything about us. There is nothing mortifying or worth minding that I can see in people's ignoring you, when they know nothing about you. And as for rudeness — that always lowers the rude person, not the object of it."

Mrs Derwent looked up quickly.

"You don't mean that any one has been actually *rude* to you, Blanchie? Was there anything this afternoon?"

Blanche hesitated. She was incapable of uttering a word that was not true; yet, again, she was determined to tell her mother nothing of Lady Marth's impertinence.

"Mamma," she said, "I am thinking a great deal about Stasy. *She* was rude, at least it was tacitly rude, this afternoon," and she related the incident we know of.

"It was unladylike and unkind," said Mrs Derwent. "Yes, I am anxious about Stasy. This uncertain position that we have got into is bad for her in every way."

"It may all come right," said Blanche cheerfully. "But I am glad you think I spoke properly to Stasy. Let us hope it will all come right, mamma, if *we* do our best to be kind and good."

Chapter Twelve.

A Sprained Ankle.

For a time it seemed as if Blanche's hopeful prognostications were likely to be fulfilled. The meeting with Lady Hebe at the vicarage led to one or two others, for though Blanche was naturally quick and orderly, it took longer than either she or her new friend had expected to initiate her into work of which the whole idea and details were completely new to her. And the more the two girls saw of each other, the stronger grew the mutual attraction of which both had been conscious since that first evening when they came together in the fog at Victoria Station.

But Hebe was powerless to do more. She found it best to avoid all mention even of the Derwents' name at East Moddersham, so evident was it that Lady Marth had conceived one of her most unreasonable prejudices against the strangers.

"It is a good deal thanks to Archie Dunstan," thought Hebe. "He made Josephine furious that day. It's really too bad of him, and if I can, I'll give him a hint about it. Of course, it doesn't matter to *him* whether people are nice to the poor Derwents or not, but he's quite worldly wise enough to know that with a woman like Josephine, and, indeed, with all these good ladies here about, *his* advocacy would do them far more harm than good. Why, I've known Josephine jealous and angry when he or Norman refused to give up an engagement of long standing, if she chose to want them. She doesn't think Archie should know any one whom she hasn't taken up."

She did speak to Archie, and he listened attentively. But at the close of her oration, when his silence was encouraging her to hope that she had made some impression, he entirely discomposed her by inquiring calmly if there were to be any more guild meetings at the vicarage before she went to town, as if so, he would make a point of looking in as he had done the week before.

"How can you, Archie?" said Hebe. "The very thing I have been trying. No," she broke off, "there are to be no more meetings, and if there were, I would not let you know."

"All right," said Archie; "it doesn't matter in the least. I've little birds in my service who are much more reliable sources of information than your wise ladyship. And one of them has informed me that there is going to be a tea-fight in the garden at Pinnerton Lodge for the damsels who have the honour to belong to the guild. And I mean to be at it."

"Archie?" exclaimed Hebe, stopping short, and looking at him in a sort of despair. "You go too far sometimes in your love of fun and amusing yourself; you do, really.

The Derwents are not people to take freedoms with. Just because Blanche—Miss Derwent, I mean—is so charming and lovely, and unlike the common run of girls, you're much mistaken if you think that you can treat her with less deference than if she—"

"If she what?" said Archie.

"Than if she—well—belonged to our set, you know. Was quite *in* everything."

"How do you know that I've not fallen desperately, in love with her?" he inquired coolly, looking Hebe full in the face.

"For two reasons," she replied. "You don't know what really falling in love means; and secondly, if such a thing had happened, you wouldn't talk about it like that."

Archie laughed.

"All the same," he said, "I am going to be at the Pinnerton Lodge tea-fight. See if I'm not."

Hebe turned away in indignation. She was fond of Archie, and they were very old friends, almost on brother-and-sister-like terms, but he sometimes made her more nearly angry than was at all usual with her.

"How glad I am Norman is not like that!" she said to herself—"turning everything into joke. I wonder if it would be any good to make him speak to Archie, and warn him not to begin any nonsense about Blanche Derwent? No, I am afraid it might lead to disagreeables; Norman would be so vexed with Archie for annoying me."

It was quite true that there was going to be an entertainment for the members of the guild at Pinnerton Lodge. The idea had been started in one of the talks on the affairs of the little society between Lady Hebe and Blanche, and Mrs Derwent had taken it up with the greatest cordiality. She was glad of anything which promised some variety for her daughters, and delighted to be the means of giving pleasure to others. Nor was she sorry to, as it were, assert her position in even so simple a way as this.

"I shall be so glad to see your Lady Hebe at last," she said to Blanche.

"I am sure you will like her as much as I do," said Blanche. "Stasy has promised me," she went on, "to be very nice indeed to those other girls, to make up for that day at the vicarage."

A few days later the little entertainment came off. It was almost the eve of the East Moddersham family's leaving for London. Hebe had been staying at Crossburn for a few days, only returning home the morning of the party, on purpose to be present at it. Rosy Milward accompanied her, in order, as she said, to see how things went off, as she had promised an entertainment of the same kind herself to Hebe's girls a little later in the season.

Rosy was a little shy of offering herself as a guest to the Derwents, for she had not succeeded in her endeavours to persuade her grandmother to call at Pinnerton Lodge. Old Mrs Milward was becoming increasingly frail, and even a small effort seemed painful to her. Yet, as is often the case with elderly people in such circumstances, she stood increasingly on her dignity, and would not hear of her grand-daughter "calling for her," as Rosy ventured to suggest.

"We know nothing of these people," she said, "except that Grace Selwyn knew the mother as a child. But no one else is calling on them, and I really don't see why we need do so."

"Lady Harriot has called," said Rosy.

"I can't help that, my dear," was the reply. "Lady Harriot has no young daughters or grand-daughters, so her calling involves nothing."

"She has a *nephew*," Rosy said to herself, for she was far too quick not to have noticed Archie Dunstan's evident admiration of Miss Derwent. But she had the discretion to keep this reflection to herself.

And, after all, Mrs Milward made no objection to her grand-daughter's accompanying Lady Hebe to Pinnerton Lodge on the afternoon in question.

"That sort of thing," she remarked, with some inconsistency, "is quite different. You can go anywhere for a fancy fair or a charity entertainment;" forgetting that her grand-daughter was sure to be specially thrown into the society of the Derwent girls on such an occasion, and little suspecting that Rosy intended to profit to the utmost by such an opportunity of seeing more of both Blanche and Stasy. For Hebe quite reassured her as to the welcome she would receive.

"They're so *thoroughly* nice, so simply well-bred," Hebe said, "so pleased to give pleasure. Otherwise, I should have felt almost ashamed to go myself, for it is much more marked for Josephine not to call, than your grandmother—an old lady, and living at some distance."

All went well. The weather was mild, almost warm; there were no threatening rain-clouds or clouds of any kind on the afternoon fixed upon; so, to Stasy's great delight, it was decided that the tea-tables should be set out in the garden, or rather on the tennis-lawn at one side of the house. Lady Hebe and her friend were the first to arrive, and were full of admiration of the way in which the Derwents had arranged their preparations.

"How pretty you have made the tables look!" said Hebe to Mrs Derwent. "It'll be quite a lesson in itself to the girls. I'm afraid our part of the country is very deficient in taste. We are so dreadfully old-fashioned and conservative."

"But many old-fashioned ways and things are in much better taste than new-fashioned ones," Mrs Derwent replied. "Good taste seems to come in cycles. I must say there was great room for improvement in such things when I was a girl."

"You lived near here then, did you not?" said Hebe. "Yes, at Fotherley, near Alderwood, you know," said Mrs Derwent. "I was so happy there, that it made me choose this part of England in preference to any other, when the time came for us to make our home here."

She sighed a little.

"It is a very nice part of the world, I do think," said Hebe. "But I suppose it takes a little time to get to feel at home anywhere. And it must seem very strange to you to come back to the same place after so many years."

"It hardly seems like the same place," said Mrs Derwent, "but that would not matter, if Blanche and Stasy get to feel at home here."

"I do hope they will," said Hebe, with such evidently sincere earnestness, that Mrs Derwent's heart was won on the spot. "If only I had anything in my power" — then she hesitated, and her colour deepened a little — "I may have before long," she added with a smile. "I mean to say," she went on, with some slight confusion, "if Miss Derwent cares to have me as a friend, I look forward to being rather more my own mistress than I am just now."

"You are very good," said Mrs Derwent simply; but at that moment Stasy came dancing over the grass, to say that the guests of the day, "the guild girls," had begun to arrive, and Lady Hebe was in request to organise the games.

"Where is Herty?" said Mrs Derwent suddenly. "I haven't seen him for ever so long!"

"He went off to the wood, to get some more ivy, just after luncheon," said Blanche. "Yes, he should have been back by now. But you needn't be uneasy about him, mamma; he's sure to be all right."

"Still, I wish he would come back," said Mrs Derwent. "He was looking forward to the fun of helping us with the tea and everything."

The next hour passed very busily — so busily, that, except Mrs Derwent herself, no one gave a thought to Herty's continued absence, and even she forgot it from time to time. But when the games had ceased for the moment, and everybody was no less busily but more quietly occupied at the tea-tables, the thought of Herty returned to Blanche's mind, as well as to her mother's.

"What can he be about?" she said to herself. "I don't want to frighten mamma, but I really think we must send some one to look for him."

She glanced round, and, thinking she would not be missed for a moment, she hastened across the lawn towards a side gate, whence they generally made their way into the woods by a short cut. There she stood listening, hoping to hear the little boys whistle, or the sound of his footsteps hurrying over the dry ground. But all was silent, save that now and then there came the distant clatter of teacups mingled with cheerful voices, and now and then a merry laugh.

"They won't hear me," thought Blanche, "if I call. And possibly Herty may, if he's still in the woods."

So she called clearly, and as loudly as she could: "Herty, Herty! where are you? Herty, Her-ty!" No reply.

Blanche waited a moment or two, and then tried again. This time she thought she heard something like a far-off whistle. It was a peculiarly still afternoon, and sound carried far. Soon, to her listening ears, came the consciousness of approaching steps, firm and decided, not the light footfall of a child like Herty. Blanche still lingered.

"It may be some one coming through the wood, who has seen him," she thought; "at least I can ask." Another moment, and the new-comer was in sight. But — Blanche had good eyesight — but for some seconds the figure approaching her set her perception at defiance. What, who was it? An old man with humped-up shoulders? A woodcutter carrying a load? No, it was not an old man — it moved too vigorously; nor was it a peasant — the step was too easy and well-balanced. And the load on its shoulders — a moment or two more, and it all took shape. The stranger was a young man, and — yes, undoubtedly, a *gentleman*, and he was carrying a child!

Then Blanche's heart leaped into her mouth, as the saying goes, with horror. The child was a little boy, and — yes, it was Herty. What, oh! what had happened to him?

She gave no thought to the person who was carrying him; she was over the stile by the gate in half a second, and rushing in frantic haste along the path, towards her little brother and his bearer.

"Herty, darling!" she exclaimed. "What *is* the matter? Have you hurt yourself?" And then, as the child did not at once reply — "Has he fainted?" she went on. "Oh, do speak!"

"Don't make such a fuss, Blanchie," came in Herty's familiar, high-pitched voice, sweet as music to his sister's ears, despite his ingratitude. "Please put me down," he went on, to the person who was carrying him; "I'm sure I can walk now. I don't like to look like a baby."

"I'm sure you can't walk, my little man," was the reply. "But you may try for yourself if you like," and the person he addressed carefully lowered the child to the ground, while Blanche, for the first time turning her attention to him, recognised in Herty's bearer the young man she had met twice before — at Alderwood, and since then at Pinnerton Vicarage, and who had been introduced to her as Mr Archibald Dunstan.

"I beg your pardon," he said, lifting his cap as soon as his hand was free. "I'm afraid we've given you a fright, but — "

"I *was* frightened for a moment," said Blanche, half apologetically, "but now I must thank you. Has Herty hurt himself? Where did you find him?"

Mr Dunstan did not at once reply; he was looking at the child, who had grown very white, and nearly fell.

"There now," he said. "It's all very well to be plucky, but I told you you couldn't manage for yourself," and he put his arm round the little fellow. — "Don't be alarmed, Miss Derwent," he went on; "it's only slight, I think — a sprained ankle; but the pain would be worse if it were bad. He was chatting quite cheerfully as we came along just now. I think the best thing to be done is for me to carry him home, if you'll allow me to do so."

"Thank you, oh thank you so much," said Blanche. "Our house is just on the other side of the gate. I will run on and open it. We are rather busy this afternoon — Lady Hebe's girls are having tea in the garden, and I shouldn't like my mother to be frightened. So perhaps if you can carry Herty straight to the house, that would be the best."

"Certainly," said Mr Dunstan, passing through the gate as she held it open. "It *is* unlucky that this should have happened when you're all so busy."

But his tone was remarkably cheerful in spite of his expressions of sympathy. And Herty, now comfortably ensconced again on the young man's shoulder, began his explanations.

"I was stretching up for a splendid spray of ivy," he said. "There was a sort of ditch, and I lost my balance and rolled in. And when I tried to get up, my foot hurt me so, I couldn't stand. So I had to lie down, but I shouted a lot. And at last, after ever so long, *he* came. — Wouldn't it have been dreadful if you hadn't?" he went on, patting Mr Dunstan affectionately: he had evidently taken a great fancy to his rescuer. "Do you think I'd have had to stay there all night?"

"It *was* lucky, indeed," said Blanche. "There is a short cut through the woods from Alderwood to East Moddersham, isn't there? You live at Alderwood, do you not? I suppose you were going to East Moddersham. You can go back the other way round if you like."

She spoke quite simply, a little faster perhaps than was usual with her, thanks to her late excitement and present relief. But there was no sort of curiosity or *arrière pensée* in her questions.

What then — or was it her fancy? — what made the young man's colour deepen slightly as she put them to him? She was *almost* sure it was so, though he was rather sunburnt, which made it more difficult to judge.

"Thank you," he said. "Yes, I was bound for East Moddersham. That is to say, not exactly — but — I promised to see Lady Hebe this afternoon," and as he looked up with the last words, Blanche caught a twinkle of fun in his eyes.

They were very nice eyes — honest grey eyes; she had not noticed them before. And after glancing at them, she turned her own away in some perplexity.

"Lady Hebe is here," she said. "I don't think she can be expecting you. It has been settled for some time that she was to come."

"Ah then, perhaps you — Mrs Derwent, that is to say — will allow me to speak to her — Lady Hebe — in your garden. That will save my needing to go to East Moddersham. Sir Conway is away, and my calls on Lady Marth are never pressing."

"He is rather queer," thought Blanche. "I know he and Lady Hebe are very old friends, but I really don't think she is expecting him this afternoon."

Mr Dunstan, however, seemed quite satisfied. He spoke cheerfully to Herty, asking him if his foot pained him still, and assuring him that it would soon be all right again.

"Shall I have to have the doctor?" asked the boy. "I don't like doctors. The old one at home made me stay in bed when it was *so* hot. I am sure it made me much iller."

"Oh, our doctors here aren't like that," said Archie. "They're very jolly fellows. But perhaps you won't need one. I'll have a look at your ankle if your sister will allow me. I'm a bit of a doctor myself."

Blanche did not speak.

"Blanchie, don't you hear?" said Herty, with a touch of querulousness. "It would be much nicer not to have a proper doctor."

"Very well, dear, we'll see," she replied tranquilly. "Mr Dunstan is very kind."

Chapter Thirteen.

Millinery.

She had spoken in rather a conventional tone, but she was really touched when they got to the house, by Mr Dunstan's extreme gentleness and concern for the boy. He put Herty on the couch in the library, which they found unoccupied, and got his boot and stocking off as skilfully as a surgeon could have done. It was not very bad, but it was a sprain, undoubtedly; and after Blanche, under Archies directions, had applied cold water bandages, and obtained Herty's promise to lie perfectly still, she went out to the garden, followed by Mr Dunstan, to explain to her mother and Stasy what had happened.

"I will send Aline in, to look after you, Herty," she said, "if she can possibly be spared."

Tea was about coming to an end when the two left the house. After all, Blanche had scarcely been missed, for all that had passed since she went to the wood gate to look for her little brother, had taken but a short time, and everybody in the garden was very busy.

But now there came a breathing-space, and more than one began to ask what had become of Miss Derwent.

"I wonder if she has gone off to look for Herty, and indeed I wonder what can have happened to him," said Stasy, with sudden anxiety. For in the bustle she had forgotten about her little brother.

She was standing beside Hebe as she spoke, and Hebe looked up to answer her.

"I hope—" she began, then stopped abruptly.

"There is your sister," she said, but a curious expression came over her face, as she went on, "and—Archie Dunstan.—What an intrusion! How dared he?" she went on, to herself, in a lower tone. Stasy did not catch the words. She only saw the annoyance, almost indignation, on Hebe's face.

But the next few minutes cleared up a good deal. Blanche hastened to her mother to tell of Herty's accident and Mr Dunstan's kindness, and Mrs Derwent was, naturally, eager in her thanks. Then she hurried in to see her boy for herself, and Blanche turned to Mr Dunstan.

"You said you wanted to see Lady Hebe; she is over there—standing by the other table."

"Oh yes, thank you," he answered. But he did not seem in any desperate hurry to speak to his old friend.

"I was thinking," he began again, "that I might perhaps be of use about the doctor. It may be erring on the safe side to let him have a look at the boy's ankle. I am driving home from East Moddersham, so I could easily stop at Blissmore on the way."

"Thank you," said Blanche. "I will see what my mother says."

"Does she want to get rid of me?" thought Archie to himself.

However that may have been, Miss Derwent certainly gave him no excuse for lingering near her, so he strolled across to where Hebe was standing alone for the moment, as the girls had again dispersed.

She would not refuse to shake hands with him, but her usually sunny eyes were sparkling with indignation.

"Archie," she said, before he had time to speak, "I could not have believed this of you. If you call it a good joke, I don't!"

Archie looked at her calmly.

"My dear little lady," he said, with kindly condescension, "it is not like you to pass judgment on a matter which you know nothing about."

"I do know about it," said Hebe. "I know what you said to me — that by hook or by crook you would manage to get here to-day. How you have managed it, I don't know. I only know that you were not justified in doing anything of the kind."

"I don't allow that," said Archie, nettled in spite of his coolness. "As it happens, *my* relation, at whose house I am staying, is the only person who has been decently civil to the Derwents at all."

The colour mounted to Hebe's face.

"You needn't taunt me with that," she said quickly. "I am not responsible, as you well know, for what Josephine does or does not do."

"Did I say you were?" he replied, raising his eyebrows. "Nor do I take my own stand on my aunt's behaviour in the matter. If you'll be so good as to listen, I will tell you how I have come to be here to-day," and he quickly related what had happened.

Hebe's face relaxed.

"It is very extraordinary," she said, half to herself. "And what were you doing prowling about the woods, pray?" she said, unable altogether to suppress a smile.

"Waiting for what fate might throw in my way," he answered calmly.

Just then they caught sight of Mrs Derwent's figure coming towards them. Archie started forward.

"If I thought he was in earnest!" thought Hebe to herself, as she followed him more deliberately.

Mr Dunstan's offer of sending the doctor was accepted, as Herty still seemed in considerable pain, and soon after the whole party dispersed; Archie accompanying Hebe and Miss Milward to East Moddersham, where he had ordered his dog-cart to meet him.

Herty's sprain proved no very serious matter; but during the next fortnight or so, it formed a plausible excuse for Mr Dunstan's calling now and then to inquire how he was, and to bring him once or twice books or toys to amuse him while he had to lie still.

Mrs Derwent took a great liking to the young man, and so did Stasy, but he did not seem to get to know Blanche any better. Indeed, on one or two occasions he came and went without seeing her at all. Still, his visits made a little break in the monotony of life at Pinnerton Lodge. During the week or two, also, which preceded the East Moddersham family's removal to town for the season, there were occasional meetings with Hebe at the vicarage, to discuss guild matters, into which Blanche threw herself with great thoroughness. Mrs Derwent, always sanguine, began to feel more cheerful as to things in general brightening by degrees.

But when Lady Hebe had left, and Mr Dunstan had no longer any excuse for lingering — Alderwood also being shut up — life seemed to return much to what it had been.

"I really don't know what I shall do with myself," said Stasy one day, "when the time comes for me to give up my regular lessons. I almost wish you were not so contented, Blanche; it is really rather irritating. If you would grumble too, things wouldn't seem so bad."

Blanche laughed.

"Do you know, I really don't feel inclined to grumble," she said, "especially now that I've got more to do I do find looking after these girls very interesting indeed."

"You're a prig," said Stasy — "a prig or a saint; I've not yet made up my mind which."

Blanche took no notice.

"Stasy," she said, "I have got an idea in my head. It's not quite a new one; some one proposed it before; but I can't manage it unless you'll help me, you're so much cleverer about that sort of thing than I am."

"What sort of thing?" said Stasy.

"Things that require neat-handedness and taste. It's a millinery class for the girls I'm thinking of. It would be such a surprise to Lady Hebe when she comes back, to see them with neat, pretty hats. It is just the time they're getting their summer ones, and they do wear such awful things."

"And I daresay they pay a lot for them, too," said Stasy.

"No doubt they do," said Blanche; "and I don't suppose one of them has the slightest idea of trimming anything neatly."

Stasy was silent for a moment; then she said, with a little hesitation: "You're very complimentary about my taste, Blanchie. But as to the actual work, I'm afraid I should not be much good. I know nothing about what may be called the 'technique' of the business. I couldn't line or bind a hat neatly, for instance."

"I've thought of that," said Blanche eagerly; and, indeed, a great part of her interest in this new idea had to do with the occupation and amusement she had hoped it would give her sister. "I've thought about that, and I feel pretty sure that little Miss Halliday would help us. I'm going to Blissmore this afternoon, and I mean to ask her if she would teach us a little. Two or three lessons would give us all we need."

Stasy brightened up.

"That would really be great fun," she said. "Do let me go with you, Blanchie. Can we pay her for teaching us, do you think? Won't it be at all like poaching on her manor?"

"Oh no," said Blanche. "These girls are not the class who would ever get things from her; and, of course, however clever we become, we mustn't leave off giving her our own work. That is to say, everything we don't get from London. She will quite enter into it, I feel sure."

And that very afternoon Blanche's idea was carried out. They walked into Blissmore, and went to see Miss Halliday, who was always delighted to have a glimpse of them; and when Blanche unfolded her plan, the little milliner entered into it heartily.

"Of course," said Blanche, "you must count it as if you were really giving us lessons. It would be quite unfair to take up your time for nothing."

Miss Halliday hesitated, grew rather pink and nervous.

"I wish, I am sure, I could refuse any payment," she said at last. "But to tell you the truth, Miss Derwent, things have not been going very well with me lately. There is a great increase of work in Blissmore, as new families keep coming, and, rather than lose the chance of increasing my customers, I had made up my mind to take a partner. After a great deal of inquiry and writing about it, I found what seemed the very person, unexceptionable in every way. She was to put a little money into the concern, and, above all, was said to be extremely clever and tasteful. Just what I wanted! For, you see, there is no denying that I may be getting a little old-fashioned; though I do think my work is always neat, and I use good materials. So I had my shop enlarged a little, and fresh painted, and a new mirror, and altogether went to a good deal of expense, when, just at the last moment, this poor girl—I can't find it in my heart to blame her—had a sudden call to Australia, owing to some family troubles. I could have held her to the bargain, or made her pay up, but it went against me to do it, so I let her off. That was nearly two months ago, and here have I been ever since trying to find some one else. The season getting on too, more work coming in than I can manage, not daring to refuse any, for fear of it getting about, and leading to some other milliners starting!"

And Miss Halliday wiped away a tear which she could not altogether repress.

The sisters were full of sympathy.

"Poor Miss Halliday!" said Blanche, "I am so sorry."

"I wish we could help you," said Stasy impulsively. "Perhaps if you find us very clever, after you've taught us a little, we might come down now and then and help you, as if we were apprentices, you know! Wouldn't it be fun, Blanchie?"

"Bless you, my love," said the old maid, wiping away another tear. "It is good of you to have such a thought, though, of course, I couldn't so presume. I'm sure you'll learn very quickly, having been brought up in France, where, they say, good taste comes with the air. Indeed, I have been thinking of trying for a French young person as a partner, and I once thought of consulting your dear mamma about it."

"I can tell her what you say," said Blanche. "But I scarcely think she would advise it. It's a risk to bring any one so far, and as for what you say of French taste—well, I don't know—in Paris, perhaps; but one sees plenty of vulgar ugliness in the provinces."

"Indeed, Miss," said the milliner, considerably impressed. "Well, I might be safer with an English girl, after all. And thank you, more than I can say, for your kind sympathy. Your visit has quite cheered me—it has indeed. You'll let me make you a cup of tea before you go. It'll be ready directly in your own parlour—we always call the drawing-room your own room since you were here, we do indeed." And the little woman started up in her eager hospitality.

"We'll stay to tea on one condition, Miss Halliday," said Stasy—"that is, that if you do find us clever, you'll promise to let us come and help you after our lessons with you are over."

"My dear Miss Anastasia," began Miss Halliday.

"Oh, but you must promise," said Stasy. "It's not all out of kindness that I want it! It would be something to do—some fun! I only wish you'd let me serve in the shop a little, it's so dreadfully dull at Pinnerton, you don't know."

Miss Halliday's face expressed commiseration.

"I'm sorry for that," said she. "I was hoping that, when you got settled down, you'd feel quite at home, and find it more lively. But, of course, about now most of the families are going up to London."

"That doesn't make much difference to us," said Stasy. "If you want to know, Miss Halliday, I think English people are horribly unfriendly and disagreeable."

The milliner looked uncomfortable; she had delicacy enough to know that any distinct expression of sympathy in such a case would be an impertinence.

"You may find it pleasanter in the winter," she said. "There are some nice young ladies in your neighbourhood—Lady Hebe Shetland at East Moddersham, now! She is a sweet young lady."

"Yes," said Blanche, speaking for the first time. "We know her a little, but still it is quite different from what it used to be when mamma was a girl here."

"Well yes, to be sure," said Miss Halliday, "for it was your dear mamma's home; and no one was more respected in all the country-side, as I've heard my aunt say, than your dear grandpapa, the late Mr Fenning. It was quite a different thing in the next vicars time; his wife and daughters were not, so to say, in the county society at all."

"Do you mean the Flemings?" asked Blanche; "yes, I have heard of them. I hope people don't confuse mamma with them; sometimes I've been afraid they may do."

Miss Halliday grew a little pink again.

"Well, Miss, as you've mentioned it," she said, "though I wouldn't have made free to speak of it myself, I'm afraid there may have been some mistake of the kind in one or two quarters, and seeing that it was so, I made bold to set it right; telling those that had made the mistake, that your dear mamma came of a very high family indeed, as my dear aunt has often told me, and that on both sides."

Blanche could not help smiling, though she was touched by the little milliner's loyalty.

"Thank you, Miss Halliday," she said. "I should certainly be sorry for mamma's family to be confused with the Flemings, not so much because they were—well, scarcely gentlepeople by birth—but because they were not particularly nice in themselves. It is misleading that the two names are so like, and I am glad you explained it."

"I won't mention names," said Miss Halliday, beaming with satisfaction; "but it will all come right in the end, you will see, my dear young ladies. And now I think tea must be ready in the drawing-room, if you'll be so good as to step that way."

"But you are going to have tea with us," said Stasy. "It would be no fun if you didn't. And we have to settle the day for our first lesson; and you've never been out to see our house yet, Miss Halliday. Mamma sent a special message about that."

"What a good little soul she is!" said Blanche, as Stasy and she were walking home together.

"Yes, isn't she?" said Stasy. "Blanche," she went on, thoughtfully, after a moment's pause, "do you ever think how nice it would be to be really very rich? Not just comfortable, as we are, but really rich, with lots to give away. What nice things one could do for other people! We could pay for a very clever assistant for Miss Halliday, for instance, so that she might get to be quite a grand milliner, and the people here would go to her for their bonnets instead of sending to London."

Blanche laughed.

"We should have to frank her over to Paris also once or twice a year. Fancy Miss Halliday in Paris!" she said. "However beautiful her bonnets were, no one could believe in her unless she went to Paris. Yes, it would be very nice to be able to do things like that. But, on the other hand—" She stopped, and seemed to be thinking.

"What were you going to say?" asked Stasy.

"I was only thinking," Blanche replied, "how little we can realise what it must be to be poor. To feel that one's actual daily bread—food and clothes and common necessaries—depend on one's work. I suppose, however, it does not seem hard or depressing to those who have always been accustomed to it."

"I have thought of it sometimes," said Stasy. "I'm not sure that there wouldn't be a sort of pleasure about it. It would be very interesting and exciting. What *I* dislike most is the being nobody in particular, neither one thing nor the other, as we have rather felt ourselves here! Nothing specially to do, and no feeling that it would matter if you didn't do it. That is so dull."

"I suppose," said Blanche thoughtfully again, "that things to do, things that you feel you could do better than any one else could do them, always do turn up sooner or later if one really wants to use one's life well."

"Oh," said Stasy, with a touch of impatience. "I don't look at things in such a grand way as you do, Blanchie. I want to get some fun out of life, and, after all, I'm not difficult to please. My spirits have gone up ever so high, just with the idea of learning millinery and teaching the girls, and perhaps helping good little Miss Halliday. Blanchie, don't you think we might plan some kind of hats that the guild girls would look very nice in—something that Lady Hebe would be sure to notice when she comes back. Perhaps if we ordered a lot of them untrimmed, you know, and got ribbon and things, we could let the girls have them more cheaply than they could buy them. There'd be no harm in that, would there? Of course, I know the guild isn't supposed to be at all a charity—"

"We may be able to do something of the kind," said Blanche. "But it wouldn't do to have them all the same, or even very like each other. The girls wouldn't care for it, and it would make a sort of show-off of the guild. We must think about it; and I want them to learn to trim their mothers' bonnets and caps and their younger sisters' things, as well as their own."

Chapter Fourteen.

Monsieur Bergeret's Letter.

The millinery lessons were begun and steadily carried on without the interest of either of the sisters flagging. For, in spite of Stasy's capriciousness, there was a good of real material in her: she would have despised herself for not carrying out any plan she had formed. And she was not disappointed in her expectation of getting some "fun" out of this new pursuit. It was a pleasure to her to find how deft and neat-handed a little practice made her. Taste in harmonising and blending colours, and a quick eye for graceful form, she had by nature.

Miss Halliday was full of admiration.

"There's nothing more *I* can teach you, young ladies," she said, at the end of a fortnight, during which time they had had about half-a-dozen lessons. "Miss Stasy — if it wasn't impertinent to say so — I would call you a born milliner. Now, I never would have thought of putting violets with that brown velvet, *never*! And yet there's no denying they go most beautifully, and you do make the ribbons and trimmings go so far, too. I've always been told it was the best of French work that it's so light — never overloaded. — And Miss Derwent, you are so neat; indeed, if I might say so, almost too particular."

Blanche smiled.

"I haven't got such fairy fingers as Stasy, I know," she said admiringly, "though perhaps I could beat her at plain-sewing. Yes, I have run on that lace too heavily, I see. Well, and so you think we're ready now to teach our girls, Miss Halliday, do you?"

"Indeed, yes, Miss; and I shall be so pleased to order the hats you want for you at any time, charging you, of course, just what I pay for them myself."

"No indeed," said Blanche; "that wouldn't be fair; you must charge a little commission. I've made out a short list of the things we want to begin with. We're thinking of having our first millinery class next Wednesday evening. We can't have more than one a week, for Miss Wandle and Miss Bracy have two other evening classes, and we don't want the mothers to think the girls are too much away from home."

"I'm sure it's better for them than idling about the lanes," said Miss Halliday, "and that's what they mostly spend their evenings in at this time of year."

"Have you got anything settled about your own plans, Miss Halliday?" asked Stasy.

The milliner shook her head, and gave a little sigh.

"Not yet, Miss Stasy," she replied; "and unless I can find a partner who could put a little money into the concern, I'm afraid I must make shift to go on alone for some time to come. I've got so behind with what I owe, for the first time in my life, all through that disappointment about Miss Green."

"I really think she should have paid you *something*," said Stasy. "I'm afraid you're too good-natured, Miss Halliday. And now you're going to be good-natured to us, and let us come in two or three times a week to help you a little."

"You're really too kind, Miss Stasy," said Miss Halliday. "I don't feel as if I could let you do such a thing. And what would your dear mamma think of it?"

"She's quite pleased," said Blanche; "she's always glad for us to be of any use we can."

"And really I have nothing to do now," said Stasy. "The dancing class and the gymnastics are given up for the summer, and my lessons don't take up long at all. I've got in the way of coming to Blissmore every day with Herty; it would be dreadfully dull to stay always at Pinnerton."

So it was settled that the sisters should come two or three mornings a week to help poor Miss Halliday as much as possible, though, of course, the arrangement was to be kept perfectly private.

It certainly did Stasy a great deal of good to have more to do and some feeling of responsibility. She became more cheerful and more equable in temper than she had yet been in their new home. She was even amiable enough to offer no objection to Blanche's consent to Florry Wandle's eager, though modest, request that she and her cousin might be allowed to join the millinery class.

"I scarcely see that we have any right to refuse them," Miss Derwent had said, "seeing that they actually belong to the guild. Anyway, it would be most ill-natured to do so, as they are good, nice girls."

"I don't mind," said Stasy, "if you and mamma think it right. So long as we are not obliged to go to their houses in return, that's to say."

But what Stasy really enjoyed was the amateur apprenticeship to Miss Halliday. It gave her the profoundest pleasure to stroll down the High Street and glance in at the milliner's window, where hats and bonnets of her own creation were displayed to the admiring gaze of the passers-by. And never had Miss Halliday's stock-in-trade changed hands so quickly. Orders multiplied with such rapidity that the milliner was scarcely able to execute them, and many were the compliments she received on the improved taste and excellent finish of her handiwork.

"You've surely got a very good assistant now," said Mrs Burgess one day. "I don't think I've seen any prettier bonnets even in Paris than some of those you've had this year."

For Mrs Burgess had now returned from her visit to the Continent, and was very full of allusions to her travels.

Miss Halliday smiled as she replied: "Yes, she thought she had been very fortunate."

But she kept her secret well, and so did her little servant. And no one noticed the frequency of the Misses Derwent's visits, as they came in and out by the long garden at the back of Miss Halliday's house, whence a door opening into the lane cut off the necessity of their passing through the entrance to the town, and somewhat shortened their walk.

Summer was advancing by this time with rapid strides. The spring had been a late one, but when the fine sunny weather did come, the delay was amply compensated for. Sunshine, blossoms, and flowers came with a burst. One could almost *see* everything growing. Mrs Derwent, who was keenly sensitive to such things, enjoyed this first spring in England, after her many years' absence, intensely, though quietly, all the more so that Stasy, her chief source of anxiety, was now so much more cheerful.

"Things *must* come right for them both," thought the mother to herself. "They are really so good! Very few girls would make themselves happy in so monotonous and isolated a life."

For even Mrs Harrowby had gone to stay with her own relations in London for a time; and Rosy Milward, who had come over to Pinnerton now and then on guild business, had taken flight, like the rest of the world.

The charms of outside nature, the peace and quiet happiness of their own home, and a fair amount of interesting occupation, made the next few weeks pass pleasantly. Afterwards, Blanche felt glad that it had been so. There was a satisfaction in looking back upon this little space of time as bright and cheerful.

"I really think," said Stasy one day, when she and Blanche were walking back together from Blissmore, "that we are getting acclimatised at last, Blanchie, or rather

I should say, *I* am, for I'm sure you've never been anything but contented. I can look forward now to going on living here with mamma and you for—oh! for ever so long, even if nothing more exciting comes into our lives."

"I'm so glad," said Blanche heartily. "Yes, we've been very happy lately, haven't we?"

"But some day," Stasy went on again, "some day, Blanchie, you must marry. Though I can't, even in my wildest dreams, picture anyone good enough for you. But you are far too pretty to be an old maid!"

"I can't imagine marrying," said Blanche musingly; "that's to say, I can't imagine any one caring enough for me, or my caring enough for any one! And I can't imagine marrying without plenty of caring."

"Of course not," said Stasy. They walked on in silence for a little, till almost in sight of their own gate.

"I thought mamma would have come to meet us, perhaps, as she often does," said Blanche. "But let's hurry on a little, Stasy, and make her come out in the wood before tea."

"And we might have tea in the garden, don't you think?" said Stasy. "We've not had it out of doors once this week, the afternoons have been so showery."

So talking, they crossed their own lawn, entering the house by one of the French windows of the drawing-room, where they half expected to find their mother.

She was not there, however, nor was she in the library.

"I hope she hasn't gone out alone," said Blanche. "Run up-stairs, Stasy dear, and see if she is in her room."

Stasy did so, Blanche remaining at the foot of the staircase.

She heard Stasy's step along the passage, a door opening, and the young girls cheerful "Are you there, mamma dear?" Then—or was it her fancy?—a sort of muffled exclamation, and the slamming to of the door, as there was a good deal of wind that afternoon, and for a moment or two nothing more.

Blanche grew slightly impatient, which was not usual with her. Was there a touch of instinctive anxiety in the impatience?

"Stasy might be quick," she said to herself. "If mamma is out, we—"

But just then came Stasy's voice.

"Blanche," it said, "come up at once. I can't leave mamma: there is something the matter."

Blanche flew up-stairs, her imagination, even in that short space of time, picturing to itself a dozen terrible possibilities. "Something the matter!" What suggestions in the simple words.

It was a relief, on entering the room, to see her mother seated on her usual chair. Pale, very pale, and looking all the more so from the reddened eyelids which told of recent and prolonged weeping. Stasy was kneeling on the floor beside her.

"Mamma, dearest," said Blanche, "what is wrong? You are not ill? No, thank God — then it can't be anything very dreadful."

For there was a strange side of comfort in the isolated position of the little family. When they were all together and well — they had caught sight of Herty playing happily in the garden — nothing, as Blanche had said, "*very* dreadful" could be the matter. Still, something grievous and painful it must be, to have thus affected the usually cheerful mother; and again, before Mrs Derwent had time to reply, Blanche's fancy had pictured every kind of possible and impossible catastrophe, except the actual fact.

Mrs Derwent tried to smile.

"You are right, Blanchie," she said; "it is 'Thank God,' as we are all together. But read this."

She held out a thick foreign letter, closely written in a clerkly hand which Blanche knew well. It was that of the lawyer at Bordeaux, Monsieur Bergeret, and though couched in a good deal of legal technicality, the general sense was not difficult to gather. The old and honourable house of "Derwent and Paulmier" was bankrupt — hopelessly ruined. Monsieur Bergeret, while expressing his deepest sympathy, held out no hopes of any retrieval of the misfortune.

"Mamma," said Blanche, looking up with startled eyes, "what does it mean? How does it affect us?"

For she knew that, besides any practical bearing on themselves, the blow to her mother would be severe. Her husband's and her father-in-law's universally respected position had for more than half her lifetime been a source of natural pride to Mrs

Derwent, and even now, though they were dead, their honourable name must be lowered.

But alas! it was worse than this.

"It means," the mother replied quietly — "it means, my darlings, that we are ruined too. Our money had not been paid out. You remember my telling you that I was a little anxious about the delay; but nothing would have made any difference: they had not got it to pay. If Monsieur Bergeret had pressed them, it would only have hastened the declaration of insolvency. I understand it all. I have read the letter over and over again, since it came by the afternoon post. Dear me," and she glanced at the pretty, quaint little French clock on the mantelpiece — "can it be only an hour ago? It came at three, and it is only just four. It seems years — years."

Her voice seemed faint and dreamy. Blanche looked at her in some alarm. She was utterly exhausted for the moment.

"Mamma dear," said Stasy, "it is impossible to take it all in at once; we must get used to it gradually. The first thing to attend to just now is *you*. You mustn't make yourself ill about it, mamma."

Blanche glanced at Stasy admiringly.

"Yes," she said, "that is the first thing to care about. I am going down-stairs to see if tea is ready. Will you come down, mamma, or shall I bring you a cup up here?"

"I will come down," said Mrs Derwent, adding to herself, in a voice which she tried to make firm: "I *must* begin to get used to it at once."

Chapter Fifteen.

Facing Things.

Derwent did not fall ill, as her daughters feared. There was great elasticity, which was, in fact, a kind of strength, in her nature, as well as a rare amount of practical common sense, and before long these triumphed over the shock, which, it must be owned, was to her a tremendous one.

For she realised, as Blanche and Stasy could not be expected to do, the whole bearing upon their lives, of this unexpected change of fortune.

For a week or two, some amount of excitement necessarily mingled with her distress. For, though Monsieur Bergeret held out no hopes of anything being saved from the crash, he yet advised her to consult the English lawyer who had had charge of her interests at the time of her marriage, and of whom the French man of business entertained a high opinion.

So Mrs Derwent and Blanche went up to London by appointment, to meet this gentleman, and had a long talk with him. His view of things entirely tallied with that of Monsieur Bergeret, but he reassured Mrs Derwent on one or two minor points. What she had in the shape of furniture, plate, and so on, was absolutely hers, and could not, as she had vaguely feared, be touched by the creditors of the firm, of whom, indeed, she ranked as first. Furthermore, there still remained to her a trifling amount of income, all that was left of the little property she had inherited from her father, as it will be remembered that, owing to unwise investment, the late Mr Fenning's capital had almost disappeared.

But anything was something in the present crisis. Even eighty pounds a year was a certainty to be thankful for.

"The best thing you can do, it seems to me," said Mr Mapleson, at the close of the interview, "is to let your house as soon as possible, thus making sure of the rent for which you are liable: I forget the length of your lease?"

"Seven years in the first place," replied Mrs Derwent. "You might let it furnished," the lawyer went on; "that would give you fifty or sixty pounds a year more—not much. Furnished houses in the country don't let for the rents they used to do, or you might have a sale, thus realising a little capital, till you have, as they say, time to turn round, and make some plan for the future. And"—he went on, with a little hesitation—"should you be short of funds at the present moment, pray do not hesitate to draw upon me. I wish with all my heart I could be of more use to you."

"You are very kind, very kind and good," said Mrs Derwent. "But I think I shall be able to manage for a little while. I will see the local house-agent at once, and put the house in his hands. I think I should prefer to be free from it altogether, if possible, and to have a sale."

"Perhaps it would be best," said Mr Mapleson. "Refer the agent to me in case of need. Furniture sometimes sells very well in the country."

"We have some very pretty things," said Blanche — "uncommon things, too; some good china that we brought from Bordeaux, and things like that."

Her voice faltered a little as she spoke, and the old man glanced at her sympathisingly.

"What a charming girl!" he thought to himself. "Too pretty to be a governess or companion or anything of that kind."

"I hope," he said aloud, "that you will be able to keep your daughters with you, Mrs Derwent. I will talk it over with my wife; she has plenty of good sense, and if any idea strikes us, I will write to you. A school — a small, select school, for instance. Your daughters must have been well educated, though, no doubt, private schools do not succeed nowadays as they used to do."

"Thank you," said Mrs Derwent; "we must think it over."

Then they said good-bye, and made their way back to the station again, feeling perhaps a trifle less depressed than on their arrival.

"Shall we stop at the agent's on our way through Blissmore, do you think, Blanche?" said Mrs Derwent, as they were nearing the end of their railway journey. "We must drive out, I suppose," she went on, with a rather wan smile, "though I want to begin those small economies at once."

Blanche glanced at her. It was a hot, close day, and Mrs Derwent seemed very tired.

"It would be poor economy to begin by making ourselves ill," said Blanche. "Of course we must drive. I will write to the house-agent to-night, if you will tell me exactly what to say, mamma. It will do quite as well as seeing him, and be far less disagreeable."

Stasy was watching for them at their own gate as they drove up. She looked bright and eager.

"Tell the man not to drive in," said Mrs Derwent; "we will get out here, poor Stasy looks so anxious to hear what we have got to say."

"She looks as if she had something to tell us, I think," said Blanche. "I must say her good spirits—for she is never low-spirited now—are a great blessing."

"She doesn't realise it," said Mrs Derwent, with a little sigh. "But at sixteen what would you have? That in itself is a blessing."

"Have you any news?" was Stasy's first question? "You don't look so—at least, not any *worse* than when you went away, except that you're tired, of course, poor dears."

"We have certainly nothing worse to tell you," said Blanche cheerfully. "And one or two things are just a little better than we feared." And she gave Stasy a rapid summary of their interview with Mr Mapleson.

"That's all right," said Stasy. "Come in: I have tea all ready for you in the library. *I* have some news for you; at least, something to tell you—two things. In the first place," she went on, as she began pouring out tea, "I've had a visitor to-day. Nobody very exciting, but it may be a good thing. My visitor was Adela Bracy."

"What did she come about?" said Blanche. "I hope they're not beginning to think they may—well, take freedoms with us, just because we've lost our money."

Blanche's tone was a trifle bitter. She was tired, and she could not bear to see her mother's pale face. For the moment, she and Stasy seemed to have changed characters.

"Take freedoms with us!" Stasy repeated. "Oh dear no! Poor Adela! if you had seen how she blushed and stammered over her errand."

"And what was it?" asked Mrs Derwent, reviving a little, thanks to Stasy's good cup of tea.

"She wanted to know," said Stasy, "if her father might call to see you to-morrow morning, mamma, on business. They have heard, you know, about our trouble, because Blanche had to tell them that we couldn't give the other guild treat that we had promised. You said it was best to be frank about it."

"Yes, I remember," said Mrs Derwent. "But both she and her cousin have been very good," continued Stasy. "They have told no one at all till this morning, and then Adela thought it would be only right to let her father know, for our sake, and it was *that* that she was in such a fright about. She thought we might be vexed."

"It doesn't in the least matter who knows and who doesn't, it seems to me," said Blanche. "Besides, I have written to Lady Hebe, to tell her I should probably have to give up the guild work, and I made no secret of our troubles. But you're so mysterious, Stasy: I wish you'd explain! What can it matter about old Mr Bracy knowing?"

"I'm coming to it," said Stasy, "as fast as I can, if you wouldn't interrupt. It's about this house. You know, mamma, you said one day you thought we'd have to sell all our things, and I think anything would be better than that."

"I'm afraid it will be the wisest thing to do, however," said Mrs Derwent, rather dejectedly.

"No, mamma, perhaps not," said Stasy. "What Adela's father wants to see you about is this. He has a brother who has been out in India for a good many years—a rich man, Adela says—and he's coming home almost immediately, with his wife and daughter, for a long holiday; and he wants Mr Bracy to find a furnished house close to theirs for a year, and it struck Adela that this might just do. She says they would take great care of everything, and, oh mamma! think how nice it would be to feel it was still ours, *in case*, you know, of some good luck turning up!"

Her mother smiled.

"My dear child, we mustn't begin to hope for anything of that kind, I'm afraid," she said. "It is better to face the reality. Still, no doubt, it would be *very* nice not to have to part with our things at once. A year from now, we should better know which of these we could keep. It was very kind and sensible of Adela Bracy to think of it, and I shall certainly be very glad to see her father. Can you send him a note to say so, Blanche? It seems to have been a very good thing that we have said nothing yet to the agent."

"I will write at once," said Blanche, rousing herself, for she felt that she had been yielding too much to her unusual depression.

She got up from her place and went towards the writing-table as she spoke.

"What's the name of the Bracys' house, Stasy—Green?—"

"Green Nest," replied Stasy.

"And will eleven o'clock be the best time, mamma?"

"Say any time that suits him, after ten," Mrs Derwent replied.

She spoke more cheerfully. It really seemed as if this new proposal had come in the nick of time, and there was something infectious in Stasy's hopefulness, little ground as there might appear for it.

"I suppose Miss Bracy said nothing about the rent her uncle would be likely to give?" asked Mrs Derwent.

Stasy shook her head.

"No," she replied, "and I didn't like to ask her, indeed I don't think I should have understood about it; but she did say he was liberal and kind, as well as rich."

"Of course I should not expect more than a fair sum," said Mrs Derwent; "the fact of its being of great consequence to us cannot be taken into consideration. Still, it is much better to have to do with people of that character, and no doubt the house is now unusually attractive in many ways, all being in such perfect order."

Blanche rang the bell, and gave orders for the note to be sent at once. Then she came back and sat down again.

"And what's your second piece of news, Stasy?" she said. "You spoke of two."

Stasy reddened a little.

"It wasn't a piece of news," she said. "It was an — an —" And she hesitated.

"What?" asked her mother.

"I'm not quite sure," Stasy replied. "I'm not quite sure but that it was an inspiration!"

Both Mrs Derwent and Blanche looked up.

"Do tell us," said Blanche, but Stasy still hesitated.

"If you don't mind, mamma dear," she began, "I think I'd rather tell it to Blanchie alone first, and see what she thinks. You *might* be a little vexed with me. It may have a little to do with what Mr Bracy says to-morrow."

"Very well, dear," said Mrs Derwent. "I'm quite content to wait, and not to hear it at all, if you'd rather not tell me after consulting with Blanchie."

She had not, perhaps, any very great faith in the practicability of Stasy's inspirations, but she was delighted to see the girl rising with such unselfish cheerfulness to meet their difficulties.

"After all," she said to herself, "troubles are often blessings in disguise. This may be the making of Stasy, and give her the stability she needs."

Mr Bracy called the next morning, behaving with so much tact and consideration as to make it easy to forget his somewhat rough and ready manner, and his frequent oblivion of the letter "h."

The terms he proposed, and which he felt sure his brother would endorse, seemed to Mrs Derwent fair and, indeed, liberal. But before committing herself to accept them, she wished to consult Mr Mapleson, a proposal which Mr Bracy at once agreed to. He was full of admiration of the house, more than once exclaiming that, as far as his brother was concerned, it was a wonderfully good chance.

"And I hope," said Mrs Derwent, "indeed, I feel almost sure that I shall have cause to congratulate myself on meeting so readily with such an unexceptionable tenant."

She spoke in the gracious and graceful way habitual to her, and the retired tradesman left her with feelings of warm sympathy and respect. Mrs Derwent had gained a friend.

Blanche and Stasy had not fallen asleep the night before without having fully discussed the younger girl's idea.

Chapter Sixteen.

Stasy's Inspiration.

Blanche did not speak for a minute or two. Then she looked up with a rather peculiar expression.

"Well, Stasy?" she said, as if expecting her sister to continue speaking.

But Stasy hesitated.

"What has all this to do with your inspiration?" said Blanche.

"I'm half afraid of telling you," said Stasy. "You're rather snubby too, to-night, Blanche, in your manner, somehow."

"I don't mean to be," said Blanche gently. "Do tell me all about it."

"Well, you see," began Stasy, "it just came into my head with a flash. Supposing *we* were to join Miss Halliday, and be milliners in real earnest. Of course it would be more you than I. I should still have to go on doing some lessons. But I could help a good deal, and we could have the same rooms in her house that we had before. We were very comfortable there. It would be better than going away to some horrid, strange place, into stuffy lodgings, where mamma would be miserable."

"You didn't say anything of this to Miss Halliday, did you?" inquired Blanche.

"Oh no," said Stasy; "of course not. But do tell me what you think of it, Blanche."

Blanche sighed.

"It is almost impossible to say all at once," she answered. "It is rather difficult to take it in—the idea of our really having to work for our daily bread, to be actually shopkeepers."

"I don't feel it that way," said Stasy eagerly.

"You are hardly old enough to realise it," said her sister.

"Yes, I think I do," said Stasy; "but it seems to me that anything would be better than being separated—being governesses or companions, or anything like that. What would mamma do without us?"

"Mr Mapleson proposed our beginning a small school," said Blanche.

Stasy made a face.

"Oh, that would be quite horrid, I think. We should be far more independent if we were milliners. And do you know, Blanchie," she went on, her eyes sparkling, "it's quite different nowadays in England. Miss Milward has a cousin who's a milliner in London, and people don't look down upon her for it in the very least. Not even regular — worldly sort of people, you know."

"I've heard of that," Blanche replied; "but in London it's different. Miss Milwards cousin probably has her own friends and relations who know her and back her up. It wouldn't be the same thing at all in a little country town, and in a neighbourhood where people have not been too kind to us as it is. And living 'on the premises,' as people say — oh no, it would be quite different."

Stasy's face fell.

"I was afraid," she said, rather dejectedly, "that you wouldn't like the idea of it at all. But, oh Blanchie, a school would be detestable! We should never feel free, morning, noon, or night; and just fancy mamma having to hear all sorts of horrid fault-findings from vulgar parents."

"They needn't be vulgar," remarked Blanche; "at least not all of them."

"They would be at Blissmore," said Stasy.

"I should never dream of beginning a school at Blissmore," said Blanche quickly. "The high school would spoil all chance of success."

"Where would we go, then?" said Stasy. "We are such strangers in England; and, of course, it would be madness to think of returning to France. No, Blanchie, I won't give up my idea yet, till you have something better to propose."

"I don't mean to snub you about it," said Blanche. "Possibly it was an inspiration. I will speak about it to mamma to-morrow, and see how it strikes her. Of course there would be a great deal to talk about to Miss Halliday. She may require more money than we should be able to give."

"I don't think so," said Stasy, "but she would tell you. Good-night then, dear. I can see you're very tired; but I'm so glad you haven't squashed the idea altogether. I think it would be capital fun! Just fancy all the people coming in and ordering their bonnets and hats. I used to long to go into the shop to take orders, when we were helping Miss Halliday."

She kissed her sister lovingly and ran off, with the light-heartedness of her age, to dream of fabricating a marvellous cap for Mrs Burgess, or some bewitching hats for Lady Hebe's trousseau.

Blanche said nothing of Stasy's scheme to her mother till after Mr Bracy's visit the next morning. But when she found that the negotiations for letting their house at once seemed so likely to go through, she thought it well to tell her mother of this new idea.

At first, there is no denying, it was very startling to Mrs Derwent. She was almost astonished at Blanche's entertaining it for a moment. But a few days passed, and gradually, as often happens in such cases, she grew to some extent familiarised with the possibility. There came two letters from Mr Mapleson, the effect of which was indirectly favourable to the realisation of Stasy's scheme.

"I have consulted my good wife," wrote the old lawyer, "as I said I would. I am sorry to say she rather shakes her head over the idea of a school. There is so much less opening for private establishments of the kind nowadays, and this applies, I fear, to some extent to governesses too, unless they have been trained in the orthodox modern way. It would, no doubt, add greatly to your troubles to be separated from your charming daughters. If you will pardon the suggestion, and not consider it impertinent, what would you say to beginning some sort of dressmaking or millinery business in which you could all keep together? This kind of thing has become rather a fashion of late years, even for women of first-rate position."

This letter arrived at breakfast-time one morning. Mrs Derwent read it and handed it to Blanche, remarking as she did so: "It is rather curious that the same idea should have struck him, isn't it?"

Stasy looked up eagerly.

"What is it? Oh, do tell me! Do read it quickly, Blanchie." And when she had got the letter in her own hands, and mastered its contents, she turned round triumphantly. "There now," she said, "I hope you'll allow in the future that I'm not a silly child. When a wise old lawyer of nearly a hundred proposes the very same thing, I should say it's worth listening to."

"I never thought it was not worth listening to, practically speaking," said Mrs Derwent. "My hesitation was simply that I didn't like the idea, and one of my reasons for disliking it is, that it would be so entirely you two, my darlings, working for me, for I am not at all clever at millinery."

"And I am not a genius at it, mamma," said Blanche. "Nothing like Stasy. It is she who has the ideas."

"But I am not nearly so neat as you, Blanche," said Stasy. "I would never have done so well without you to fasten off my threads, and that sort of thing."

Blanche smiled.

"What I was going to say, mamma," said Blanche, "is that there would be a great deal to do besides the actual millinery. All the business part of it—ordering things and keeping accounts, the sort of thing you're so clever at. You know grandpapa used always to say that you were as good as a head-clerk or private secretary any day. And if the business were extended, as Miss Halliday hopes, there would be a great deal more of that side of it."

"Yes," said Stasy. "She told me the last time I saw her that that is one of her difficulties. She's not very well educated, you know, poor little woman, and her accounts, such as they are, are rather a trouble to her. Indeed," she went on, looking preternaturally wise, "I've a great idea that she is cheated sometimes."

"I can quite believe that she cheats herself," said Mrs Derwent. "I was always finding out things she had forgotten to put down in our weekly account. That reminds me, Blanche, of some things that came into my mind in the night—I didn't sleep very well—about the arrangements we should have to make with Miss Halliday, if—if," with a little hesitation—"this idea really goes farther. We should have to guarantee Miss Halliday against any risk to a certain extent; for, you see, she would have to give up ever having any lodgers if we went to live there."

"Yes," said Blanche thoughtfully; "and yet we could not now afford to pay as much as when we *were* her lodgers."

"Perhaps we should pay half the house rent," said Mrs Derwent, "and, of course, a larger proportion of the housekeeping. All that, I could guarantee out of capital for a time—the first year or so—till we saw how we got on. Miss Halliday is such an unsuspicious creature that I should be doubly anxious to be fair to her."

"Perhaps it would be best to consult Mr Mapleson," said Blanche.

"Yes, I think it would be quite necessary," her mother agreed. "I should like to have a talk with Miss Halliday before doing so, however, so that we might know our ground a little; and then, again, I can't say anything definite till I hear more from Mr Bracy."

She got up from her seat as she spoke, and crossed the room to the window, where she stood looking out.

It was a perfectly lovely, early summer morning. The grounds at Pinnerton Lodge were now beginning to reward the care that had been bestowed on them when the Derwents first took the house. The view from the window across the neat lawn, its borders already gay with flowers, was charming.

No wonder that poor Mrs Derwent sighed a little.

"I think almost the worst part of this sort of trouble," she said, "is waiting to see what one should do; though in some cases, no doubt, this goes on for months."

At that moment the click of the gate was heard.

"I don't think we are going to be kept very long waiting," said Blanche cheerfully — she too had left her seat, and was standing beside her mother — "that's the Bracys' page coming up the path; he must be bringing a note."

Her conjecture was correct. Two minutes later the note was in Mrs Derwent's hand.

"They are really very kind and considerate," she said, looking up after she had read it. "This is to ask if Mrs Bracy may come to look through the house more particularly, as they have quite made up their minds about it. Fancy, Blanche, he has actually telegraphed to India, and has got a reply. I do believe he has done it more for our sake than for their own, for I said to him we wanted to know as soon as possible. They are very rich, I suppose, but they are certainly also very kind."

"And how *horrid* I was to Adela Bracy the first time I saw her," said Stasy, contritely. "Well, never mind, I'll make up for it by fabricating the loveliest hats that ever were seen, for her, if she patronises our millinery establishment."

"Stasy," said Blanche softly, "I wouldn't joke about it if I were you; and you know it isn't the least settled yet. At least not before mamma," she went on, in a lower voice, seeing that her mother was not listening, as she was again reading Mr Bracy's note.

An answer was sent, arranging for Mrs Bracy to see the house that same morning, and by that afternoon the negotiation was virtually concluded. The rent Mr Bracy proposed to pay would in itself have been a sufficient income for the mother and daughters to have lived upon very modestly, had Pinnerton Lodge been their own; but deducting the amount Mrs Derwent was responsible for, as the tenant of the house unfurnished, a very small income was to be counted on, and that but for one year.

"We may feel sure of two hundred," said Mrs Derwent, "for I have still a good balance in the bank, and I have *almost* paid everything we owe, up to this."

"You are counting, of course, the eighty pounds a year that Mr Mapleson spoke of as quite certain," said Blanche.

"Oh dear, yes," her mother replied; "it is indeed our only certainty in the future, except what we would realise by selling the furniture and plate, and so on."

"And I'm sure it is better not to do that in a hurry," said Blanche. "Don't you think, mamma," she went on, "that we know enough now to justify us in having a talk with Miss Halliday?"

Mrs Derwent considered.

"Yes," she said, "I think that is the first thing to be done now, for I have practically promised to give possession of the house early next month."

"Would you like me to see her first, mamma?" Blanche proposed. "Could it make it any less disagreeable for you if I were to sound her, as it were?"

"Oh no, dear," said her mother. "I shall not feel it disagreeable, and even if I did, why should I not take my share when you and Stasy are so good about it all? You would hardly be able to go into it definitely without me. I must make a rough calculation as to what ready money I could promise her at once, subject, of course, to Mr Maplesons approval."

"And he should be written to without delay," said Blanche. "Yes, mamma, if you're able for the walk, I think we should certainly see Miss Halliday to-day. If we go rather late in the afternoon, she would be better able to speak to us uninterruptedly."

They found the milliner in rather low spirits, though the flutter of nervousness at the honour of Mrs Derwent's visit made her forget her own troubles for a little. She was full of sympathy, yet afraid of presumption if she expressed it. But before long Blanche and her mother managed to put her at her ease.

But the calm was only of a few minutes' duration. When Mrs Derwent laid before her with quiet composure the object with which they had sought her, Miss Halliday's excitement grew uncontrollable. She cried and laughed, thanked them and apologised to them, all in a breath, till Mrs Derwent at last made her see that the proposal was for their interest as well as for hers, and managed to calm her down by matter-of-fact discussion of ways and means, and pounds, shillings, and pence.

"It is too good to be true," said Miss Halliday. "I have got silly lately with brooding over things all by myself. Since the day Miss Stasy talked to me, I have not said a word of my troubles to any one, and knowing, of course, how much worse anxieties you dear ladies had to bear, I couldn't have troubled you by asking for advice."

Her confidence in Mrs Derwent was touching. She would have agreed to almost anything proposed, so that Blanche and her mother left her, empowered to tell Mr Mapleson that the milliner was ready to accept any arrangement he thought fair and equitable.

Chapter Seventeen.

A Visitor.

Two months later. A sunny day towards the end of July, the sort of day on which one longs to have nothing to do but to saunter about a garden, or lounge under trees with the lightest of light literature in his hands. It was rather hot in the milliner's shop in the Blissmore High Street, though the sun-blinds had been down since the early morning to protect the few, though pretty, bonnets and hats tastefully displayed in the window. These sun-blinds were a new addition to Miss Halliday's frontage, and she was very proud of them.

"Such a convenience," she said, "making such a nice shade, and yet not stopping passers-by seeing what was to be seen. Not that that would matter," she went on, complacently. "If we had nothing but a plain front door, customers would come in plenty, I feel sure, now that we're getting such a name."

It was quite true. Even during the few weeks that had passed since the Derwents had joined her, Miss Halliday's connection had steadily increased, though just at this season it consisted mainly of the residents at Blissmore itself.

Some came out of curiosity, no doubt, for no secret had been made of the change in the Derwents' position and the courageous step they had taken. It was a new sensation, in a provincial town, at least, to be waited upon by "ladies," and very charming ladies too; though, to tell the truth, the adjective was chiefly drawn forth by Blanche, whose sweet grave face and perfect patience and courtesy of manner rarely failed to win her customers' hearts. But if curiosity brought several of these in the first place, real satisfaction at the way in which their orders were executed was pretty sure to lead to repeated visits. And added to the increasing conviction that not many milliners out of Paris had prettier wares, and "so moderate too," was a sensation, agreeable to the Blissmore ladies, that somehow or other they were acting in a praiseworthy fashion by lending a helping hand to the "poor things."

Yes, as far as the town was concerned, there was no doubt that the new departure was a decided success, though the very success brought certain difficulties in its train, the management of which called for considerable tact.

"You mustn't let yourselves be patronised, dear young ladies," said Miss Halliday, when an invitation to a small evening party was left one day for "Miss Derwent" by Mrs Burgess's parlour-maid. "She wouldn't have dared do it, if you had been at Pinnerton Lodge; and, to my mind, it's a greater freedom now than it would have been then."

"She counts herself an old acquaintance, I suppose, as she called upon us at first," said Blanche; "and Dr Burgess was very good to Stasy when she was ill, you know, Miss Halliday. Still, of course, I would never dream of accepting this. Only we must not risk offending any one, and I believe, in her way, Mrs Burgess has done her best to help us by recommending us."

Miss Halliday gave a little snort, Mrs Burgess being no very great favourite of hers.

"I will answer her note quite civilly," said Blanche, "and just say we do not intend to go out at all. To begin with, mamma would certainly not let me go alone."

"And they'd scarcely venture to ask *her*," said Miss Halliday with satisfaction. "But I wish you wouldn't say you don't mean ever to go anywhere, for when the county ladies are home again, there's no saying but that you may have invitations of quite a different kind."

Blanche smiled.

"The county ladies didn't trouble themselves about us much before," she said. "I can scarcely think it likely they will now, though I certainly hope they will come to us for their bonnets."

"I've not much fear but what they'll do that," said Miss Halliday, whose impressionable nature now saw everything on its bright side. "And even more than that, my dear Miss Blanchie, people are 'funny'—you can't count upon them. Anything that makes a sensation is the thing nowadays;" for the milliner was, in her way, a shrewd observer of human nature. "And there's many nice ladies among them too—real ladies—who'd feel with you more truly than such as Mrs Burgess. There's that sweet Lady Hebe, now!"

A deep sigh from the farther corner of the shop seemed to come in appropriate response to her last words.

"Stasy!" exclaimed Blanche. "What are you sighing so about? I thought you were working up-stairs beside mamma. What is the matter?"

"Oh, a lot of things," replied Stasy dolefully. "I'm so hot, and I can't get these *beastly* flowers to go the way I want them. My fingers seem all thumbs this afternoon."

"*Stasy!*" said Blanche again, this time in a tone of reproof. "Is that the way Blissmore young women talk?"

"I'm a Blissmore young woman myself, now," said Stasy. "So what can you expect?"

"You're overworking yourself," said Blanche. "Instead of doing less, now that your classes are over for the holidays, you're fagging yourself out; and it is really not necessary just now. We got on very well when you only helped us part of the day, didn't we, Miss Halliday?"

"Of course we did," said Miss Halliday, "though we couldn't do without Miss Stasy's taste in anything. But do go out into the garden for a little, my dear; you'll only make your head ache, and not be pleased with what you do in the end, when you're feeling so."

Stasy looked regretfully at the hat on her knee.

"I meant to make it so pretty," she said. "And so you will, if you put it away in the meantime. There's no hurry for it—there isn't, really. Miss Bracy's not leaving home till the end of the week," said Miss Halliday.

Blanche had crossed the room to her sister, and took up the hat to look at it.

"It is pretty already," she said, "and it is going to be quite charming, I can see. So uncommon!"

Stasy looked up with tired eyes.

"Do you really think so?" she said more cheerfully. "I am so glad, for I do want to make it very nice."

It was an uncommon hat, even in these modern days of eccentricity without end—uncommon, but still more, perfect in taste—and in imagination Blanche already saw Adela's piquant face and beautiful dark eyes looking their best under its shade.

"I want the roses to droop over a little on to her hair, do you see?" said Stasy. "And they will look rather sprawly."

"They will come all right in the end, I am quite sure," said Blanche encouragingly, as Stasy rose half reluctantly from her place.

"I just wish you'd go out with her too, Miss Blanchie," said the milliner. "It is hot in here, and you're looking pale yourself. I can call you in a moment when you're wanted. I'll tell you what," she went on, with a sudden inspiration, "shall I tell Aline to take your tea out into the garden? Your dear mamma might like it, for she's been writing all the afternoon, and Master Herty will help Aline to lay it."

Aline was the only servant who had been added to the High Street establishment, and with her happy French faculty of adapting herself to varying circumstances, she had proved so far a real boon to the little family.

So Miss Halliday opened the door leading to the kitchen and gave her directions, while Blanche and Stasy made their way out to the long, pleasant strip of walled-in garden at the back of the old-fashioned house.

"Blanche," said Stasy, as they slowly walked up and down the gravel path, "it wasn't only about the hat I gave that sigh. I do feel so hurt at Lady Hebe, and I do so wish Miss Halliday hadn't put her into my head again."

"She doesn't know anything about Hebe a not answering my letter," said Blanche. "There was no use speaking of it."

"No, of course not," Stasy agreed.

"And I feel certain there must be some reason for it," Blanche resumed. "She is the very last girl in the world to change to us because of all this. Besides, I think it was quite as difficult for her before to be nice to us, as it would be now."

"Perhaps so," said Stasy, rather absently. "Blanche, I do feel so dull and cross now, somehow. It isn't, after all, as much fun as I expected. I do so dislike some of the people that come with their orders."

"Yet, I think, on the whole, they have been wonderfully kind," said Blanche. "Kind, and even delicate."

"Oh, I daresay they have," said Stasy. "But they have such ridiculous ideas! That woman yesterday, who wanted a bonnet that would 'go' with everything. And yet it wasn't to be black or any neutral colour."

"Yes, but Stasy," said Blanche, "I was trembling for fear she should find out that you were making fun of her, when you proposed a— What is it, Aline?" she said, as the maid came out with the tea-tray, which she hastily deposited on a garden seat.

"Some one is at the front door," replied Aline. "The bell rang as I left the kitchen. Will mademoiselle excuse my leaving the tray there? I must answer the door, for that stupid little girl has not yet dressed herself," and she hastened off.

Just at that moment Herty put his face out at the glass door, which was slightly ajar.

"Where is Aline?" he said. "She promised I was to help her to carry out the tea things."

"She has gone to open the door," said Blanche. "She will be back in a moment. Come out here and help us to lay the table. — We may as well, Stasy," she said to her sister; "the tray is not very secure on that chair."

She began unfolding the little table-cloth which Aline had brought out.

"Herty must have run to the door," said Stasy with some annoyance. "I am afraid he is getting rather common in his ways, Blanche, now that we live so plainly. I think we must be more particular with him. It does seem so vulgar for a child to be peeping out to see who is at the door."

"I doubt if Herty will content himself with peeping," said Blanche. "I wonder if all little boys are as inquisitive as he is."

At that moment Herty's shrill voice was heard in eager excitement.

"Blanchie, Blanchie," he cried; "Stasy — somebody's come to see you. — Come along, do," he added to some one, as yet invisible in the drawing-room. "We're going to have tea in the garden; won't it be jolly? You're just in time."

Some inaudible words of remonstrance must have been addressed to him by the unfortunate individual he had under his convoy. But Herty was not to be so easily balked of his prey.

"You *must* come out," they heard him say. "They'll be as pleased as anything to see you."

And apparently the invisible new-comer judged it wiser to resist no more, though it was with somewhat heightened colour, and less appearance of being equal to the occasion than was usual to him, that Mr Archibald Dunstan followed, or, more correctly speaking, allowed himself to be dragged out into the garden by the irrepressible Herty.

"I do beg your pardon, Miss Derwent," he said as he shook hands, "but I couldn't help myself, Herty is such a determined young person."

Blanche looked up at him, serenely enough to all appearance, though in her heart she was not sure how this unexpected visit should be regarded.

"I had no idea you were in the country," she said. — "Herty, go and tell mamma that Mr Dunstan is here. We are just going to have tea, as you see; we hoped it would be a little cooler in the garden than in the house."

"It has been very hot lately," Archie replied, slightly disconcerted, he scarcely knew why, and disgusted with himself for finding nothing more original to say; though Blanche was to the full as self-possessed as if she were receiving him in the pretty little home in which she had last seen him, as if no crash had completely broken the tenor of their life.

Archie almost felt as if he were dreaming, and yet — there could be no doubt that all he had heard was true. The facts spoke for themselves. Here the Derwents were, installed in the back rooms of the Blissmore milliner's house.

And yet how nice it was! The sunny afternoon and the old garden; nothing to jar even upon the ultra refinement with which he was often taxed. Was it that Blanche Derwent, by the perfect sweetness and dignity of her presence, shed harmony and beauty about her wherever she might happen to be? He almost thought that herein was to be found the secret of it all.

"Why are we all standing?" said Stasy, with her rather incisive, girlish abruptness. Her voice recalled the young man to matters of fact. He hastily turned to draw forward some of the seats that were standing about.

"I daresay mamma won't come down for a minute or two," Stasy continued. "She told me just now that she had two or three letters that she must finish for the post."

Mr Dunstan looked rather guilty.

"I do hope she will not hurry on my account," he said. "I am in no hurry, but I do want to see Mrs Derwent. I have a" — and he hesitated — "a message for her from an old friend. At least I promised to give her news of him the first time I saw her."

"Indeed," said Blanche, who, if she felt curious as to who the old friend might be, for her own reasons repressed her curiosity.

But Stasy was less self-contained.

"An old friend," she repeated eagerly. "How interesting! I wonder who it was. Do tell us, Mr Dunstan."

Archie was by no means reluctant to do so. Anything to get out of the stilted commonplace-isms which had begun the conversation.

"It is no one you know personally," he said, turning rather pointedly to Stasy; "though you have probably heard of him, as he was your grandfathers greatest friend — I mean old Sir Adam Nigel."

Stasy almost clapped her hands.

"Oh, how glad I am," she exclaimed, "and how delighted mamma will be! She has been longing to hear of him again. Is he in England? He was to have come in the spring."

"No," Mr Dunstan replied, "I came across him at Cannes. I ran down there for a week last month to see an old relation of mine. Sir Adam has not been in England for two years, but he hopes to come over before very long, and he is sure to stay at Alderwood with my aunt, if he does so, as Mrs Lilford has suggested it. He asked me if I had met Mrs Derwent when I was staying there, and he was so pleased to hear about you all. I am staying at Alderwood again just now, you know, for a day or two by myself."

Blanche suddenly raised her eyes and looked at him.

"Does," she said—"did Sir Adam know, when you saw him, of—of what had happened to us? That we had lost all our money?"

"No," said Archie. He could not hesitate or feel awkward, when the girl was so straightforward. "No, he certainly had heard nothing about it. I doubt if he has heard it even now."

"I am glad of that," said Blanche, "for he has not written."

"I did not know myself—I had not the slightest idea of it—till two days ago, when I came down here," said the young man; "and I cannot tell you how dreadfully sorry I was, for I suppose it is all quite true?"

"Quite true," replied Blanche. "Thank you for being sorry about it. I am rather surprised at your not having heard of it before. Not, of course, that our affairs are of general interest. But have you not seen Lady Hebe lately? I wrote to tell her about it, because it affected the work I had undertaken to do for her."

"And has she not written to you direct?" inquired Mr Dunstan quickly.

Blanche shook her head slightly.

Archies face darkened.

"I don't understand her," he said, as if speaking to himself. — "No," he went on aloud, "I have not seen her for some time; she has been away for several weeks at Coblenz, of all places in the world at this time of year. She is back in London now, but I didn't call before coming down," he finished, rather abruptly.

"I thought you were such very great friends," said Stasy, looking him full in the face. "Have you had a quarrel?"

"*Stasy!*" said Blanche, her colour rising as she spoke.

But before she had time to say more, the rustle of a skirt across the grass made her start up. Their mother had just come out to join them.

Chapter Eighteen.

Herty's Confidences.

Derwent greeted Mr Dunstan with quiet courtesy, scarcely, however, amounting to friendliness. He was instantly conscious of the slight change in her manner, and at exerted himself to regain the ground he found he had somehow lost. This, under usual conditions, would have required little effort on the young man's part, for he was gifted with that charm of manner which springs from a really unaffected and unselfish character. "Spoilt" he might well have been, and to some extent, in fact, he was so. But the spoiling did not go far below the surface. Yet it was second nature to him to feel himself more than welcome wherever he chose to go. Awkwardness of any kind was a perfectly novel sensation.

What was the matter this afternoon? He felt embarrassed and self-conscious, as if treading on ground where he had no right to be.

Mrs Derwent's attitude was that of tacit expectation, as if waiting to hear the reason of his visit, so Archie's preliminary remarks about the heat in London, and the refreshment of getting a day or two in the country, fell rather flat.

So at last he plunged abruptly into the only tangible explanation of his visit he could lay hold on.

"I have just been telling Miss Derwent," he began, "that I met a very old friend of yours the other day at Cannes. He is an old friend of some of my people's too — Sir Adam Nigel — who used long ago to live at Alderwood, you know."

Mrs Derwent's manner grew more cordial, and her face lighted up.

"Oh," she exclaimed, "I am so glad to hear about him. He spoke of us — of me — then, to you?"

"Oh dear, yes," said Archie, delighted at his success. "He asked me no end of questions about you, when he heard I had had the pleasure of meeting you. And he begged me to give you all kinds of messages, as I told him I was sure to see you again before long. I'm always turning up in this neighbourhood," he went on, "though my own home is in another county, for my uncle Dunstan was my guardian, and they've been at Alderwood for fifteen years or so now. Mrs Lilford has never really settled there."

"Dear me," said Mrs Derwent, "that makes it seem still longer since it was almost like home to me," and her face saddened again a little. "Did Sir Adam say nothing about coming over this year?" she added. "I had hoped to see him before this."

"Mamma," said Blanche gently, "Mr Dunstan tells us that Sir Adam had no idea of what has happened, or that we had left Pinnerton Lodge."

"No indeed," said Archie eagerly.

Mrs Derwent's face cleared again.

"I am not surprised," she said. "Indeed, I felt sure of it, from his not having written again."

"He is pretty certain to be in this neighbourhood before the winter," added Archie, "and then, of course." But he hesitated. It was not his place to assure Mrs Derwent that her old friend would look her up.

"Yes; then, of course, I shall see him," she said, finishing the sentence for him. "But I think perhaps I will write, as, no doubt, Mr Dunstan, you can give me his present address."

"Certainly I can," the young man replied. "That's to say, I can give you the Cannes address, and from there his letters are sure to be forwarded."

Just then Herty reappeared, carefully carrying a plateful of buttered toast.

"There were no tea-cakes," he said apologetically; "so Aline and me have been making this."

"Buttered toast in July!" exclaimed Stasy contemptuously. "And you look as if you'd been toasting your face too, Herty; you're as red as a turkey-cock."

Herty's beaming face clouded over.

"I thought you'd like it so much," he said. "You generally do, Stasy."

"Of course we like it," said Blanche, as she began to pour out the tea.

"I think there's nothing better than buttered toast at any time of the year," said Archie heartily, at once following Blanche's lead.

He was beginning to feel quite himself again. More than that, indeed, when Blanche glanced at him with an approving smile such as she had not yet favoured him with. How lovely she looked! He had always thought her lovely, but never, it seemed to him, had he seen her to such advantage as now; the afternoon sunshine adding a glow to her fair hair, and a touch of warmth to the delicate tints of her face, which had struck him as rather pale when he first saw her. Yet nothing could be simpler than the holland dress she was wearing. What made it so graceful in its folds? He had often condemned holland as too stiff and ungracious a material to be becoming, for Archie was a great connoisseur in such matters. Its creamy shade even seemed to deepen her blue eyes, lighted up by the transient smile. He had been a little doubtful about the colour of her eyes before, but now he was quite satisfied. They were thoroughly blue, but never had he seen so rich a shade in conjunction with that complexion and hair. He forgot he was looking at her, till a slight flush, for which the sunshine was not responsible, creeping over the girl's cheeks, made him realise his unconscious breach of good manners.

The little bustle of handing cups and plates covered his momentary annoyance with himself.

"Really," he thought, "what's coming over me? I must be losing my head."

The next quarter of an hour or so, however, passed very pleasantly. Mr Dunstan began to hope that he might feel himself re-established in the little family's good graces.

"Are you going to be at Alderwood for some time?" asked Mrs Derwent in the course of conversation. "Isn't it rather dull for you?"

"I don't mind it," replied Archie. "I'm rather used to being alone — in the country, that's to say. I've no one but myself at my own home. I've been an orphan, you know, since I was a little fellow, and my only sister has been married for several years. Her husband is Norman Milward's half-brother, Charles Conniston. They live in Ireland. By the way, you must have seen them that — that first afternoon I met you at Alderwood. They were staying at Crossburn then."

"No," said Blanche, whom he seemed to be addressing. "I don't think I remember any one except old Mrs Selwyn that day, though I have seen young Mr Milward — Lady Hebe's *fiancé* — once or twice, and his sister several times."

"Oh, Rosy!" said Mr Dunstan. "Isn't she nice? But isn't she plain — almost odd-looking?"

Blanche did not reply.

"Blanche never thinks people that she likes, plain," said Stasy.

"I beg your pardon," said Blanche, "I'm not so silly. But the word doesn't seem to me to suit Miss Milward, she has such wonderful eyes."

"Yes indeed," agreed Archie, almost too evidently eager to endorse whatever Blanche said. "I quite agree with you. They are really beautiful eyes, because there's no sham about them. She is as good as they would lead you to believe."

Again the same bright smile of approval came over Blanche's face, and Mr Dunstan felt himself rewarded. Just then Aline appeared at the door.

"Mademoiselle," she said; then coming closer, she spoke to Blanche in a lower voice, though unluckily Mr Dunstan was so near that he could not but overhear what she said.

"Some ladies are in the shop. Miss Halliday is very sorry, but she fears you must come."

"Of course," said Blanche, springing to her feet—for the moment, she had begun to forget the present facts of her daily life, and she gave herself a sort of mental shake— "of course," she repeated, "I'll come at once.—Mr Dunstan, will you excuse me?" and she held out her hand, as if in farewell.

The young man's face had grown visibly redder.

"Good-bye," he said, repressing the effect that Alines words had had upon him.

Then turning to Mrs Derwent:

"Will you allow me to call again?" he said very clearly. "I intend to stay at Alderwood for two or three days longer."

"Oh, certainly, if you happen to be anyway near," she replied simply.

Then a bright idea struck Archie, as his glance fell on Herty.

"I wish you'd allow this young man to spend a day with me," he said. "I'd take good care of him, and it is holidays just now, I know. I shall be driving in to-morrow morning in my dog-cart, and I will call for him, if he may come."

"Oh mamma, mamma," said Herty, ecstatically, "do say I may!"

It would have required a heart of stone to refuse the poor little fellow, and Mrs Derwent's heart was by no means of that material.

"It is very good indeed of you, Mr Dunstan," she replied; "and I am sure Herty would enjoy it immensely. Of course he has not nearly so much to amuse him here as at Pinnerton."

"Then I will call for him at—let me see—shall we say eleven o'clock? and I'll bring him safe back in the afternoon. Between four and five, if that will do?"

"Perfectly," said Mrs Derwent, and then Mr Dunstan left taking care not to glance into the shop as he passed its open door on his way out.

Herty was ready the next morning betimes. Long before eleven had struck he was fidgeting about, asking every one half-a-dozen times in a minute what o'clock it was, so that it was a relief to everybody when the dog-cart drew up to the door and Herty was safely hoisted up to his seat beside his friend.

"I was so afraid it would rain or something, and that perhaps you wouldn't come," said the little boy.

"I would have come all the same if it had rained," said Archie. "I could have wrapped you up in a mackintosh, and I daresay we'd have found something to amuse you at Alderwood."

"These holidays are very dull," said Herty with a sigh. "I have got no rabbits, nor nothing like I had at Pinnerton. I'd almost rather go back to France."

"There's no chance of that?" said Mr Dunstan quickly.

"Oh no," said Herty. "Blanchie says we must stay here for—always, I suppose. Anyway, till I'm a man; and then I mean to make money for them. You know we've got no money now, at least scarcely any except what they make with having a shop. It's rather horrid, don't you think?"

"Yes," agreed Archie, somewhat incautiously; "I think it's exceedingly horrid. And I can quite understand that you feel in a great hurry to be a man, so as to be able to help them."

"It'll take a good while, though," said Herty prudently, and then he began talking about the horse, extracting a promise from Archie that he would let him hold the reins when they got to a perfectly quiet part of the road.

But with some skill Mr Dunstan managed to bring him back to the subject they had been discussing.

"Do you think your sister minds much?" he asked, when Herty had been retailing some of his own grievances.

Herty considered.

"Well," he said, "she hadn't any rabbits, you see, and I think she likes making bonnets. They made them for the girls at Pinnerton, you know. But I think she does rather mind not having such a nice garden; she minds it for mamma, you see. And Stasy gets awfully cross sometimes! I heard Blanche speaking to her one day about being cross to the people in the shop."

"And is Blanche never cross?" inquired Mr Dunstan, with great interest.

"Not like Stasy," said Herty. "But she was very angry with me once when I was little. It was when I cut some hairs off Flopper's tail. Flopper was grandpapa's dog, an English dog, and those hairs are very particular, and then—and then," said Herty, very slowly, "I said I hadn't done it. It was that made Blanchie so cross. Telling a story, you know."

"Yes," said Archie, with preternatural gravity. "But that was a long time ago; of course you know better now," he went on, cheerfully. "You never vex your sister now."

"No, not as badly as that," said Herty. "But one day, not long ago, I did see her crying. It wasn't my fault, but I was very sorry; I think she had a headache, perhaps."

The horse gave a spring forward at that moment, nearly dislodging Master Herty from his seat.

"I say, Mr Archie," he exclaimed reproachfully, "what are you whipping him for? He's going along quite nicely! I nearly tumbled out, I really did."

"I beg your pardon, Herty," said Mr Dunstan. "I'll be more careful in future. I suppose I wasn't thinking."

Herty's visit was a great success, the day passing to his complete satisfaction; and between four and five that afternoon the pair of friends found themselves at Miss Halliday's door. Not this time in the dog-cart, for Mr Dunstan had left it at the "George," a little way down the High Street.

"I won't come in, I think, Herty," he said, as Aline appeared in answer to the bell.

But Herty clung on to him.

"Oh, you must, just for a minute," said the child. "I'm sure mamma would like to see you."

"Madame is in the drawing-room," put in Aline discreetly.

So, between the two, Archie allowed himself to be over-persuaded.

As Mr Dunstan, an hour later, passed the post-office on his way to the "George," it suddenly struck him that he might call for the afternoon letters. There were two for himself, forwarded from his club—one of no special interest; the other a few hurried words from Norman Milward, whom he had not seen for a considerable time. "Hebe wants to see you," he wrote. "She is back in London, but we have been in great anxiety lately. She wants to tell you about it herself. Do come as soon as you can."

Chapter Nineteen.

Something Important.

The very next afternoon found Mr Dunstan standing at the door of the Marths' house in London.

"Is Lady Hebe at home?" he inquired at once when it was opened, glancing up with some anxiety as he asked the question.

But nothing was to be learned from the man-servant's impassive face, though—yes, it was surely unusually grave, for Archie was no stranger to him.

Her ladyship was at home, he replied, and expecting Mr Dunstan. For Archie had telegraphed that he would call at a certain hour.

Then he was ushered up-stairs to Hebe's own little sitting-room, where many a happy half-hour had been spent by the circle of young "old friends."

"Well, Hebe," he said, as the door closed behind him, "here I am. I only got Norman's letter yesterday afternoon, for I have been out of town for a few days. What an age it is since I have seen you!"

He had hardly as yet noticed her face, for the room was very dark; but as she came forward, holding out her hand, he almost started. She was unusually pale.

"You've not been ill, have you?" he said. "Its surely not that that has been the matter?"

"Then Norman did tell you something was the matter?" were her first words. "No, I have not been ill, at least not exactly. But, sit down, Archie, dear; I've a good deal to tell you."

The young man drew a chair near her—she sat with her head to the light—with a feeling of increasing uneasiness.

"You make me feel quite frightened, Hebe," he said. "What is this mysterious trouble?"

To his distress Hebe—happy Hebe—gave a little gasp that was almost like a sob.

"Archie," she said, "it is a very great trouble that has come upon me, or rather upon us, for I am sure it is quite as bad or worse for Norman. Do you know there have been, there still are, grave fears that I am going blind? That is what I have been at Coblenz for. You know there is a very great oculist there."

Archie's bright, sunburnt face had paled visibly.

"Good heavens!" he exclaimed. "My poor child—my dear little Hebe. It *can't* be true; those specialists are always alarmists as well."

"No," she said. "I will tell you all about it, for I quite understand. They've not hidden anything from me. My guardian has been *very* kind, and Josephine—I did not think there was so much tenderness in her. It is not hopeless. It has come on gradually. But till this summer I did not realise it at all; I have always been so strong and well, you know, in every way. Then the glare and the heat of London seemed to make it worse suddenly. I began to think it must be something more serious than short-sightedness."

"You *never* were short-sighted," Archie interrupted. "You had splendid sight."

And indeed, as he looked at her eyes now, deep and lustrous, but with a sadness in their brown depths which he had never seen there before, it was difficult to believe that there could be anything wrong.

"Yes," she agreed; "but for some time I have not seen so well, and I got in the way of thinking I must be short-sighted. But this summer pain began, very bad sometimes, and then we consulted our doctor, and he sent me to Coblenz."

"And the opinion you got there was?—"

"I will tell you exactly," said Hebe, "for I know you care."

And she gave him a rapid *resumé* of the whole. It had ended in an operation being decided upon, in the anticipation of which she was already under a course of treatment.

"We are going back to Germany in a fortnight," she said. "It is to be in about a month or six weeks from now. The Marths can't stay with me all the time, but when Josephine leaves, Aunt Grace will come; and if all goes well—or, indeed, in any case—I hope to be back at East Moddersham some time in October. But what I wanted to see *you* about. Archie, was to ask you to look after Norman. He is so miserable, and it is much better for us not to be together. It breaks my heart to see him, and he says it breaks his heart to see me."

"What can I do?" said Archie.

"I thought," said Hebe, with some hesitation—"I thought perhaps, if it didn't interfere too much with your own plans, you might propose taking him off to Norway, or something like that."

Archie did not at once reply.

"You are such very old friends, you know," said Hebe. "I wouldn't ask such a thing only for my own sake."

There was just a touch of hurt feeling in her tone. She had been so sure of the heartiest response from him. She was changed—her happy, almost childlike confidence seemed to have deserted her, and as Archie glanced up at her pale face, he felt disgusted with himself for his even momentary hesitation.

"My dear Hebe," he exclaimed, "as if I wouldn't do far more than that, for you as well as for Norman! I was just considering if I could explain everything to you! But I can't just yet. Of course you may count upon me for Norway. I will set about it at once, and plan it so that Norman shall not in the least suspect that you had suggested it."

"Oh, thank you," said Hebe, in a tone of great relief.

"Let's see," Archie went on. "We might start in ten days or so, and you'd like me to keep him away till after—"

"Yes," said Hebe calmly, "till after the operation. That is to say, till its result can be known. I am not afraid of the operation itself—nowadays those things are managed painlessly—but it is the afterwards. Oh Archie, I mustn't cry, they say it is so bad for my eyes; but if I am going to be blind, I *can't* marry Norman. He's so young and full of life, it would be terrible for him to be tied to—"

She drove the tears back bravely, but it was all Archie himself could do to reply cheerfully.

"He would never give you up, I feel convinced," he said. "But I am quite certain that what we have all got to do just now is to be hopeful. I will see you again soon, Hebe, when I've got things into shape a little. Trust it all to me. I must go back to—the country again to-night, for a day or two."

He rose as if preparing to go.

"Where are you staying?" said Hebe—"at Saint Bartram's?"

"N-no, I'm at Alderwood," he replied. "I had some things to see to about there."

Hebe's brown eyes looked at him curiously.

"At Alderwood," she repeated. "Oh, by-the-bye," and she sighed, "I am so sorry never to have replied to a letter I had from Blanche Derwent. It was a private letter, and I have not been allowed to write at all."

"Yes," said Archie coolly, "I know about it. She told me."

"You know all about their troubles, then—their loss of money?" asked Hebe, with some surprise.

"Yes, I heard it when I went down there. And then I saw them. They have left Pinnerton; they are living at Blissmore. They—no, I hate talking about it—they've actually joined that funny old milliner there; they are working for their daily bread."

Hebe gasped.

"Is it so bad as that?" she said. "But how splendid of them, how brave, and oh how horrid I must have seemed! Oh Archie, could you explain about me if you see them again? I can't write myself, and there is really no one I can ask to do so, especially now, after what you've told me."

"Certainly I can do so," replied Archie briskly. "Nothing can be easier. I will make a point of seeing Miss Derwent as soon as possible."

"Thank you very much," said Hebe, but some amount of reservation crept into her tone; something in Archie's voice and manner struck her, and revived her former misgivings.

"It was thoughtless of me to propose it," she said to herself. "Archie," she began again, "I—"

"No," interrupted Mr Dunstan, with some impatience. "Don't ask me anything, Hebe, for if you do, I can't answer. You blamed me before undeservedly, and I deserve it still less now."

His words startled Hebe still more. She looked very grave.

"I didn't blame you, Archie," she said. "I only wanted you to be careful. You have always treated some things so lightly, it makes it difficult to believe you could be in earnest. And in this case—under the circumstances"—She did not like to say what was in her mind—that serious attentions on the part of the rich and much-made-of Archie Dunstan to Blanche Derwent, however charming personally, would appear in the eyes of the world highly improbable. Doubly so considering the change in the latter's position. "I mean," she went on hesitatingly, "you must be very careful."

Archie smiled at this somewhat lame conclusion to her warning.

"You may trust me, dear Hebe," he said, as he pressed her hand in farewell, and then he was gone.

But Hebe sat thinking deeply for some time after he had left her.

"*What* would Josephine say?" she thought to herself. "What a romantic goose she would think me. But I have never seen Archie quite like this before. And if such a thing came to pass—if I could be sure he is in earnest for once—it would be delightful in many ways. But"—and here a new view of the subject struck her—"I don't believe Blanche would accept him," she thought. "She is proud, rightly proud, and she has seen so little of him. She is not a girl to marry a man without thoroughly caring for him. No, I don't believe she would accept him. But if he is in earnest now, he has certainly never been so before."

Mr Dunstan returned to Alderwood that same evening, having already written to Norman Milward with some suggestion of the proposed plan, and promising to see him in London early the following week.

"It would have been perfectly impossible to refuse Hebe," he thought to himself, as he was sitting alone in the small room where dinner had been served for him, "but it does seem dreadfully unlucky. I don't see my way at all, and yet can I go away for an indefinite time and leave things as they are? I must trust to chance, I suppose. I *must* call there to-morrow, for I promised Hebe to give her message. Beyond that, I see nothing."

Mr Dunstan's visit had not made any great impression on the members of the little household in the High Street, with the exception possibly of Miss Halliday and Herty.

An unexpected and rather important order coming at a dull season had made the milliner and her young assistants unusually busy, and it was not without a feeling almost amounting to annoyance that Blanche found herself called away from the workroom the day after Archies return from London, to join her mother in the drawing-room.

"Do you want me particularly, mamma?" she said as she went in. "I am so busy just now. I could come in half an hour or so."

As she spoke she suddenly became aware that her mother was not alone. Mr Dunstan was standing by the window.

"I did not know any one was here," she went on, with an instinct of apology, "I had not heard the bell ring."

"I am exceedingly sorry for interrupting you," said the young man as he came forward, "but I could hardly help myself. I promised to see you personally to give you a message from Lady Hebe. I have been telling Mrs Derwent about it, but I know it would be a satisfaction to Hebe to hear that I had seen you, yourself."

Blanche looked perplexed, and glancing at her mother's face, she saw that it was unusually grave.

"Is there anything the matter?" she said quickly.

"Yes," said Mrs Derwent. "You will be very sorry for poor Lady Hebe. A great trouble has come upon her."

"Has anything happened to Mr Milward?" asked Blanche, and somehow Archie felt pleased that this was her first idea.

"No," he answered. "Norman is all right. The trouble has come to Hebe herself, though, of course, it is terrible for him too."

And then he went on to give the details of the grievous loss with which the young girl was threatened.

Blanche's face grew graver and graver as he spoke. "Oh dear!" she exclaimed, when he had finished. "How dreadfully sad! Those pretty, happy eyes of hers. I can't believe it. May I write to her, Mr Dunstan, do you think? I do feel so inexpressibly sorry for her. Mamma, our troubles don't seem much in comparison with this, do they?"

"No, indeed," Mrs Derwent agreed heartily. "But still it is not hopeless by any means, is it, Mr Dunstan?"

"I trust and believe not," he replied. "But then I have only Hebe's own account, you see. I shall know more after I have seen Norman and the Marths. — About writing to her," he continued, turning to Blanche, "I don't quite know. I don't fancy she's allowed to read at all, and you might not care for your letter going through other hands."

Blanche looked disappointed.

"Then will you tell her from me?" she began, but he interrupted her.

"I'll tell you what," he said, "if you won't think me officious—if you like to write to her and will give me the letter, I'll take it myself, and she can have it read to her by some one you would not mind—Rosy—Rosy Milward, perhaps."

"Thank you," said Blanche. "I would like to write a little, however little, if I were sure she would get it herself. I can write it at once," she went on, "if you don't mind waiting a few minutes;" and she left the room as she spoke. She had hardly done so, when Stasy made her appearance.

"Blanche," she said, as she came in, "Miss Halliday does so want you—How do you do, Mr Dunstan? I did not know you were here.—Where is Blanchie, mamma?"

"She is writing a note," Mrs Derwent replied—"something rather particular. Can I not do instead of her?"

"Oh, well, perhaps you can; it's about a letter she is wanted," said Stasy. "If you could come, Miss Halliday will explain about it." And with a word of apology to Mr Dunstan, Mrs Derwent left the room with her younger daughter.

"What a life of slavery for women in their position!" said Archie to himself. "To be at the beck and call of all the Blissmore shopkeepers. It is insufferable!"

He strolled restlessly to the window and stood looking out, feeling very indignant with the world in general and, most unreasonably, with Miss Halliday in particular.

He had not stood there long when Blanche returned with an envelope in her hand.

"This is my little letter," she said, holding it out to him. "Thank you for taking charge of it, though it does not say half—not a hundredth part—of what I feel for her."

"I know that she will value your sympathy," said Archie, wishing he could think of something less commonplace to say.

He stood there, feeling, if not looking, uncertain and embarrassed, Blanche's evident expectation—for she did not sit down again—that he was on the point of going, not tending to set him more at his ease.

Suddenly he spoke.

"I know you are busy, Miss Derwent," he began. "I've no doubt you are wishing I would go. But the truth of it is, I can't go without saying something more to you."

Blanche looked up, a gleam of surprise in her face.

"I am busy," she said, smiling a little. "But if it is anything important, I can wait a few minutes."

Archie glanced irresolutely towards the window.

"*Would* you mind," he said, "coming out into the garden. It *is* something important, and if we stay here they will be calling for you immediately."

Chapter Twenty.

A Nephew and an Aunt.

Blanche did "mind," for she was anxious to go back to the workroom. But Mr Dunstan had been very kind, and it was not in her nature to be unyielding in small lings.

"Perhaps he has something more to tell me about, Hebe," she thought, as she led the way out through the open glass door.

"Miss Derwent," began Archie again, when they had strolled towards the farther end of the long strip, "the fact of the matter is—and you must forgive me if it seems impertinent—I cannot stand this."

"What?" asked Blanche, looking up in bewilderment.

"This—this position for you," he said. "This horrid slavery."

"Oh," said Blanche, somewhat coldly. "I couldn't think what you meant. It's very good of you, but you really needn't trouble about it. On the whole, I think we are very fortunate indeed. Lots of people have far worse things to bear. I thought you were going to tell me something about Hebe."

"I see you do think me impertinent," Mr Dunstan resumed, with some slight bitterness in his tone. "You don't understand. I don't care about 'lots of people's' troubles. It is *you* I care about. It is for *you* I can't endure it."

Blanche looked up again, this time with slightly deepened colour.

"Thank you again," she said, "for your kindly meant sympathy. But if you knew me better, or had known me longer, you would understand that there are many kinds of troubles which would be much worse to me. I am really not unhappy at all—none of us are. Indeed, in some ways, the having more to do makes life more interesting." And then she stopped, at a loss what more to say—feeling, indeed, that there was nothing more to be said.

Archie grew desperate.

"You are not like any girl I have ever met," he said; "you won't understand me. Can't you see that the reason I mind it so much is that I care so much for you?"

"Mr Dunstan!" exclaimed Blanche, and in the two words a calmer hearer would have detected some indignation as well as the astonishment which was unmistakable. "No, I don't understand you," she went on. "We are almost strangers."

"Strangers!" he repeated reproachfully. "You have never seemed a stranger to me since the first day I saw you, for since then you have never been out of my thoughts. You *must* understand me now. Can I speak more plainly? I don't want to vex you by seeming exaggerated, but I care for you, and have done so all these months, as much, I honestly believe, as it is possible for a man to care for a woman. I did not mean to have said this so soon. Of course I don't ask you to say you care for me as yet, but don't you think you might get to do so in time? I could be *very* patient."

It was impossible to reply with any feeling of indignation to a suit so gently urged.

"I am very sorry," was all Blanche could say.

"I would do anything," he went on—"anything in the world that you wished. I am perfectly independent, entirely my own master, and I have no one very near me. Your family would be like my own to me. It would be a delight to be able to release them from any necessity like this present arrangement."

"You are very good," murmured Blanche, really touched, "but—"

"Don't say 'but' just yet; let me finish," he went on. "I am leaving England almost immediately, for two months at least. I won't ask to see you again till I come back. I won't say anything if you feel that you must stay on here in the meantime, though I would give worlds to see you back in your own home. If you will only agree to think it over, to try to get accustomed to the idea? That is all I ask just now."

Blanche stopped short. They had been walking on slowly.

"Please don't say any more," she said. "Mr Dunstan, I can't agree to anything, I don't care for you—I mean, I don't love you in the *very* least. I never dreamt of your having thought of me in any way. You must see, under the circumstances, it would be perfectly impossible for me to say I would try to get to care for you, except as a friend. Your very goodness and kindness make it impossible. I do thank you most heartily for what you have said about us all I am not proud in some ways. If—if I loved anybody, it would not be painful to me to accept whatever he was able to do for those I love. But you wouldn't have me try to care for you because of that?"

"It might come to be for myself," said Archie. "Certainly, I agree with you that nothing I could possibly do would deserve such a reward."

"I don't mean that," said Blanche. "I could never disassociate the two. I should always feel that pity and sympathy had made you imagine your own feelings deeper than they were."

"No, no," he almost interrupted. "It was long before I knew of all this. It is hard upon me that you will not even give me the chance, which you might have done had circumstances been otherwise."

Blanche shook her head.

"I want to be quite fair," she said. "Honestly, I can't imagine myself ever caring for you in that way, putting all secondary feelings out of consideration."

"You are so young," he said, "you can't judge."

"I think I can," she replied. "I am older in some ways than you imagine. Good-bye, Mr Dunstan," she went on. "I am glad you are going away, for I hate to feel myself ungrateful, and yet, what could I do? Good-bye."

She held out her hand.

"Good-bye, then," he repeated, and in another moment he was gone.

She was wanted indoors, Blanche knew. A quarter of an hour before, she had felt almost feverishly anxious for Mr Dunstan to leave, for she was much interested in the important order they had unexpectedly received. Nevertheless, when she had seen the young man's figure disappear into the house, she turned again and slowly retraced her footsteps along the gravel walk to the farther end of the garden, feeling that for a few minutes she must be alone.

Every sensation seemed absorbed for the time in an intense, overpowering rush of pity for the disappointment she felt she had inflicted.

"I wonder if all girls feel like this when this sort of thing happens," she said to herself. "If so, I pity *them*; it is quite horrible. I feel as if I had been so terribly unkind and ungrateful. But how could I have guessed that such a thing was in his mind! It seems too extraordinary. And why should he have thought of *me*, among the crowds of girls he must meet?"

She went on musing to herself a little longer. Then, though not without some amount of effort, she made her way slowly back to the house.

"I will not tell mamma," she decided. "I don't think it would be wrong not to do so, and though she is so good and unworldly, she might feel, considering everything, a little disappointed that I had been so decided about it."

Five minutes later she was in the middle of a discussion as to the prettiest shade of blue for Miss Levett's bridesmaids' hats.

The next few weeks passed, on the whole, quickly; for though it was what Miss Halliday described as "between the seasons," the good woman had never, even in her palmiest days, been so busy. She was overflowing with delight; her most sanguine dreams bade fair to be realised.

It was an unusually fine and hot summer, and early autumn crept on imperceptibly, so mild and genial did the weather continue. Blissmore and the neighbourhood broke out into an unprecedented succession of tennis and garden-parties, picnics and the like. And whether the entertainers and the entertained on these festive occasions belonged to the exclusive county society or to the inhabitants of the town itself, the practical result, so far as the milliner and her friends were concerned, was the same.

Everybody needed new hats and bonnets, for a fine and prolonged summer necessarily makes great havoc with such articles of feminine attire, and orders succeeded orders from all directions with almost overwhelming rapidity.

The secret of the young milliners' extended fame was not long left undivulged. For one day, a week or two after young Mr Dunstan's visit, a carriage from Alderwood drew up again at the door in the High Street, and from it descended, without any preliminary summons by bell or knocker, the short stout figure of Lady Harriot in person.

She walked straight into the shop, looking round as she did so with short-sighted eyes. The first person they lighted upon was Miss Halliday.

"Oh – ah," began the visitor, "I came to see Miss Derwent. Is she not here?"

Blanche emerged from the farther part of the shop and came forward.

"How de do?" began the old lady, holding out her hand with what she intended for marked affability. "I'm pleased to see you again. Well, now, I don't exactly know whether I should say that. At least, I mean, I should rather have seen you at Pinnerton than here. I'm very sorry for what's happened – I am indeed. Mrs Selwyn told me all about it, and I promised her I'd look you up as soon as I came back. I think you're a very brave girl, I do indeed, my dear. I wish you success with all my heart."

"Thank you," said Blanche cordially. "It was very good of Mrs Selwyn to think of us. And is there anything I can do for you, Lady Harriot?" she went on, with a twinkle of fun in her eyes. "I do hope you want a new bonnet."

The fun was lost upon Lady Harriot, whose density was her predominating characteristic, but the practical suggestion was quite to her mind.

"Yes," she said, "that's just what I do want. I've gone through such a number this year in London, with the fine weather and the sun and the dust. And I was going to bring down one or two new ones with me, just when I saw Aunt Grace; so then I said to her I would wait till I came back here, and see what you could do for me. And I hope to get you some more customers, but the best way to begin is by getting something for myself. One's head shows off a bonnet so, you know."

Blanche glanced up at the good woman's headgear with some trepidation. She felt rather caught in her own trap, for Lady Harriot's bonnets were remarkable, to say the least. Like many stout, elderly ladies, she loved bright colours, and was by no means amenable to her milliners suggestions, and Blanche's misgivings were great as to the desirability of Lady Harriot in the shape of an advertisement.

An amusing consultation followed. Blanche would have liked to summon Stasy to her aid, but she dared not.

"What would happen," she asked herself, "if Stasy made fun of the old woman to her face? *I* couldn't keep my gravity, even if Lady Harriot didn't find it out."

And probably her own tact and powers of persuasion were far more effectual than Stasy's rather despotic decisions on all questions of taste or arrangement.

And Lady Harriot departed in immense satisfaction, firmly convinced that the bonnet was to owe its success to her own suggestions, and that Blanche Derwent was really "a sensible girl, with no nonsense about her."

"And really very pretty," she added to herself. "I must call on their mother the next time I am in the town, and I mustn't forget to speak about them everywhere. I do hope, for their sakes as well as my own, that she'll remember all I said about the bonnet."

Two or three days later saw her again at Miss Halliday's. The bonnet was ready, and this time Stasy was with her sister, having faithfully promised to behave with immaculate propriety. Blanche's face was very grave as she lifted out her handiwork—or more strictly speaking, Stasy's, for it was the young girls clever fingers that were usually entrusted with orders of special importance — out of its nest of tissue-paper, and held it up for their visitors inspection.

Out came Lady Harriot's *pince-nez*.

"Very nice, very nice indeed, so far as I can tell before trying it on. I will do so at once." And she proceeded to divest herself of the bonnet she had on, a creation which Stasy's eyes took in with silent horror.

"Stasy!" said Blanche, when the new erection was placed on Lady Harriot's head, and there was a decided touch of triumph in her tone.

Stasy came a little nearer.

"It must be just a shade farther forward," she said, skilfully touching it as she spoke.

Lady Harriot submitted, but looked at the girl with surprise.

"Do you mean to say?" she began, hesitating.

"Oh yes," said Blanche, replying to the unspoken inquiry. "My sister's much cleverer at millinery than I am. She always does our most particular things."

"Really," said Lady Harriot; but she could not say more, for by this time she was absorbed in her own reflection in the looking-glass.

"Doesn't it look nice?" said Blanche gleefully. "You *are* pleased with it, aren't you, Lady Harriot?"

"Yes; it really does you great credit. I like it better than any bonnet I've had in London this year. You have so thoroughly carried out all my suggestions — that is a great point for young beginners."

"And, of course, we have the benefit of Miss Halliday's experience, too," said Blanche, glancing towards their good little friend, who, she was determined, should not be left altogether out in the cold.

Miss Halliday smiled back to her. It was a proud day for the milliner when a woman of Lady Harriot's position patronised her shop, but she was well content that all the honour and glory should fall to the sisters' share.

"Ah yes, of course," Lady Harriot replied civilly. "Now, my dear Miss Derwent, I shall make a point of wearing this bonnet everywhere. I wish my nephew could see me in it. He is very particular about what I wear, and he's really quite rude about my bonnets sometimes. I must get my winter ones from you, and then he will see them, for he is out of England just now for some time. — Is Mrs Derwent at home this afternoon?" she went on. "Do you think she could see me?"

"I am sure she would be very pleased," said Blanche readily. "She is in the drawing-room," and as she spoke she led the way thither.

Lady Harriot exerted herself to be more than agreeable, and Mrs Derwent was really won over, by her visitors praise of her daughters, to meet her present cordiality responsively.

"By-the-bye," said Lady Harriot, as she rose to take leave, "I expect a few neighbours the day after to-morrow at afternoon tea. I shall have some people staying in the house by then, and we like to have tea in the garden in this lovely weather. Couldn't you manage to come over?"

Blanche glanced at her mother doubtfully.

"We are really very busy," Blanche began; but her mother interrupted her.

"I think you might give yourselves a holiday for once," she said, and the old lady hastened to endorse this.

"Yes, indeed," she said good-naturedly. "All work and no play. Oh dear, I forget the rest, but I'm sure it meant it wasn't a good thing. Won't you bring them yourself, Mrs Derwent? Your younger daughter is not out, I suppose; but you know this sort of thing doesn't count, does it?"

Mrs Derwent smiled.

"We can't think much about questions of that kind, now," she said. "But I shall be very glad to bring Stasy too."

"That's right," said Lady Harriot, increasingly pleased with them because she was feeling so very pleased with herself. "Then I shall expect you between four and five. You may like to walk about the grounds a little if you come early," she added to Mrs Derwent, "as you used to know the place so well. — And remember, my dear," she said to Blanche in conclusion, "that whomever I introduce you to, it will be done with a purpose. It will be an excellent thing for you to see some of the people about, especially as I shall make a point of wearing my bonnet."

Blanche's face looked very grave when their visitor had taken leave, and her mother glanced at her anxiously, fearing that Lady Harriot's eminently clumsy remarks at the end had annoyed her.

"You mustn't mind it, dear," she said. "She is a stupid, awkward woman, but she means to be kind now, and we must really take people as we find them, to some extent."

Blanche started as if recalling her thoughts, which had, indeed, been straying in a perfectly different direction.

"Of course we must," she said cheerfully. "I don't mind what she said in the very least. I don't particularly care about going there, it is true; but if it amuses Stasy, and if you don't mind it, mamma, I daresay I shall like it very well. We may see Miss Milward, and hear about poor Lady Hebe." And then for the moment the subject was dismissed, though Mrs Derwent had her own thoughts about it.

"It is strange," she said to herself, "how things come about. To think that our first invitation of any kind from the people I used to be one of, should have come in this way — almost out of pity."

Chapter Twenty One.

Mrs Burgess's Caps.

Blanche's hope or expectation of meeting Miss Milward at Alderwood was not fulfilled. She had not, however, been there many minutes before she caught sight of Mrs Harrowby, the wife of the Pinnerton vicar, among the guests, and of her she made inquiry as to Rosy's absence.

She was away, paying visits, for a few weeks, Mrs Harrowby replied; and something in her manner made Blanche feel that it was better to hazard no further inquiry, as she had been half-intending to do, about Lady Hebe herself. For some slight allusion to the East Moddersham family only drew forth the remark that the Marths were expected back some time in October.

"Either," thought Blanche, "she doesn't know how bad it is, or she has been asked not to speak of it."

"The guild girls are getting on wonderfully well," volunteered the vicars wife, "thanks to Adela Bracy and her cousin, though, in the first place, thanks to you. They miss you very much—indeed, we all do, at Pinnerton. Adela says you have been most kind in allowing her to apply to you about some little difficulties that occurred;" as was the case.

"I was so sorry to have to give it up," said Blanche simply. "I only wish I could help Miss Bracy more."

Just then Lady Harriot appeared with some of the numerous members of the Enneslie family in tow, to whom Miss Derwent was introduced with great propriety. Some irrepressible allusions to the bonnet followed on the good hostess's part, which Blanche minded very much less than the Misses Enneslie minded them for her. They were nice girls, ready to be almost enthusiastic in their admiration of Blanche and of her sister, whom the youngest of them took under her wing, with the evident intention of making her enjoy herself. And the sight of Stasy's brightening face was enough to make her sister's spirits rise at once, more especially when she saw how, on her side, her mother was enjoying a tour of the grounds under old Mr Dunstan's escort.

Other introductions followed, several of them to families whose names were not altogether unfamiliar to the girl, for as they sat working together, Miss Halliday was not above beguiling the time by a little local gossip of a harmless kind. And Lady Harriot's good offices did not stop with "the county." Blanche was trotted out, so to say, for the benefit of some of the Alderwood house-party, her hostess challenging their admiration, not only of the *chef d'oeuvre* reposing on her own head, but of the charming "confections," which she described as to be seen in the High Street at Blissmore.

"You must really drive in with me one day, before you leave," she would exclaim to some special crony of her own. "You would think yourself in Paris, you really would. — And yet none of your things have come from there as yet, have they, Miss Derwent?"

"None of those you saw, I think," Blanche replied, "though I did write for a few models to a shop we used to get our own things from. The hat I have on is copied from one of them."

"I was just thinking how pretty it was," said the mother of some daughters, standing beside her. "I should extremely wish to have one like it for each of my girls, if we may call some day soon. That's to say, if you don't mind our copying yours, Miss Derwent. It isn't as if we lived in this neighbourhood; we're only here for a few days."

"I shall be delighted to make them for you," Blanche replied pleasantly.

And the perfect good taste of her manner increased the favourable impression she had created.

Indeed, that afternoon at Alderwood bade fair to see her and her sister exalted into the rank of heroines. It was plain that "taking up" the Derwents was to be the fashion in the neighbourhood, and to a less entirely single-minded and well-balanced nature than Blanche's, the position would not have been without its risks. But, without cynicism, she appreciated the whole at its just value. The neglect and indifference and stupid exclusiveness shown to them during their first few lonely months in England had been a lesson not lost upon her, all the more that she had in no way exaggerated its causes.

"There are lots of kind people in the world, I suppose," she said to Stasy, whose head was much more in danger of being turned than her own. "But there are not many who go out of their way to make others happier, like dear Lady Hebe, or to help them practically, like kind Mrs Bracy; and the sort of attention that comes from ones being in any way prominent is really worth very little."

"I know," Stasy agreed. "People are very like sheep; still, Blanche, the Enneslies are very nice girls. You are not going to advise mamma not to let me go to see them, when they asked me so very kindly, and not at all in a patronising way. You have always wanted me to have nice companions."

"Mamma can judge much better than I," said Blanche. "I should not think of advising her one way or the other, though I hope she will let you go to spend a day with the Enneslies."

"Really," said Stasy, "if it's to be made such a fuss about, I'd much rather not go; if I were a poor apprentice, I should be allowed 'a day out' now and then, I suppose."

For Stasy's temper just now was, to say the least, capricious. She was growing tired of the steady work required of her, now that the first blush of novelty and excitement had worn off. And this invitation to the Enneslies, a simple and informal affair, such as there could be no possible objection to for any girl of her age, was but the precursor of others, which, while they gratified Mrs Derwent to a certain extent, yet gave her cause for a great deal of consideration and some anxiety.

"Stasy is too young," she said to Blanche, "too young and excitable to go out, even in this ungrownup way, as much as would now be the case if we laid ourselves out for it. And for her it would not be the simple sort of thing that it is for girls in an ordinary position. Wherever we go, you would just at present be more or less picked out for notice and attention, and however kindly that may be meant, it would not be good for Stasy."

"Nor for me either, mamma," said Blanche. "I dare say I should get very spoilt. I know I feel dreadfully lazy after these garden-parties and things of the kind, and disinclined to do anything at all."

"My darling," said her mother, "I can scarcely imagine anything spoiling you. The spoiling would go deeper with Stasy than in the common sense of the word, for immediately people began to make less of her, she would be exaggeratedly embittered and cynical."

"We must save her from that," said Blanche eagerly; "and it is just what would happen. Still, mamma, I think we should let her have all the change and recreation possible, for she does work so hard — harder than she needs. She throws herself so intensely into whatever she is doing. She gets as flushed and nervous over a hat as if her life depended upon it."

"It is even better when she is doing some lessons," said Mrs Derwent, "and the classes will be beginning again soon. We must just take things as they come, Blanchie, and do our best."

So a great part of the invitations that were sent to them was courteously declined on the plea of want of time, none being accepted save such as it was desirable for Stasy to take part in, and which did not involve the expense of long drives or of much loss of working hours.

One day early in October, "business" — to use Miss Halliday's expression — "being rather slack just then," Mrs Burgess made her appearance in a great state of excitement. She wanted some caps at once, as she was going off unexpectedly on a visit.

It was late in the afternoon. Blanche had persuaded her mother to go out for a little stroll. Miss Halliday, in her corner of the shop, had, to confess the truth, been indulging in a little nap, and Stasy, some lace-frilling in her hands, which she was working at in a rather perfunctory way, glancing between times at a story of thrilling incident in a volume lent her by the Enneslies, was feeling unusually restful and contented.

"I do hope no one else will come to-day," she thought to herself. "It is nice to have a little breathing-time before the winter season begins, which Miss Halliday expects to be such a success."

Suddenly the shop door opened. Miss Halliday started up, looking and feeling very guilty.

"Good-afternoon, Miss Halliday," said Mrs Burgess, the new-comer. "Dear me, what a colour you are! I hope you're not going to get apoplectic! Where is Miss Derwent? I must see her at once;" and she proceeded to explain the reason of her visit, and the urgency of her wants.

Now, Mrs Burgess's caps were even more marvellous works of art than Lady Harriot's bonnets. They had indeed set Stasy's teeth on edge to such an extent that Blanche had taken them altogether into her own hands, especially since some over-plain-speaking of Stasy's on the subject had gone very near to deeply offending the doctor's wife.

No visitor could have been more unwelcome. What imp had suggested to Blanche the desertion of her post that afternoon?

"I am sorry," Miss Halliday replied, as she collected her scattered faculties, speaking with unusual dignity as she took in the sense of Mrs Burgess's uncalled-for remark on her own appearance — "I am sorry, but Miss Derwent is not in at present. If you will kindly explain to me what you want, I will do my best, and I will tell Miss Derwent all particulars as soon as she comes back."

"No," interposed Stasy, coming forward, before Mrs Burgess had time to reply. "You are tired, Miss Halliday: I know you had a bad headache this afternoon. Let me take Mrs Burgess's orders;" and she darted a wrathful glance at the visitor. "Miss Halliday apoplectic indeed!" she thought inwardly; "*she* looks far more so herself."

The doctor's wife looked at Stasy rather dubiously. She had not the same faith in the young girl as in her elder sister, and at the bottom of her heart she was a little afraid of Stasy, whom she was given to describing to her own friends as an impertinent, stuck-up little monkey. But her friends did not always agree with her – that is to say, not those among them who had benefited by the girls cleverness, or been fascinated by the charm of manner Stasy could exert when it suited her.

Furthermore, there was no choice. The caps must be had by a certain hour the next day, and as Mrs Burgess expected a guest to dine at her house that evening, she knew she would have no time to call again.

"I'm sure Miss Anastasia's taste will please you," said Miss Halliday, full of gratitude to Stasy, and recalling dire failures of her own in time past, anent Mrs Burgess's head-dresses.

"Ah well," said the lady, "you will do your best, I have no doubt, my dear, and I will explain exactly, so that you scarcely can go wrong. See here" – and she drew out a little parcel from the voluminous folds of her cloak – "I have brought one of my old caps as a pattern. This one was made by a French milliner in London, and was a great beauty in its day."

"Indeed," said Stasy, as she took up the crumpled and faded article gingerly by the tips of her long delicate fingers. "That was a good while ago, I suppose, though of course fashions change quickly. You do not wish this to be copied exactly?"

"You couldn't do it if you tried," said Mrs Burgess, already on the defensive, as she scented danger.

"No," replied Stasy, with apparent submissiveness, "I don't suppose I could. But if you will be so good as to take off your bonnet and put this cap on, it will be a guide as to the size of your head and the fit. Then I can show you some lace and flowers, or whatever you prefer."

It took some little time for Mrs Burgess to divest herself of her bonnet and veil, as precautions had to be observed lest the remarkable addition to her somewhat scanty locks, which she called her "chignon," should come off too. But at last the feat was safely accomplished, Stasy standing by and eyeing her the while with preternatural gravity.

Then the cap was hoisted to its place and adjusted with the help of a hairpin or two, Stasy marching round and round her victim, so as to get a view from all sides, with no more regard for Mrs Burgess, who was hot and flurried, and very doubtful as to the behaviour of her chignon, than if the poor woman had been a hairdresser's block.

"Yes," she said at last, composedly, "I quite see how it should be. Miss Halliday, please give Mrs Burgess her bonnet. — Now as to the lace you would like the caps to be made of, and the colours? I forget how many you said you wanted?"

Mrs Burgess had made up her mind to have three. But something quite indescribable in Stasy's tone aroused her spirit of contradiction.

"I didn't speak of more than one," she said.

"I beg your pardon," said Stasy, with extreme deference. "I must have been mistaken. I thought you alluded to *some* caps."

"Well, and what if I did?" said Mrs Burgess, growing illogical as she waxed cross. "I came, hoping to see Miss Derwent, and there's no saying how many I mightn't have ordered if she had been in. But as it is, I don't know but what I'd do better to wait till I get to London. I'm not at all sure that you'll be able to manage it."

"That must be as you prefer," said Stasy, preparing to replace the lid on a box of tempting-looking laces which had just caught Mrs Burgess's eye. The girl knew quite well that the doctor's wife did intend to order the caps, and in her heart she was beginning to feel some interest — the purely disinterested interest of the artist — in fabricating something which should for once show off her customer's plain features to the best advantage; but she was determined to reduce Mrs Burgess in the first place to a proper attitude of humility and deference. Her air of profound indifference was perfect.

"You may as well let me see those laces," the doctor's wife began again. "You needn't be quite so short about it, Miss Stasy; it's natural I should like to see what you can do. I won't go back from having *one* cap, and, if it's all right, I'll let you know about another."

Stasy looked at her calmly.

"I must have misunderstood you again," she said.

"I thought you wanted them at once. I could promise two, or even three, to-morrow, if you decide upon them now, but not otherwise."

"And perhaps you will allow me to mention," said Miss Halliday, coming forward, "that even if Miss Derwent had taken the order, ten to one but Miss Stasy would have carried it out. There is no one like her for quick work. She knows in an instant what's the right thing to do, and her fingers are like a fairy's. — I *will* say it for you, my dear!"

Mrs Burgess's respect for Stasy rapidly increased, though the girls air of calm superiority made her try her best to hide the fact.

"Ah well," she said, in what she intended to be a tone of condescending good-nature, but which Stasy was far too quick not to interpret truly, "suppose we fix for two caps, one for morning and one for evening. Yes — those laces are very nice. You have some pretty flowers, I suppose?"

"For the evening head-dress, you mean," said Stasy. "These thick laces are for evening caps, and, *of course*, without flowers. I should propose a few loops of black velvet with this lace."

"Black velvet!" exclaimed Mrs Burgess. "That will be dull. I like a bit of colour in my cap. It sets off a dark dress, and Mr Burgess likes me best in dark things since I've got so stout."

"If you particularly wish it, you can have crimson velvet," said Stasy; "but, of course, black would be the right thing."

"Well, I'll leave it to you," secretly convinced, but determined not to show it, was the reply, and, feeling herself triumphant, Stasy could afford to be generous. She drew out a box of beautiful French flowers of various shades, in which she allowed Mrs Burgess to revel with a view to the evening cap. And just as the doctor's wife, having recovered her usual jollity, was impressing upon her that she *must* have the caps — *must*, whatever happened — to try on by eleven o'clock the next morning, the shop door softly opened.

"Mind you," repeated Mrs Burgess in her loud, rather rough tones, intending to be jocular, "you'll have them back on your hands, Miss Stasy, unless you keep to the time."

The name "Stasy" fell on ears to which it had once been very familiar.

"Stasy," their owner repeated to himself inaudibly, as he stood unnoticed by the door. "Can that be my little girl's child, and in such a position? Good heavens! how careless I have been."

Chapter Twenty Two.

The Tall Old Gentleman.

"Ahem!" followed by a slight cough, drew the attention of the three in the shop wards the door, whence the sound proceeded.

There stood a tall, rather bent, grey-haired old gentleman. Miss Halliday stared at him dubiously, but Mrs Burgess started forward.

"Good gracious!" she exclaimed. "Sir Adam! Who'd have thought it? I had no idea, sir, you were in the neighbourhood."

The new-comer glanced at her coldly.

"Oh," he said, after a moment's pause, "Mrs Burgess, is it not? I hope your good husband is well—But"—and he stepped forward—"may I ask," addressing Miss Halliday, "if it is the case that—that Mrs Derwent and her daughters are living here for the present?"

"It is so," said the milliner, with gentle and half-deprecating courtesy. "I am sorry."— Then remembering Stasy's presence, she turned to her. "This is Miss Anastasia. She can explain better. Perhaps, Miss Stasy, you will take the gentleman into the drawing-room till your mamma returns. I daresay she will not be long now."

Stasy put down on the counter a trail of roses which she was still holding, and laid her pretty little hand, with almost childlike confidence, in Sir Adam's, already extended to meet it. The old man looked at her with a curiously mingled expression. Something about her, as well as her name, recalled her mother; still more, perhaps, her grandfather. For, though Stasy was at what is commonly called the "awkward age," in her very unformed, half-wild gracefulness there was the suggestion of the underlying refinement and courtliness of bearing, for which Sir Adam's old friend had been remarkable.

"My dear child; my poor, dear child!" he exclaimed.

Then the two disappeared—the young girl's hand still held firmly in the old man's grasp—through the door at the end of the shop, which led into the Derwents' own quarters, to Miss Halliday's intense satisfaction, and Mrs Burgess's no less profound discomfiture and amazement.

"Dear, dear!" she ejaculated. "What's going to happen now?" and she turned to Miss Halliday.

"I don't understand you, ma'am," she said quietly.

"Why, it's plain to see what I mean," returned the other. "Old Sir Adam Nigel treating Stasy Derwent as if she were his grand-daughter! How does he know anything about them?"

"She is not that, certainly," said Miss Halliday, referring to the first part of Mrs Burgess's speech, "but she is the grand-daughter of his very oldest and dearest friend, Mr Fenning—the Honourable and Reverend—and of his wife, Lady Anastasia Bourne, to give her maiden name," rolling out the words with exquisite enjoyment. "If you'll excuse me, Mrs Burgess," she continued, "I think, from the first, you've just a little mistaken the position of my dear ladies, if I may make bold to call them so."

For a worm will turn, and all Miss Halliday's timidity vanished in indignation, hitherto repressed, at the behaviour of the doctor's wife.

"Bless me!" exclaimed Mrs Burgess, "how was I to know? But what about my caps?"

"You shall have your caps; no fear of that," replied Miss Halliday. "It's not real ladies that break their word." And with a little bow of dismissal, which Mrs Burgess meekly obeyed, she opened the door for the latter to make her way out.

"I've done no harm," thought the little woman, with satisfaction; "she's too pleased to have got hold of some gossip, to mind my plain-speaking."

Half-an-hour or so later, Mrs Derwent and Blanche, who had been tempted by the loveliness of the autumn afternoon, to go farther than they had intended, made their way home through the fields at the back of the house, entering by a door in the garden wall, of which Blanche had the key. Half-way up the gravel path, the sound of voices reached them through the open glass door of the drawing-room.

"Dear me!" exclaimed Blanche, "whom can Stasy have got in there? She seems to be talking very busily, and—yes, laughing too. Listen, mamma."

"It must be Herty," Mrs Derwent replied, half indifferently, for she was feeling a little tired, and, as could not but happen now and then, for all her courage, somewhat depressed. "Herty, or Miss Halliday," she added.

"No," said Blanche, standing still for a moment. "Miss Halliday must be in the shop, as Stasy isn't Mamma," with a quick and slightly nervous misgiving, "I'm sure I hear a man's voice.—Surely," she thought to herself, "it can't be—oh no, he would never come again in that way."

"Who can it be?" said Mrs Derwent, for her ears, too, were quick.

They hastened on, Stasy's cheerful tones banishing any apprehension. As they got to the door, Blanche naturally fell back, and Mrs Derwent stood alone on the step outside, looking into the room.

There was Stasy on a low seat, drawn up closely to her mother's own pet arm-chair, in which was comfortably ensconced a figure, strange, yet familiar. Stasy's face was turned from Mrs Derwent, but the visitor at once caught sight of her, and, as her lips framed the words, "Sir Adam!" he started up from his place and hastened forward.

"Stasy!" he exclaimed. "My little Stasy, at last!" And Stasy the younger, glancing up, saw the words were not addressed to her.

"Mamma, mamma!" she exclaimed. "You see who it is, don't you? Isn't it delightful? We have been longing for you to come in; but I've been telling Sir Adam *everything.*"

For a moment or two Mrs Derwent could scarcely speak. Meeting again after the separation of a quarter of a century must always bring with it more or less mingled emotions, and in this case there was much to complicate Mrs Derwent's natural feelings. It was not all at once easy to throw aside the apparent neglect of her once almost fatherly friend, which for long she had explained to herself by believing him dead; and yet here he now stood before her, her hand grasped in both his own, the tears in his kind old eyes, as moved as herself—to outward appearance, even more so.

"Stasy," he repeated; "my dear little girl, can you ever forgive me? I have not really forgotten you." This appeal to her generosity was all that was required.

"Dear Sir Adam," she said, "I never really doubted you."

"Until quite lately, you know," he went on, "of course I thought things all right with you, always excepting, of course, your great sorrow some years ago. And I was pretty ill myself for a good while. I am stronger now than I have been for years past, thanks to all the ridiculous coddling the doctors have insisted on, as if my life was of much value to any one."

"I am so glad," said Mrs Derwent fervently.

"Well, upon my soul," he replied, "I think I shall begin to be glad of it myself. I feel as if I'd got something to do now, besides running about from one health-resort to another."

He started, as at that moment Blanche entered the room.

"And this is Blanche!" he exclaimed, with undisguised admiration. "Stasy, my dear, you did not prepare me for two such daughters."

"But I did," interposed the younger Stasy, from behind her mother; "at least about Blanche. Didn't I tell you how lovely she was, Sir Adam?" she went on, mischievously, rewarded by the sight of the rosy colour which crept up over Blanche's fair face.

Stasy's high spirits, and the touch of impishness which generally accompanied any unusual influx of these, were a godsend at this moment, helping to tide over the inevitable constraint accompanying any crisis of the kind, in a way that Blanche's calm self-control could not have achieved. The younger girl was simply bubbling over with delight, and it was very soon evident that she had completely gained Sir Adam's heart; while the amount of information she had managed to impart during their half-hour's *tête-à-tête* perfectly astounded her mother.

"I know all about everything," said Sir Adam, sagely shaking his head. "You're to have no secrets from me—none of you, do you hear? And if I suspect you, Stasy number one, or you, Miss Blanche, of concealing anything from me, I shall know where to go for all I want to hear;" and he patted little Stasy's hand as he spoke. But his eyes had somehow wandered to Blanche. Why did she again change colour? She almost bit her lips with vexation as she felt conscious of it.

Soon after this, Sir Adam left them. He was staying at Alderwood, but was dining that evening at East Moddersham.

"Oh, have they come back?" exclaimed Blanche impulsively. "And how is—" She stopped.

"Hebe Shetland, you're thinking of?" he said quickly, for his instincts were keen. "I know all about it, as I fancy you do. Yes, she has come back too, only the day before yesterday."

"And?" said Blanche eagerly.

"They are very hopeful," he replied. "I don't know that one dare say more as yet. I shall hear further particulars there to-night, and then I'll tell you all about it. I shall see you again very shortly. I want to think over things. Good-bye, my dear children, for the present I haven't seen the boy yet."

As he reached the door, he turned round again.

"By-the-bye," he said, "don't mind my asking, have the Marths been civil to you? You were such near neighbours. Josephine is a peculiar woman, but there's good in her."

"There is in nearly every one, it seems to me," answered Mrs Derwent with a smile. "Lady Marth had no special reasons for noticing us."

"That means she was—ah well, the very reverse of what she might have been," he said, with a touch of severity. "However—"

"But Lady Hebe was all she could *possibly* be," said Blanche quickly. "We felt drawn to her from the very first."

"That's right," said Sir Adam, and with the words he was gone.

They were but a small party at East Moddersham at dinner that day. A few of Sir Adam's particular friends, got together to welcome him back again, even if but for a short time, among them.

He drove over with Lady Harriot and her husband, to whom had not been confided the whole gravity of poor Hebe's troubles. And the old lady chattered away rather aggravatingly as to reports which had reached her of Norman Milward's *fiancée* having grown hypochondriacal and fanciful.

"The poor fellow's been in Norway for ever so long," she said, "because she wouldn't agree to fixing the time for their marriage. Aunt Grace was with her about then, but even she couldn't make her hear reason. It's not what I'd have expected of Hebe, I must say."

"Did Aunt Grace tell you so herself?" inquired Sir Adam drily.

"Well, no, not exactly," Lady Harriot allowed. "It was something I heard in London about Hebe's being so changed, and poor Norman looking so ill. It must have been true, for our Archie has been away with him all this time. I do hope he'll be back soon, for he's so useful in the autumn."

"Norman Milward has come back," said Sir Adam. "He was expected at East Moddersham to-day, so you will hear all about your nephew from him, and I can take upon myself to set your mind at rest as to any misunderstanding between Hebe and her *fiancé*!"

"I'm glad to hear it, I'm sure," said Lady Harriot. "By-the-bye, Sir Adam," she went on, "I think you might do your friends the Derwents a good turn by speaking of them to Josephine Marth. She's almost the only person about here now who hasn't taken them up."

Sir Adam winced slightly at the expression.

"*You* have been very kind to them from the first, Lady Harriot," he said. "I shall always feel grateful to you for it. But as to Lady Marth—no, I don't care to bespeak her good offices, as she had not the sense or kind-heartedness to show them any civility before."

Almost as he finished speaking, the carriage drew up at the hall door, and no more was said.

As they entered the drawing-room, Lady Harriot a little in advance of her husband and her guest, she gave a sudden cry of astonishment.

"Archie!" she exclaimed. "You here, my dear boy! and not with us at Alderwood! I didn't even know you were back in England."

"Nor did I myself, auntie, till I found myself in London yesterday morning," the young man replied. "I came down here with Norman to-day, meaning to look you up to-morrow."

"That's right," said Lady Harriot, but there was no time just then for further explanations, as Lady Marth came forward.

But it struck Sir Adam, as he shook hands cordially with the younger Mr Dunstan, that there was something forced in his tone and manner.

"Archie Dunstan's spirits failing him *would* be something new," thought the old man. "I must have my wits about me," and a moment or two later he found an opportunity of saying a few words without risk of their being overheard.

"I'm particularly glad to meet you to-night, Dunstan," he said. "I have never thanked you for looking up my old friends the Derwents again, and giving them my message. But for you, I should have felt even more ashamed of myself, for my carelessness towards them, than I do. I have been a selfish, self-absorbed old man, not worth calling a friend."

"You have seen them, then," said Archie eagerly.

"Yes, this afternoon. It has been almost more than I could stand to see them where and as they are, and to think how I might have saved it all I shall never forgive myself. Those two girls are perfectly charming, worthy to be their mother's daughters."

A new light seemed to come into Archies face, though he only murmured some half-inaudible words of agreement.

"At least," he thought unselfishly, "this looks like an end of that hateful life for her, and once clear of that, who knows what opportunities might turn up? She would surely look on things differently."

"And how is Hebe?" asked Sir Adam, still in a low voice.

"Better, really better," replied Archie. "I saw her a few minutes ago, and she is hoping to see you after dinner. They will have to be awfully careful of her for some time; but still, Norman is ever so much happier."

"Poor dear child!" said Sir Adam, and then he found himself told off to conduct his hostess to the dining-room.

He would have preferred another companion, for his feelings towards Lady Marth were not of the most cordial. They had some common ground, however, in the good hopes, now sanctioned, of Lady Hebe's recovery; and in the interest of discussing these, the first part of the dinner passed more to Sir Adam's satisfaction than he had anticipated.

Chapter Twenty Three.

At East Moddersham.

"It was all so touching," said Lady Marth. "I cannot tell you how patient Hebe was, thinking of every one more than of herself. I don't know any one else who would have behaved so beautifully through such a trial."

And her somewhat hard though handsome features softened as she spoke, and her dark eyes looked almost as if there were tears in them.

Sir Adam, on his side, felt that he had perhaps been judging her too sharply.

"Of course," he thought to himself, "but for their being friends of my own, I would never have known or cared whether she was kind to the Derwents or not. And I suppose one should try not to be personal; still—"

At that moment a slight pause in the conversation at the other end of the table allowed Lady Harriot's rather harsh, unmodulated voice to be heard very distinctly. She was speaking to a lady seated opposite to her, a visitor at East Moddersham, and not a resident in the neighbourhood.

"Yes," she said, "you positively must get Lady Marth to drive you into Blissmore to see their things. I have been getting them all the custom I could, and I do think, now they have made a good start, they may get on well, poor things."

"I'll make a point of giving them an order," the lady replied good-naturedly. "One does feel so sorry for them."

Sir Adam was an old man, and a man of the world; but his face reddened perceptibly.

"Excuse me, Lady Harriot," he said very clearly—and somehow every one stopped speaking to listen—"If you are alluding to Mrs Derwent and her daughters, I must not leave any misapprehension about them. There will soon be no need for any one to patronise them, however kind the motive. Their being in their present position has been the result of a complete misapprehension, for which, I must confess, I am myself to blame."

Lady Harriot stared.

"My dear Sir Adam," she said, "why didn't you tell me so before?"

But Sir Adam had already turned to Lady Marth, and did not seem to hear the question. Lady Harriot nodded across the table confidentially.

"Never mind," she said in a low voice. "Be sure you go to see their things, all the same."

Lady Marth had looked up in astonishment at Sir Adam's speech.

"Are you talking of some people who took a house on Pinnerton Green and have left it again already?" she said. "I had no idea they were friends of *yours*! I remember Hebe rather took up the daughters in connection with that guild of hers that she's so enthusiastic about."

Sir Adam's face was grave and his tone very cold as he replied.

"You cannot possibly have *met* them," he said, "or your discrimination would have shown you that, whether friends of mine or not, they are very different from what you have evidently imagined them."

"Why, you seem quite vexed with me," said Lady Marth, trying to carry it off lightly. "How can I be expected to know all about the good people on the Green, or to have guessed by instinct that the Derwents had anything to do with you?"

"Lady Hebe found out enough to make her show them all the kindness in her power," he replied. "Lady Harriot called on them, poor dear soul, meaning to do her best, and Mrs Harrowby surely mentioned them to you?"

"Perhaps she did," replied Lady Marth carelessly; "but the vicar's wife, you know, Sir Adam, doesn't count in that way. It's her rôle, or she thinks it is, to ignore all class distinctions."

"In this case there were none to ignore," said Sir Adam, still more frigidly.

"I don't say there were," she replied. "Of course not with friends of yours. But how was I to know that? Now, you're not to be vexed with me, for you've really no cause to be." But as she said this, a certain afternoon in the vicarage drawing-room recurred to her memory—a beautiful, fair-haired girl, standing near her, a faint flush rising to her face as she—Lady Marth—drew herself back with words, to say the least, neither courteous nor amiable. Her tone to Sir Adam softened still more. "Of course," she continued, "I shall be more than delighted to pay any attention in my power to Mrs Derwent—that is to say, if you wish it."

"Thank you," he answered, gratified, in spite of himself, by her evident sincerity. "I will tell you more about them some other time. I may see Hebe after dinner, may I not?" he went on. "Archie said something about her wishing it."

"Oh yes," replied Lady Marth. "She is counting upon it, I know. If you will follow us into the drawing-room a little before the other men, I will take you to her. She is really quite well in herself, but we daren't risk any glare of light for her as yet. Isn't it nice to see poor Norman looking so much happier?"

"Yes; of the two, I think he does more credit to their travels than young Dunstan," Sir Adam replied thoughtlessly.

He regretted the remark as soon as he had made it, but a glance at Lady Marth's face reassured him. She was in utter unconsciousness that Archie Dunstan and Blanche Derwent had ever met.

"Not that I have much ground for the idea, though," he said to himself. "I wonder if Hebe can possibly enlighten me."

They were approaching the end of dinner, and the rest of the conversation between himself and his hostess was on general subjects. But as she followed her guests to the drawing-room, she touched him gently on the arm.

"I shall expect you in a few minutes," she said; and a quarter of an hour or so later, Sir Adam found himself following her up the first flight of the broad oak staircase, along a passage, the rooms of which, since her first coming there as a little child, had always been appropriated to Sir Conway's ward.

"Poor dear child," thought the old man to himself. "Things don't seem so unequal, after all, in life. Stasy's children have had more than Hebe, heiress though she is. She has never known what 'home' really is as they have done?"

But it was a very happy Hebe who rose from a low seat near the fireplace in her pretty boudoir, to greet him as he followed Lady Marth into the room.

"Now, I shall leave you alone," she said. "I'm sure you've heaps to say to each other."

They had more to talk of even than the lady of the house suspected. For long after Hebe had replied to all her old friend's inquiries about herself — the result of the operation, and the still necessary precautions to be observed — and had told him the happy hopes for the future she now dared to entertain, they still went on talking earnestly and eagerly.

"I think our marriage will be early in the spring," Hebe had said, and the allusion seemed to send Sir Adam's thoughts in a further direction.

"Hebe," he said, "I want to speak to you about my friends the Derwents, whom I am delighted to find you've got to know on your own account."

The girl's face lighted up with the keenest interest. "I too want to talk about them to you," she said. "I have just been wondering if I may speak to you *quite* openly."

"Certainly you may do so—it is just what I have been hoping for," replied Sir Adam, and the hands of the pretty clock on Hebe's mantelpiece had very nearly made their accustomed journey of a full hour before it suddenly struck Sir Adam that he was scarcely behaving with courtesy to his hosts in spending so much of the evening away from the rest of the party.

Just then Norman Milward put his head in at the door.

"I'm most sorry to interrupt you," he said. "But Lady Marth thinks that perhaps—"

"Of course," said Sir Adam, rising as he spoke; "I had no business to stay so long.— Then you'll expect us to-morrow afternoon, my dear child? I will explain it to Lady Marth.—You'll stay up here, I suppose, Milward?"

"Yes," the young man replied; "I've scarcely seen her yet. It seems all too good to be true."

Sir Adam glanced back at them as he left the room, standing together on the hearthrug, the firelight dancing on the two bright heads, on the two young faces so very full of happy gratitude.

"I scarcely feel like a childless old fogy, after all," he thought, as he made his way down-stairs. "It seems to me I have a good many children. That little Stasy now— Blanche is charming, but Stasy is perfectly irresistible."

About four o'clock the next afternoon the Alderwood brougham might have been seen on the road from Blissmore to East Moddersham. There were two people inside it—Blanche Derwent and Sir Adam. It was a cold day, for the autumn was now advancing rapidly.

"Dear me," said Blanche, with a slight shiver, as she glanced out of the window at her side, "this road is beginning to look quite wintry. It is just about a year since mamma and Stasy and I drove along here for the first time, the day we came down to look at Pinnerton Lodge—only a year!"

Sir Adam stooped and drew the fur rug a little more closely round her.

"Blanche, my dear," he said, "you are a sweet, good child, I know, but I'm *very* angry with you, nevertheless. You really might have helped me to make your mother see things more reasonably."

"But if I don't see them 'reasonably' myself?" said Blanche. "I can't help quite agreeing with what mamma feels; and after all, Sir Adam, it is only a few months' delay."

"But a few months mean a good deal at my age," he persisted. "Your mother promises to look upon me — for the years, certainly not many, that still remain to me — entirely as a father. Why should we put off acting upon this at once, for a scruple which, after all, need be of no importance?" Blanche hesitated.

"I can't feel that," she said. "To me it seems so much better, from every point of view, to carry out our plan for the time arranged. And you know, Sir Adam, it will not practically make much difference. You couldn't risk all the winter in England, and mamma thinks it better not to interrupt Herty's and Stasy's lessons, though, of course, these are secondary reasons; the real one is our promise to Miss Halliday and — "

"And what?"

"Perhaps it is selfish," said Blanche. "But somehow it seems to me more dignified not to give up what we are doing, so hurriedly, as if — almost as if we were at all ashamed of it;" and she blushed a little.

"There's something in that perhaps," replied her old friend. "Perhaps in my heart I agree with you to some extent. But I am tired of wandering about by myself. I am longing to feel I have got a home again, and daughters to care about me in my last days."

"Dear Sir Adam," said Blanche, "you don't know how I love to hear you speak like that! The winter will seem as bright as possible to us with the looking forward to going back to Pinnerton in the spring. You're going to see our house to-day, aren't you, while I am with Lady Hebe? You mustn't be disappointed in its size. It isn't at all large, you know, but those half-finished rooms mamma was telling you about can easily be made very nice."

"Yes, I'm sure of it," said Sir Adam. "I've no love for very big houses and the worries they entail. The Bracys are very good-natured, and will let us make plans beforehand, so as to lose no time. They turn out in May next year, don't they? And by then your beloved Miss Halliday will have found an assistant to suit her — not as difficult a matter as a moneyed partner, which she will not now require. Then, as I was saying, I shall take a house in London for a short time, and all of you must join me there. We must give Stasy a pleasanter impression of London than she has, poor child. But here we are — "

Blanche looked up with interest at the fine old house. It was the first time she had seen more of it than its gables and chimneys through the trees, even though for several months they had been within a stone's-throw of the lodge gates.

"I will take you up at once to Hebe's room," said Sir Adam, "as she is expecting you;" and he led the way across the hall to the wide staircase.

"And how shall I meet you again?" said Blanche, who was not above a certain sensation of nervousness at the thought of encountering the formidable Lady Marth in her own house.

"It will be all right," Sir Adam replied, laying his hand lightly on her shoulder as he spoke. "Hebe will look after you," for he was quick enough to perceive her slight timidity, and liked her none the less for it. His kind tone reassured her, but had she known who was at that moment crossing the hall below them, it is very certain that Blanche's habitual calm would have been still more seriously disturbed.

She forgot all about Lady Marth and everything else for the moment in the pleasure of seeing Hebe Shetland again — her "girl with the happy face," chastened perhaps, somewhat paler and thinner than she remembered her, but sweeter still, and best of all, with the same bright sunny eyes, bearing no traces of the suffering they had gone through.

Hebe caught her by both hands and kissed her.

"Dear Blanche," she said.

The words and gesture surprised Blanche a little, but pleased her still more; while to Hebe it was an immense gratification to feel that she and the girl she had instinctively chosen as a friend could now meet on equal ground, with no constraint.

"It is so good of you to come," she said to Blanche.

"So good of Sir Adam to bring you" — But Sir Adam had already disappeared. "I have been looking forward so very much to seeing you again. I only wish you were at Pinnerton Lodge, and then you would come to see me often, wouldn't you?"

"Yes, indeed," said Blanche heartily, thinking to herself with satisfaction that, thanks to Sir Adam, there could no longer be any complication in the matter. "But we shall not be at Pinnerton for a good while — not till next summer; however, I will come to see you whenever I can, you may be quite sure."

"I'm afraid I shan't be allowed to go as far as Blissmore just yet," said Hebe; "I have to guard against any chill. But I had quite hoped you were coming back to the Lodge soon, from what Sir Adam said last night."

"Dear Sir Adam," said Blanche. "I could never tell you how good he is to us! But still, things must stay as they are for a while." And then she went on to explain to Hebe the position of affairs with regard to Miss Halliday, and how much they felt themselves indebted to her, adding simply: "At that time she really seemed our only friend."

Hebe stroked Blanche's hand.

"I quite understand how you feel," she said, "and I have no doubt you are right. But Sir Adam was so full of it last night, he was sure he'd get your tenants to turn out at once, and—he's such an old man now, Blanche—he can't have many years to live. Don't you think perhaps, for his sake, you should not be *quite* so scrupulous?"

"It may be possible to arrange things a little sooner," said Blanche. "Of course his wishes will be almost our first thought now. But, you see, in any case he must not risk the winter in this climate."

"I was forgetting that," said Hebe regretfully. "He seems so much stronger lately."

Then they went on to talk of other things, Hebe giving a few details of all she had gone through.

"I can bear to think of it now that it is all so happily over;" and in the interest of their conversation time passed rapidly.

Hebe started when the silvery sound of a gong reached them from the hall below.

"That's the tea-gong," she said. "I am allowed to go down to tea, for Josephine keeps the room in a half-light for me. I had no idea it was so late."

The two girls went down the staircase together; the drawing-room door stood open, and a hum of voices reached their ears before they entered the room. Then Lady Marth's clear, decided tones rang out conspicuously above the others.

"Nonsense!" she was saying. "You can both stay if you choose—you know you are always welcome."

"That must be Norman," said Hebe gladly, "and—"

But Blanche heard no more, for by this time they were inside the room, and Lady Marth was addressing her.

"How do you do, Miss Derwent? My hands are full of teacups, you see. I persuaded Sir Adam to stay to tea."

Some one came forward from the little group near the fire. It was almost too dark to distinguish faces at the first moment, but Hebe's, "This is Norman, Blanche," prepared her for his cordial greeting.

"Here's a nice corner for you both," said Mr Milward. "No foot-stools to stumble over!"

"I see better in the dark than the rest of you, I think," said Hebe laughingly; "it is too bad for you all to suffer for my sake. — Oh," she exclaimed, "is that you, Archie? I didn't know you were coming back again to-day."

"Norman brought me over," Mr Dunstan replied.

"And he's pretending he can't stay to dinner," put in Lady Marth. — "As if your aunt would mind, Archie!"

He did not at once reply. He was shaking hands with Blanche.

"How do you do, Miss Derwent?" he said easily. "I hope Mrs Derwent is well, and that famous little brother of yours?"

"Yes, thank you," said Blanche, in a tone which she endeavoured to render unconstrained, though feeling for once nervous, and ill at ease and disgusted at herself for being so, especially as Mr Dunstan struck her as his airiest, most conventional self.

"I really can't stay," he went on, turning again to Lady Marth. "Auntie is counting upon me, as she has got a man too few, and some people are coming to dinner."

"It's only to take in Rosy," said Norman, with a brother's brutality.

"Only Rosy!" repeated Lady Marth. "My dear Norman, if Rosy were any one but your sister, I don't think you would be quite so much at a loss to account for Archie's obstinacy."

Archie laughed a hearty unconstrained laugh. "Archie's taste is not peculiar; every one loves a *tête-à-tête* with Rosy, when they have a chance of it," said Hebe, with apparently uncalled-for warmth.

"Of course they do," said Sir Adam, speaking for the first time. — "And now, my dear Blanche, if you've had a cup of tea, I think we must be off — I have to get back to Alderwood in time for dinner, too, Master Archie. By-the-bye, we've got the large brougham — will you come with us *viâ* Blissmore, though it is rather a round?"

"Well no, I think I prefer Norman's cart, which is here," said Mr Dunstan lightly. "Though many thanks, all the same."

"And how is Norman going to get home, then?" said Lady Marth. "You're not going to force him away too?"

"The cart can come back," said Archie.

"Thank you," said Norman, somewhat grimly. "*Pray*, be on no ceremony."

"There comes our brougham," said Sir Adam, shaking hands with Lady Marth, Blanche following his example.

Then came a more affectionate farewell from Hebe, who accompanied them to the drawing-room door.

"I mustn't go farther," she said; but Norman Milward crossed the hall to see them off, Mr Dunstan having contented himself with a regulation hand-shake, when standing beside his hostess on the hearthrug.

The air outside felt chilly as they stepped into the carriage, but not so chilly as a strange, unreasonable breath of disappointment, which seemed to pass through Blanche, though, even to herself, she would have shrunk from calling it by such a name.

Chapter Twenty Four.

Hebe's Good News.

May again! A later spring this year than last. As Blanche Derwent stood at the window of a house in a broad, airy street, at one end of which the trees of the Park were to be seen, she could scarcely believe it was same time of year, the same date, actually, as the day on which the news of their reversal of fortune had reached her mother at Pinnerton Lodge.

"That was such a lovely summery day," she said to herself. "I remember it so well; Stasy and I walking home from Blissmore, laughing and talking—I even remember what we were talking about—how Stasy was flattering me;" and Blanche's colour deepened a little. "And then to find poor mamma as she was when we got home! It was dreadful. And yet, how wonderfully all that side of things has come right! I *should* be grateful, and I think I am;" but still she gave a little sigh.

Sir Adam had carried out his scheme. He had taken a house in London for a part of the season, and had got his god-daughter and her children with him, excepting Herty, whom it had been thought wiser to leave under Miss Halliday's care, not to interrupt his lessons.

Just then Stasy joined her sister.

"What are you doing, Blanche?" she said brightly.

"I thought it was against your principles to stand idle at the window. Even though these lovely London streets are delightful to look out on."

Blanche smiled.

"How you have changed, Stasy! London used to be a synonym with you for everything dreary and miserable."

"Yes, I daresay. London in November, with a fog, in a horrid hotel, and without a creature to speak to, isn't exactly the same thing as London in May, in a bright open street like this, and with—really, I must say, everything one could reasonably wish to have."

"London means a great many things—worlds and worlds of different lives," said Blanche soberly. "I was just thinking how bare the trees are, Stasy, compared with this time last year;" and she reminded her sister of the date.

Stasy seemed impressed.

"It should make us awfully thankful," she said, "and I'm sure it does. But I don't quite understand you lately, Blanchie. You so often seem rather depressed, and just a little gloomy."

She looked at her sister anxiously as she spoke.

"I wonder," she went on—"I wonder if it is that you kept up too well when we were in such trouble. You were always so cheerful, and I used to be so cross. Do you remember my raging at Mrs Burgess's caps?"

"No," said Blanche decidedly. "You were always as good as could be. I don't know how we should have got on without your fun and mischief, and I know I've grown horrid lately."

"Are you not well, perhaps?" said Stasy. "I don't think you have been quite yourself for a long time. I remember noticing it first, that Christmas week at Alderwood, when I did so enjoy myself. Even Lady Marth couldn't freeze me up."

"On the contrary, I think you're rather a favourite of hers," remarked Blanche.

"Oh, I don't mind her," said Stasy. "She's not bad, after all; only she wants to manage every one's affairs for them. I wonder if she'll ever succeed in her match-making?"

"What do you mean?" said Blanche.

"Oh, you know, you must have forgotten about it. Rosy Milward and Archie Dunstan, of course."

Blanche turned on her sharply.

"I do hope, Stasy, you're not going to get into that odious habit of calling men you scarcely know, by their first names."

Stasy opened her eyes very wide.

"I do know him, very well, I consider, and so do you, only you don't like him. We saw a great deal of him at Christmas time, and *I* shall always consider him a true friend, whether you do or not. And so will mamma, I'm sure; the way he stuck to us, and was so kind to Herty at the time when no one else troubled their heads about us at all. Indeed, I'm by no means sure that Sir Adam would have found out about us as he did, not for a long time anyway, but for Mr Dunstan the younger. Does that suit you, Blanchie?"

Blanche took no notice of Stasy's sarcasm.

"I know he was very good at that time," she said. "I think he has most kind and generous impulses, but I don't think his character can be very deep."

"I think you are perfectly unfair and very censorious," said Stasy indignantly. "Because you don't personally like the man, and *cannot* give any good reason for your dislike, you imagine qualities, or no qualities, to justify your own prejudice."

"Well, what does it matter what I think?" said Blanche, in a tone which she intended to be light and indifferent. "Rosy Milward's opinion of him is, I suppose, the thing that signifies."

Something in her voice struck Stasy. She eyed Blanche curiously.

"I don't know that," she said, speaking more slowly than was usual with her. "I'm not at all sure that Archie Dunstan does care in any special way what dear Rosy thinks about him."

"Do you not think so?" said Blanche, with involuntary eagerness; but before Stasy had time to reply, they were interrupted by their mother's entering the room.

"Quick, dears," she said. "You must get ready. Sir Adam will be waiting for you."

For the kind old man was devoting himself to "doing" London for his adopted grand-daughters' benefit, two or three times a week, in the earlier part of the day.

At that very moment, at no great distance from the spot where Blanche and Stasy Derwent had been discussing Archie Dunstan's character, the very person in question was sitting beside Lady Marth in her boudoir, listening to a very solemn oration discoursed, for his benefit, by that somewhat dictatorial lady herself.

She had summoned him by a note the evening before, and as he felt himself in duty bound to obey the behest of an old friend, he had made his appearance punctually. He was not without some suspicion as to the nature of the good advice she intended to bestow upon him, but saw no advantage in evading the interview.

"I must put an end to it, once for all," he thought to himself. "Why will women meddle in such matters? But Josephine is honest and trustworthy when she feels herself trusted, so I'd rather have to do with her than with many would-be match-makers."

So he sat in silence, patiently enough, to all appearance, while Lady Marth unbosomed herself of what she considered her mission, prefacing her advice with the usual excuses for interference, on the ground that, sooner or later, both of the principals concerned would thank her for having acted as a true friend in the matter.

Archie bent his head in acknowledgment of her kind intentions, but beyond this, neither by word nor look did he help her out with what she had to say.

This attitude of his made her task by no means easier. For some little time she floundered about in unusual embarrassment; but once fairly under weigh, her words flowed fluently. She dilated on Archie's lonely position—the advisability of his making up his mind to marry, instead of remaining a target for the aims of designing mammas or rich husband-hunting daughters, and possibly some day finding himself pinned by their well-directed arrows. She hinted at the satisfaction and security of being cared for, "for himself," and by one who had known him long and thoroughly, to all of which Archie listened unmoved, with the utmost deference and attention, till her ladyship at last pulled up short, partly through breathlessness, partly because, without the encouragement of a responsive word or gesture, she had really nothing more to say.

Then he looked up, but nothing in his face helped her to any conclusion as to the effect of her exordium.

"I must thank you," he said, "for your great interest in my welfare. Believe me, I shall always remember it." Which statement was certainly well founded, though the glimmer of a smile danced in his eyes as he made his little speech.

The smile, however, Lady Marth was too engrossed to perceive.

"But"—and at this word, for the first time, her heart misgave her as to what was to follow—"but it is best for me at once to make you understand my position. I am not likely to marry. It seems to me at present almost certain that I never shall."

"Archie!" exclaimed Lady Marth, startled and surprised, "why not?"

"Simply for this reason. There is only one woman in the world whom I can imagine myself caring for in that way, and she"—here, even Archies calm somewhat deserted him—"she," he went on, with a touch of bitterness quite new to him, "won't have anything to say to me."

"I can scarcely believe it," exclaimed his hearer.

"There *must* be some mistake!"

"Thank you for the inferred compliment," he replied. "But no—it is quite true; there is no mistake."

Then a wild idea struck Lady Marth, suggested by her irrepressible belief in her own powers of discernment.

"You don't mean to say," she began. "Is it possible that we are both thinking of the same person! It can't be that *Rosy* has refused you."

Archie laughed, quite unconstrainedly.

"As things are," he said, "I suppose I may be quite frank. Rosy!—oh dear, no; we are the best of friends, as you are aware, but thoroughly and completely like brother and sister. And it is by no means improbable that she suspects the real state of the case, as Hebe is in my confidence."

"Then who in all the world can it be?" said Lady Marth, completely nonplussed, "for somehow you seem to infer that it's some one I know."

"I don't mind telling you," said Archie. "You do know her—it is Blanche Derwent."

For a moment or two Lady Marth did not speak. Then she said, half timidly:

"It must have been very sudden. You have seen very little of her? Oh yes, there was that Christmas week at Alderwood."

"It all happened long before then," said Archie.

"It is true, I had not seen much of her, but it doesn't seem to me now that time is required in such a case. It was soon after they left Pinnerton, and took up that millinery business."

"Before Sir Adam came home?"

"Of course," said Archie drily.

"And she refused you—*then*?"

"Naturally, as she didn't care for me."

Lady Marth again relapsed into silence. The confusion of ideas in her mind was too great to find expression in words. She had read of such things; in novels, perhaps, they seemed credible and rather fine. But in real life—no, she couldn't take it in.

Archie showed no inclination to say more. He rose, and held out his hand.

"Good-bye," he said. "Thank you for your interest in me."

"Good-bye," she replied, "and—no, perhaps I had better say nothing. Except, yes—honestly, Archie, I should like to see you happy."

"Thank you," he repeated.

When Archie found himself in the street again, he looked about him vaguely, and sauntered on, scarcely knowing why or whither, thinking over the interview which had just taken place, and recalling, not without a certain grim humour, Josephine Marth's blank amazement.

Suddenly the sound of his own name not far from him made him start, and looking up, on the opposite pavement he caught sight of three familiar figures, Sir Adam and his two "grand-daughters."

"Where are you off to?" said the old man. "You don't look as if you were bound on anything very important. Come with us — we're going to see some of the pictures."

Mr Dunstan hesitated.

"Yes, do come," said Stasy, with whom he was on the friendliest of terms. "Three is no company, you know, and I'm always getting left behind by myself."

He glanced up, still irresolute, but at that moment he caught Blanche's eyes, and something — an impalpable something in their blue depths — brought him to a sudden determination.

"If I won't be in the way," he said, "I should like nothing better."

And the four walked on together.

"Norman," said Lady Hebe that same evening, when they met for a few moments before dinner in her guardian's house — it was within a week or two of the date fixed for their marriage — "Norman, I've something wonderful to tell you. Archie Dunstan rushed in late this afternoon to see me for a moment —"

"Well?" said Norman, as she paused. "Do you want me to guess?"

"No," said Hebe, "I want to tell you straight off. Archie knew how I should enjoy doing so. Its all right, Norman — between him and Blanche, I mean. Just fancy! *Aren't* you pleased?"

And never had Hebe's face looked happier than as she said the words.

End of "Blanche."

Chapter Twenty Five.

One Sunday Morning.

The Rector of a large West-end church was ill. His illness was not very serious, nor did it threaten to be protracted, but it fell at a bad moment. It was the middle of the season, the time at which his church was more crowded than at any other of the year. He was an earnest and thoughtful man, and one who, despite much discouragement, laboured energetically to do his best; but on the Friday evening, preceding the second Sunday in June, he was obliged to acknowledge that for some days he would be unfit to officiate in his usual place.

"What shall I do?" he said in distress. "What shall I do about the sermon on Sunday morning? The curates can manage the rest, but it will be as much as they *can* do. I cannot ask either of them to prepare another sermon so hurriedly. And the one I had ready has cost me much time and thought—I had even built some hopes upon it. One never knows—"

"Your sermon will keep till another Sunday. That is not the question," said his wife.

"No, truly," he agreed, with some bitterness; "my sermon, as you say, will keep. Nor can I flatter myself that any one will be the loser if it never be preached at all. Do sermons ever do good, I sometimes ask myself? Yet many of us—I could almost say most of us—do our best. We spare neither time nor trouble nor prayer; but all falls on stony ground, it seems to me. And we are but human—liable to error and mistake, and but few among us have great gift of eloquence. It is easy, I know, to pick holes and criticise; but is the fault all on the side of the sermons, I wonder?"

"You misunderstood me, Reginald," said his wife gently. "No, truly; the fault must lie in great part with the hearers. All other efforts to instruct or do good are received with some amount of respect and appreciation. No popular lecturers, for instance, are listened to with such indifference or criticised so captiously as the mass of English clergy. It is the tone of the day, the fashion of the age. Though one rose from the dead—nay, if an angel from heaven came down to preach one Sunday morning," she went on with sad impressiveness, "he would be found fault with, or sneered at, or criticised, and accused of having nothing to say, or not knowing how to say it; yes, I verily believe it would be so."

Her husband smiled, though his smile was a melancholy one, at her earnestness.

"I have it," he exclaimed suddenly; "I will write to Lyle by to-night's post. He will come if he can, I am sure, and I know he only preaches occasionally where he is."

The letter was written and despatched. Mr Lyle was a young clergyman doing assistant duty temporarily at a church in the suburbs while waiting for a living promised to him. His answer came by return. He would be glad to do as his friend asked. "But I shall go straight to Saint X's on Sunday morning," he wrote. "I shall not probably be able to reach it till the last moment, as I have an early service here. Ask them to count on me for nothing but the sermon. I shall look in after the service and shall hope to find you better."

"He will be here at luncheon, then, I suppose?" said the Rector's wife — Mildred was her name.

"Doubtless; at least you will ask him to come. You can wait to see him after the service," her husband replied. "With you there he will have *one* attentive hearer, I can safely promise him," he added, with a smile.

"I cannot help listening, even when it is not you, Reginald," she said naïvely. "It seems to me only natural to do so and to try to gain *something* at least. We cannot expect perfection in sermons surely, even less than in lesser things. And if the perfection were there, could we, imperfect as we are, recognise it?"

Sunday morning rose, bright and glowing over the great city — a real midsummer's day.

"How beautiful it must be in the country to-day!" thought Mildred, as she made her way to church; "it is beautiful even here in town. I wonder why I feel so happy to-day. It is greatly, no doubt, that Reginald is better, and the sunshine is so lovely. When I feel as I do this morning I *long* to believe that the world is growing better, not worse, that the misery, and the ignorance, and the sins are lessening, however slowly; I feel as if I could give my life to help it on."

There was scarcely any one in the church when she entered and sat down in her accustomed place. Gradually it filled — up the aisles flecked with the brilliant colours of the painted windows, as the sunshine made its way through them, the congregation crowded in, in decorous silence. There were but few poor, few even of the the so-called working classes, for Saint X's is in a rich and fashionable neighbourhood, yet there was diversity enough and of many kinds among those now pressing in through its doors. There were old, and middle-aged, and young — from the aged lady on her son's arm, who, as she feebly moved along, said to herself that this might perhaps be her last attendance at public worship, to the little round-eyed wondering cherub coming to church for the first time. There was the anxious mother of a family, who came from a vague feeling that it was a right and respectable thing to do, though it was but seldom that she could sufficiently distract her mind from cares and calculations to take in clearly the sense of the words that fell upon her ears. There was the man of learning, who smiled indulgently at the survival of the ancient creeds and customs, while believing them doomed. There were bright and lovely young faces, whose owners, in the heyday of youth and prosperity, found it difficult to put aside for the time the thoughts of present enjoyment for graver matters. There were some in deep mourning, to whom, on the other hand, it seemed impossible that aught in life could ever cheer or interest them again.

There were men and women of many different and differing modes of thought, all assembled for the avowed purpose of praying to God and praising Him in company, and of listening to the exhortation or instruction of a man they recognised as empowered to deliver it. And among them all, how many, think you, prayed from the heart and not only with the lips? how many thrilled with solemn rejoicing as the beautiful words of adoration rose with the strains of the organ's tones? how many ever thought of the "sermon," save as a most legitimate subject for sharp criticism or indifferent contempt?

The service went on with the usual decorum. From her place Mildred could see all that passed. She noticed that the two curates were alone and unaided.

"Mr Lyle cannot yet have come," she thought nervously. "Surely nothing can have detained him?" and a slight misgiving, lest he should not have got away in time, began to assail her. But when the moment for commencing the Communion service came, the sight of a third white-surpliced figure removed all her apprehensions, and with a sigh of relief she knelt again, joining her voice to the responses. She observed that the new-comer took no active part in the service; he remained kneeling where she had first perceived him. But it seemed to her that the music and the voices had never sounded so rich and melodious, and once or twice tones caught her ears which she fancied she had not before remarked.

"I wonder if it can be Mr Lyle singing," she thought. "I do not remember if Reginald ever mentioned his having a beautiful voice."

And when the time came for the preacher to ascend the pulpit, she watched for him with increased interest. It needed but the first few syllables which fell from his lips to satisfy her that his was the voice which she had perceived; and with calm yet earnest expectancy she waited to hear what he had to say.

At the first glance he looked very young. His face was pale, and he was of a fair complexion. There was nothing in him to strike or attract a careless or superficial observer. But when the soft yet penetrating tones of his voice caught the ear, one felt constrained to bestow a closer attention on the speaker, and this, once given, was not easily withdrawn. For there was a power in his eyes, though their habitual expression was mild, such as it would be vain for me to attempt to describe—a strength and firmness in the lines of the youthful face which marked him as one not used to speak in vain.

"Is he young?" thought Mildred more than once. "It seems in some way difficult to believe it, though his features are in no way time-worn; and those wonderful eyes are as clear and candid as the eyes of a child that has scarcely yet learned to look out on to this troubled world."

And her perplexity was shared by many among the hearers.

They had settled themselves comfortably to listen or not to listen, according to their wont, as the preacher ascended the pulpit steps.

A momentary feeling of surprise—in a few cases of disappointment—passed through the congregation on catching sight of the unfamiliar face.

"Another new curate, no doubt," thought a portly and pompous churchwarden. "And what a boy! Well, if the Rector chooses to throw away his money on three when two are quite enough for the work, it is no business of ours. Still, it would be more becoming to consult us, and not to set a beardless youth like that to teach us. I, for one, shall not irritate myself by listening to his platitudes."

And he ensconced himself more snugly in his corner to carry out his intention. But what was there in that vibrating voice that *would* be heard?—that so often as Mr Goldmain turned his thoughts in other directions, drew them back again like a flock of rebellious sheep, constraining him to hearken? Then his mood changed: annoyed, he knew not why, he set himself to cavil and object.

"Arrant Socialism!" he called the sermon when describing it afterwards. "Shallow, superficial, unpractical nonsense, about drawing all classes together by sympathy and charity. It sounds plausible enough, I daresay; so did many of the theories and doctrines of the first movers in the great French Revolution, I have no doubt. No, no! Let each do his duty in that station of life where God has placed him; that is *my* interpretation of religion. Our great charitable institutions must be kept up, of course, so that the *deserving* poor may be helped when they really need it; though even among the respectable, in nine cases out of ten, my dear sir, you may believe me, it's their own fault. But as for this dream of universal brotherhood, 'of the rich mingling in the daily life of the poor, weeping with them in their sorrows, rejoicing in their joys,' it is sentimental twaddle. It would revolutionise society, it would break down all the barriers which keep the masses in their places. And to have this nonsense preached to us by a chit of a boy, it makes me lose my temper, I confess. I have not seen our worthy Rector yet, but when I do, I must tell him plainly that if he is not more careful whom he puts in his pulpit when he is absent or ill—hypochondriacal fellow he is, I fancy—I shall look out for seats in some other church than Saint X's."

Such was Mr Goldmain's impression of the sermon. For though he closed his eyes in order that those about him might think he was asleep, he did not succeed in achieving even the shortest of dozes. Nay, more, he felt as if mentally stung by nettles for the rest of the day, so irritated, and, though for worlds he would not have confessed it, ill at ease, had the strange preacher's discourse left him. But the soil of his conscience was choked with thorns; there was room for naught beside. Mr Goldmain was of this world, worldly, and such he remained.

He might have spared himself the trouble of thinking of how he appeared to those around him. They were none of them paying any attention to him. In the next seat sat some richly-clad ladies of uncertain age. They had become members of the Saint X's congregation because they had been told they would find its Rector's views in no way "extreme." For these worthy women had an exaggerated horror of everything "high," or, as they expressed it, "verging on papistry." That God could be worshipped "in spirit and in truth," in any but their own pet "evangelical" fashion, was a possibility that had not yet suggested itself to their dull brains. And they too, this Sunday morning, felt a shock of disapproval when, looking up at the sound of the vibrating voice, the fair face of the strange preacher met their gaze.

"Like a young novice, or whatever it is they call those who are going to be priests; looks as if he fasted and half-starved himself," whispered one to the other. "The Rector should be more careful. Who knows but what he is a Jesuit in disguise?" replied the third.

And at intervals during the sermon little groans or ejaculations of disapproval might have been heard from the seats of the wealthy spinsters.

"I did my best not to listen," said the eldest candidly, as they were walking home, "for I knew in a moment what it was going to be. But no doubt he had a persuasive tone and manner. Poor deluded young man—he will be over to Rome in no time! Did you hear—all that about 'the Church?'—"

"The 'invisible' Church, he spoke of also, I think," suggested the younger sister timidly.

"Ah, I daresay, just to hide their real meaning; but I can see through it. There was all that in favour of images, too—symbols he called them. What was it he said, Janet? You have the best memory."

"'The childlike expressions of human yearnings after the Divine, which is not for you to condemn or despise,'" quoted Janet.

"Ah, yes—all very fine. We shall be having Madonnas and rosaries and graven images in our English churches next," said the eldest sister somewhat confusedly.

"He seemed to me a conscientious young man, very much in earnest, I should have said," observed the younger sister humbly.

"Of course, they take that tone; that is the very danger of it," answered the elder lady. "I really must ask the Rector to be on his guard."

And yet by another group seated just across the aisle the stranger's sermon had been criticised in a very different fashion. By some among his hearers his views were pronounced to be, not too "high," or "leading to Rome," but dangerously "broad."

"I dislike those allusions to 'evolution' and 'development' in the pulpit. It is not the place for science; our preachers should keep to the Bible, and not give heed to all the talk of the day about matters which have nothing to do with religion," said an elderly gentleman dogmatically.

His companion smiled; they, too, were walking down the street. "Yes, religion or teachers of religion get rather out of their depth when they touch upon science, certainly," he said.

"But if science be true, and religion be true, *truths* cannot disagree," said a young girl, who was walking between the two, her bright intelligent face raised to the last speaker, her brother, as he spoke. "You are a very clever and learned man, Gerald, and I am only a very young and ignorant girl, but yet I *feel* you are wrong, and I never felt this more intensely than when listening to this stranger this morning. Why should we refuse to believe what we cannot understand? Is it not the very height of presumption, and even stupidity, to do so? I cannot remember his words, but they seemed to me to say it as I have never heard it said before. And—I hoped you felt it so, too."

But the philosopher only shook his head. The two were some paces in front of the old gentleman by now; they knew that such talk annoyed him, hedged in, in his "orthodoxy."

"I am glad if you were pleased, my dear child," said the brother; "but I must keep to my old opinion. Reality and dreams *cannot* be reconciled. We can only know that which we have experience of. Still, I allow that he put it in rather an original way."

"You mean," said the girl, eagerly, "when he said that our refusing to believe in God and the spiritual universe, because we cannot see and touch them, is like a deaf-mute refusing to believe in music — that we complain of the things of God not being proved and explained to us before we have learned the alphabet of the spiritual language."

"That we complain of not being treated as gods before we have learned to live as men. Yes, that was rather fine," the other allowed. "But still, my dear child, I cannot see that these discussions are profitable. We have plenty to do and learn about matters as to which we *can* arrive at certainty. Why not be content to leave those matters as to which we *know* nothing? I don't quarrel with the clergy for trying to bring us to a different way of thinking; it is their business, and as long as there are priests, we must submit to their platitudes. But what can a young theologian, determined to see things in but one way, know of the researches of science, the true spirit of philosophy?"

The girl looked grievously disappointed, and tears filled her beautiful eyes.

"Gerald," she said, "I could not live in the negation of all belief that you advocate; still less," she went on in a lower voice, "could I die in it. Uncle thought the preacher dangerously 'liberal;' *you* think him narrow and ignorant. For me, I can only say, if I may use the words without irreverence, that my heart burned within me as I listened."

"Little enthusiast!" said her brother, smiling. Mentally he thought to himself that it would really be a pity if Agatha went too far in "that direction," and his eyes wandering across the street, caught sight of a party of young people, laughing and talking, though in well-bred fashion, as they went along. "She should be more like other girls of her age," he reflected, as his glance again fell on the thoughtful young face at his side.

"You should be pleased and flattered, Agatha," he said, "that I gave so much attention as I did to this pet preacher of yours."

"I don't know him, Gerald," she replied. "I never saw or heard him before."

"Really," he said, "I had half an idea that you had some reason for so particularly asking me to go to church this morning."

"Oh, no. I expected the Rector would be preaching himself," she said. "But I am glad you came, Gerald. You do allow that it was a remarkable sermon."

"Ye-es," he replied, smiling again, and with that Agatha was forced to be contented.

Across the street the same subject was being discussed.

"I feel quite tired," laughed one of the pretty girls to the man beside her. "Do you know, for once in my life, I really listened to the sermon?"

"You don't mean to say so," he replied. But something in his tone made her glance up at him archly.

"Why do you seem so conscious?" she said. "Were you asleep?"

"No, I scarcely think so. I was very sleepy at the beginning, it was so hot. But there was something rather impressive in that fellow's voice. To confess the truth, I caught myself listening, like you."

"If one could always listen, it would make church-going less wearisome," said the girl. "As a rule, I never attempt it; they always say the same thing."

"And there was nothing particularly new in what that pale-faced young man had to say this morning, after all," said her companion. "It was the mere accident of his having an unusually good voice."

"Yes, I suppose so," replied the young lady, indifferently, "though I've really forgotten what it was about—there are too many other things to think about when one is young and—"

"Lovely," interrupted her companion. "Yes—and for my part I don't see what we're in the world for, if it isn't to make ourselves as happy as we can. That's *my* religion."

"A very pleasant one, if it has no other merit," the girl replied, with a laugh.

At that moment a carriage passed them. It had but one occupant—an elderly lady. Her face, though worn and even prematurely aged, was sweet and calm. Her glance fell for an instant on the upturned laughing face of the girl.

"Something in her recalls my Margaret," thought the lady; "but Margaret was more serious. How is it that they all seem to have been so near me to-day? All my dead children who have left me—I am so glad I went to church. I have not felt so near them all for years. I could almost fancy that young man knew something of my sorrows, his glance rested on me once or twice with such sympathy. How beautiful and how strengthening were his words! Yes — we are not really separated — I am content to wait while God has work for me to do here. And I am glad I am rich when I feel how many I can help. God bless that preacher, whoever he is, for the strength and comfort he has given me to-day."

Mildred in her place sat quietly waiting till the congregation had dispersed. Then she rose and went forward to speak to the verger.

"Will you tell the clergyman," she said, "Mr Lyle is his name — that I hope he will return with me to the rectory to luncheon. I will wait here till he comes out."

The man went with her message. But in a moment or two he reappeared looking somewhat surprised.

"He has gone, ma'am," he said. "I can't make out how he went off so quickly. No one seems to have seen him."

"He must have hurried off at once. No doubt I shall find him at home," she said, feeling nevertheless a little disappointed. She had looked forward to the few minutes' talk with the preacher who had so impressed her; she would have liked to thank him without delay.

"I shall feel too shy to say it to him before Reginald, I am afraid," she thought. "I am a little surprised he did not tell me more of this Mr Lyle."

And she set off eagerly to return home. At the church door she almost ran against one of the curates, an honest and hard-working, but dictatorial young man, with whom she did not feel much sympathy. He accompanied her a few steps down the street.

"And how did you like the sermon?" he said.

Mildred replied by repeating his own question, hoping thus to escape a discussion she felt sure would not be to her mind.

"How did *you* like it, Mr Grenfell?" she asked.

He smiled in a superior way, conscious to his fingertips of his unassailable theology.

"I daresay he may come to be something of a preacher in time," he said. "But he was crude — very crude — and I should say he would do well to go through a good course of divinity. He evidently *thinks* he knows all about it; but if I could have a talk with him I could knock his arguments to shivers, I could — "

"Mr Grenfell," said Mildred, feeling very repelled by his manner, "do you think religion is only theology of the Schools? If you could not feel the love of God, and love to man—the 'enthusiasm of humanity,' if you like to call it so—breathing through Mr Lyle's every word and look and tone, I am sorry for you."

Mr Grenfell grew very red.

"I am sorry," he began, "I did not mean—I will think over what you say. Perhaps it is true that we clergy get into that way of thinking—as if religion were a branch of learning more than anything else. Thank you," and with a shake of the hand he turned away.

A step or two further on, Mildred overtook a young man—a cripple, and owing to his infirmity, in poor circumstances, though a gentleman by birth. She was passing with a kindly bow, when he stopped her.

"Might I ask the name of the clergyman who preached this morning?" he asked, raising his face, still glowing with pleasure, to hers.

"Mr Lyle," she replied; "at least," as for the first time a slight misgiving crossed her mind, "I feel almost sure that is his name."

"Thank you," the cripple said. "I am glad to know it, though it matters little. Whoever he was, I pray God to bless him, I little knew what I was going to church to hear this morning; I felt as if an angel had unawares come to speak to us."

And in the relief of this warm sympathy Mildred held out her hand.

"Thank *you*, Mr Denis, for speaking so," she said; "you are the first who seem to have felt as I did."

Then she hurried on.

She found her husband on the sofa, but looking feverish and uneasy.

"How?" he began, but she interrupted him.

"Is Mr Lyle not here?" she said.

"Mr Lyle!" Reginald repeated. "What do you mean? You had scarcely gone when a special messenger brought this from him;" and he held out a short note of excessive regret and apology from the young priest, at finding the utter impossibility of reaching Saint X's in time for the morning service. "I have been on thorns," said the

Rector, "and I could do nothing. There was no one to send. Did Grenfell preach, or was there no sermon?"

Mildred sat down, feeling strangely bewildered.

"I cannot explain it," she said. "Reginald, tell me what is Mr Lyle's personal appearance? Can he have come after all? even after despatching his message? Is he slight and fair—rather tall and almost boyish-looking, but with most sweet yet keen eyes, and a wonderful voice?"

The Rector could hardly help smiling.

"Lyle," he replied, "is slight, but short, and dark—very dark, with a quick lively way of moving, and a rather thin, though clear voice. He has not a grain of music or poetry in his composition."

Nothing could be more unlike the preacher of that morning.

Mildred told her husband all she could recollect of the sermon. Its vivid impression remained; but the words had grown hazy, and curiously enough she could not recall the text. But Reginald listened with full sympathy and belief.

"I wish I could have heard it," he said. "Were the days for such blessed visitations not over, I should think." But there he hesitated.

Mildred understood, and the words of the cripple, Mr Denis—"an angel unawares"—returned to her memory.

The events I have related were never explained, nor of the many who had been present that Sunday morning at Saint X's did any ever again look upon the fair face of the mysterious stranger.

But—till the matter had passed from the minds of all but two or three—the Rector had to listen with patience to much fault-finding with the sermon, and with its preacher.

The End.